SCORCHED EARTH

A DALTON SAVAGE MYSTERY
BOOK 2

L.T. RYAN

WITH
BIBA PEARCE

LIQUID MIND MEDIA

For information contact:

contact@ltryan.com

http://LTRyan.com

https://www.facebook.com/groups/1727449564174357

THE DALTON SAVAGE SERIES

Savage Grounds

Scorched Earth

Cold Sky

The Frost Killer (Coming Soon)

Join the L.T. Ryan reader family & receive a free copy of the Rachel Hatch story, *Fractured*. Click the link below to get started:

https://ltryan.com/rachel-hatch-newsletter-signup-1

Love Savage? Hatch? Noble? Get your very own L.T. Ryan merchandise today! Click the link below to find coffee mugs, t-shirts, and even signed copies of your favorite L.T. Ryan thrillers! https://ltryan.ink/EvG_

ONE

EDDIE YOUNGBLOOD HAD A BAD FEELING. Something about the message didn't make sense, but he couldn't put his finger on it. It was too abrupt, too succinct. Not her usual style. But he'd come, anyway. He had to. It was *her*. Eyes the color of pine needles after the rain, dewy skin, and a smile that warmed him like the sun on a summer's day. How could he not come?

Still, every sense was tingling. His friend Tomahawk had taught him well. A tracker and member of the tribal police, Tomahawk had taught him how to be silent. How to listen and be aware of his surroundings. To trust his instincts, now telling him to get the hell out of there.

But what if she was in trouble? What if she needed him?

Her words this morning had been confusing. "There's something I need to tell you, but now's not the time. Let's talk tomorrow. Meet me at the usual place?"

And he'd agreed. Her eyes had glistened as she'd spoken, and she'd turned her head away, as if what she had to tell him was somehow over-whelming, or too much for her to bear. He'd reached for her hand, but she'd run off, with only a tearful backward glance to sustain him until tomorrow.

And then this message.

"Can you meet tonight? Same place. 6:30 pm."

Why had she changed her mind and brought their meeting forward? What did she want to tell him that couldn't wait?

His heart hammered as he waited in the shadow of the massive excavator. Its dirty yellow claw dangled above him, silent and menacing in the hazy half-light of dusk. The construction site was deserted. The workers had finished their shift for the day and were already in their barracks, or out on the town.

The ground beneath him was dusty from the dry weather, coating his boots with a fine red powder. Soon the leaves would turn, painting the landscape in bronze, gold, and copper. Fall was his favorite time of year. There was a sliver of a moon rising, but it didn't offer much in the way of light.

The excavator was one of many machines, all lined up ready for the next day's work. The construction site was vast, a huge stretch of land running from the foothills of the mountains to the Southern Ute Reservation, where he lived.

Billy Nighthawk, the ex-chief of police on the reservation, had told him this was sacred land that used to belong to the Ute. Before Billy had died, he'd tried to lobby the government to return it to the Ute people, but his pleas had fallen on deaf ears.

Instead, the land had been sold to a developer from Denver, and the sacred ground would soon house a shopping center and accommodation for the expanding population of Hawk's Landing. Right now, however, it simply looked like an excavation site. The ground was pockmarked with gaping holes and punctured with metal pylons. Ropes crisscrossed the site, demarcating the planning areas. In some places, the holes had been filled with concrete and smoothed over. A band aid on a scar that would never heal.

He'd written about it in *The Drum*, the tribal newspaper that he worked for. Eddie loved writing, much to his grandparents' bewilderment. They were old-school. His grandfather had worked in a hardware store his whole life, while his grandmother taught the local preschool kids how to read and write. She was smart, but not worldly. When he'd been orphaned, they'd taken him in and raised him as their own. Despite his difficult start in life, he'd had a loving home and a good education.

It was here, in one of these cordoned-off areas, that he was supposed to meet *her*. The foundation had been laid and was hardening, although it still felt wet when he put his foot on it. That much cement took a long time to dry.

A rustling sound behind the machines made him swing around, but there was nobody there. He called her name, his voice measured, not too loud, but not so soft she wouldn't hear him.

Yet he got no reply.

Then he saw it. A dim glimmer of light on the other side of the concrete rectangle. It wasn't moving, just flickering in one spot like a hovering firefly. It must have been her.

Eddie took off, rounding the concrete slab, his breath shallow with anticipation. He waved, but the motion was swallowed up by the encroaching darkness. The fluttering light didn't waver. He rounded the concrete slab and headed down the final stretch toward the light.

There was a figure there, holding what looked like a candle. It was hard to make out who, but the shape looked larger, heavier than hers. Frowning, he picked up the pace. "Hello?"

The figure disappeared into the tree line. He sped up, breaking into a run. "Hey, wait."

Something snared his ankle, and he fell forward, sprawling onto his hands and knees.

"What the—?"

Eddie glanced down and saw a fine length of string stretched across the ground. It ran from a metal pylon to a tree several feet away. A tripwire.

He sensed the shadow loom over him. The person's silhouette blocked the stars. Swiveling, Eddie gasped. "You!"

The man glared down at him. "Hello Eddie."

Eddie looked around, trying to find her. Where had the flickering candle gone?

"She's not here," the man said.

"What?" Eddie looked up. The man was holding something in his hand. Was it a gun? No, it wasn't big enough. "Where is she? What have you done with her?"

"Nothing. It's you I'm here to see."

"I—I don't understand." The message. The request. Had it been a con?

"I sent that text message," the man said, as if reading his mind.

A cold chill descended over Eddie. "Why?"

"I wanted to talk to you."

"About the protest? I'm afraid you're too late. We'll be back tomorrow, and the day after that, and the day after that. You can't stop us. What's happening here isn't right."

"I don't care about the protesting," the man scoffed. "Do you really think all that prancing about is going to change anything? If you do, you're more stupid than I thought."

The look on the man's face made Eddie's blood boil. Anger rose up to choke him. "This is sacred ground!"

"Was. It now belongs to the corporation."

The man came closer. Eddie kicked out, but he wasn't fast enough. The man sat down on his legs, rendering them useless.

"Get off me!" Eddie yelled, thrashing about.

"Steady." The man was too strong, too big. His weight made it impossible to move.

Eddie tried wriggling out, instead feeling the hard, pebbly ground graze his calves. He was going nowhere. "What are you doing?" he spluttered.

"Isn't it obvious? She told me, you know. I made her. You know too much."

"I don't know what you mean," Eddie whimpered.

The man's face was contorted like he'd tasted something bad. With his one free arm, he held Eddie back in a semi-reclining position. He couldn't sit up but lying down wasn't an option either. He was helpless.

"She told you everything, silly bitch. So now I have to silence you."

"Told me what?" Then Eddie thought about what she'd said.

There's something I need to tell you.

"No, you're wrong. I don't know anything."

"Liar."

It was a syringe. Eddie couldn't make out what was inside. Whatever it was, it wasn't good.

The man held it up, getting ready to plunge.

"What is that?" Eddie blurted out. "What are you doing?"

"Relax," the man said. "You may as well enjoy the ride."

"I don't—"

The man grasped his left arm, pulling him in. Eddie fought to push him off, his right hand palming the man in the face. His assailant grunted, turning his head, but the needle kept coming. Eddie tried to smack it out of his hand. It fell to the ground. Growling, the man picked it up and lashed out. Eddie blinked as a blow to the head stunned him. His vision blurred.

"Stop moving," the man hissed.

Eddie fought harder. "No, stop it. You don't have to do this."

"Oh, I do. It's the only way to keep it from coming out."

"Keep what from coming out?" Then he knew. The realization shot through his body like electricity. His eyes widened.

"You do know," the man said.

The needle came down, plunging into the inside of his arm. A burning liquid shot into his bloodstream. Eddie cried out.

Soon, a river of euphoria washed over him, a tingling, then a rush of adrenaline unlike anything he'd ever known. His eyes rolled back in his head, his heart pounded like a jackhammer. He was afraid it would burst right out of his chest.

He began shaking uncontrollably. The man's weight left him and he was floating, drifting on the air currents like the bald eagle he'd watched that morning. The stars twisted into a cosmic mash-up of flickering lights, which then exploded inside his head.

He groaned as it consumed him. He was a leaf in a tornado, swirling around, and there was no way to stop it. He rode the whirlwind and felt his touch with reality lessening with every ripple, every wave of euphoria. Finally, he couldn't handle it anymore. The stars began to fade, his vision went black.

Nausea engulfed him and he gagged. His whole body convulsed, but he was powerless to stop it. It didn't last long. A few final spasms and he began drifting again. This time it was quieter, more peaceful. He was a leaf on the creek now, drifting with the flow of the current.

He took one final breath, and let it wash him away.

TWO

SHERIFF DALTON SAVAGE surveyed the footprint in the drying concrete. "This belong to the victim?"

"Yeah," answered James Thorpe, one of his newest deputies, who'd arrived first at the scene. "He's lying on the other side of the slab there, but this is his print."

The foreman, a beefy guy by the name of Angus Harmon, had discovered the body shortly after sunrise and called it in. Savage had gotten here after Thorpe, followed by Sinclair. They'd all come from home, given the early hour. The cacophony of sirens had woken most of the builders who lived in barracks on the construction site, and who now clustered around, talking in low voices.

It was easier that way, the foreman had told Savage. It kept them out of town and away from the bars. Instead, they frequented Zeb's girls at the nearby trailer park and drank at Mac's Roadhouse, a rowdy biker bar not far from here. In Savage's opinion, this wasn't the better option.

"Can we get these guys out of here?" he said to Harmon, trying unsuccessfully to hold the builders back. "They're contaminating the scene." Dozens of pairs of heavy boots were churning up dust from the dry ground, obliterating everything.

Savage turned to Thorpe. "You think he tried to cross the concrete, then realized it was wet and went around?"

"It's possible." Thorpe pushed his glasses up his nose. A Tennessee native, he'd transferred to Hawk's Landing Sheriff's Department nearly a year ago and had become an invaluable member of Savage's rookie team. Thorough and meticulous, he wasn't the type to commit to a theory unless he was certain. It was one thing Savage liked about him.

Another was his mettle. Back in the spring, when a local girl had gone missing in the mountains, Thorpe had proven he had what it took to get her back, despite his lack of field experience. "I can't think of another reason his print would be here."

Savage squinted across the slab at the figure lying on the other side. The young man's body was unnaturally still. Something was wrong. His bright yellow T-shirt stood out like a beacon against the dry dirt and the backdrop of green trees, beckoning Savage.

There was a loud cry followed by a gaggle of young voices as a group of long-haired youths descended on the crime scene. The protesters had arrived.

Bad news sure traveled fast.

"Is it him?" asked a shrill voice, while another cried, "Oh my God. That's his T-shirt. It is Eddie."

A shocked murmur, and then someone began sobbing.

"Is he dead?" asked another voice.

Savage gestured to Sinclair. "Get their names and contact details. I want to talk to everybody here, including the laborers." She nodded, then gestured to the foreman to help her set up a cordon. It would have to be big, spanning this entire section of the site, as well as the other side of the concrete foundation, which was the size of a basketball court.

Savage and Thorpe trudged around the cemented zone, their boots crunching on the gravelly ground. They skirted a large excavator, its boom paused in the air, waiting to get back to work. Fragmented sunlight filtered through the treetops, dappling on the hardening ground. The soft light took the edge off the ugliness of the building site.

Several yards from the body stood a man Savage recognized as Tomahawk Winter. Jet black hair, a slender build, and dark, probing eyes. Tomahawk, or Tommy as he was known to his friends, was a law enforcement officer for the tribal police, based in the Southern Ute Reservation half a mile south of here.

"Tomahawk." Savage greeted him.

Thorpe studied the stranger.

Tomahawk responded with a sullen nod.

"What are you doing here?" Savage asked, even though he knew. The victim was a Native American, probably from the reservation. That made it Tomahawk's business.

Savage bent down to take a closer look at the body. Young, early twenties, with what was once a handsome face, now had the waxy complexion of the dead. His eyes had rolled back in his head and stayed that way upon his death, giving him a zombie-like appearance. Unlike Tomahawk who wore his hair long, the victim had short, cropped hair in a modern style. He was dressed in jeans and sneakers with an Eco Warrior logo on his bright yellow T-shirt.

"You know him?"

"Eddie Youngblood." Tomahawk's haunted gaze moved from the victim to Savage. "He lives on the res." He cleared his throat, his voice tightening. "Lived."

Savage pulled a pair of latex gloves out of his pocket. This would complicate things. The Ute were already furious about the development. Hell, only last week the sheriff's department had been called out to break up a protest that got out of hand.

"Was he a protester?" Savage glanced up, pulling the gloves on. He noticed that Tomahawk also wore gloves. Had he touched the body?

The tribal officer gave a stiff nod. "Yeah, and a reporter. He was one of the more vocal protesters."

Savage looked across at the group of construction workers who Sinclair had managed to push back behind the police tape. Was one of them responsible? Had an altercation got out of hand?

There was a shout and a couple of the protesters surged forward. They were getting rowdy. He heard Sinclair yelling at them to stay back.

The group was growing in number. People from the reservation were arriving, joining the protesters. One of their own had died. This could get out of hand. They didn't have much time.

"Who's in charge?" Savage asked, knowing the tribal police officer would know.

"A guy called Kushner," said Tomahawk. "But he works for Douglas Connelly, the head of Apex Holdings. Connelly is not on site much. He prefers to work from his fancy hotel room outside of town. Kushner's here every day. He runs things."

Apex Holdings was the name of the property development company. "You seem to know a lot about what goes on here."

The young deputy sniffed. "It is my business to know. This is our land. It belonged to our ancestors."

Savage didn't disagree. Unfortunately, there was nothing he could do about that. He didn't make the rules, just enforced them.

"What's that around his mouth?" Savage leaned in closer.

"It looks like he's thrown up," said Thorpe.

Savage scanned the hard ground. No blood. Possibly some vomit. "Was he sick?"

There was a soft sigh, and Tomahawk held out a gloved hand. "I found this." In it was a used syringe with dark, amber liquid congealed at the bottom. It looked like heroin or methamphetamine. "It was among the trees, about twenty yards over there." He nodded behind his shoulder.

Savage stared at the syringe, then at the tree line. "You were going to show me this, right?"

"I just did."

Savage wasn't surprised the officer had cased the scene. The man was like a bloodhound, he could sniff out anything. Before he'd been a lawman, Tomahawk had been a tracker, a skill passed down from his father. Despite the new development, Hawk's Landing and its surroundings were still largely rural. Flanked by mountains and state forest, it boasted some of the best hiking trails in the county. It also meant that people who didn't want to be found could disappear into the hills, which was when Tomahawk's skills were really useful.

"Are you saying he OD'd?" Savage asked.

Tomahawk gave him a hard look. "Eddie did not do drugs. He was a good kid, if a little overzealous. I admired his passion." Sadness flashed across his swarthy features. "If this was used on him, it was not by choice."

Savage frowned. "He was murdered then?"

Thorpe took an evidence bag out of his backpack. "Maybe we can pull some prints off it," he said.

Tomahawk dropped the syringe into the bag. "Maybe."

Savage inspected the young man's arms. "This is the site of the injection. It certainly looks like he shot up."

"Why would he throw the syringe over there?" asked Thorpe.

"I don't know. Perhaps he didn't want anyone to know what he'd done. Maybe he just wanted to dispose of it. He wouldn't have expected to overdose."

"Or someone injected him to make it look like he'd OD'd," Tomahawk suggested.

Savage studied Tomahawk. "It's a possibility."

"The ME will be here shortly," Thorpe pointed out. "I called him as soon as I arrived. Maybe he can shed some light."

An owl, disturbed by the commotion, took off from among the trees and swooped low over the crime scene. Its haunting cry set Savage's teeth on edge. He saw Tomahawk glance up and frown. The Ute considered the owl a bad omen.

There was a crunch of tires and a black SUV glided to a stop behind the protesters, who huddled around the vehicle, shouting and banging on its doors. Savage could hear them thumping on the hood from way over here.

"That would be Douglas Connelly," murmured Tomahawk. "Boss of Apex Holdings."

Savage gestured to Thorpe. "We better get over there. Looks like it's about to kick off." He turned back to Tomahawk, but the tribal police officer had vanished into the forest.

Thorpe gave an uncertain nod. "Who was that guy?"

"Tribal police. The Southern Ute Reservation land borders the construction site and extends south for nearly a thousand miles. Tomahawk is Billy Nighthawk's cousin."

Thorpe's eyes widened. "That explains a lot." Billy Nighthawk was the former Chief of Police for the reservation. He'd been killed by a couple of poachers a while back.

"Yeah. Tomahawk's a tracker too, and a damn good one. There aren't many people he can't find."

Thorpe raised his eyebrows. "Pity he doesn't work for us."

"I asked him once, but his duty is to the Ute."

They got back to the SUV where two men in suits were talking to Sinclair, while a third, a big bastard towering above everyone else, was speaking to the foreman and construction workers. Savage put the suits in their forties, but while one had brown hair graying at the temples and an arrogant, forthright gaze, the other was taller, thinner, and wore glasses. The giant was just the muscle. It wasn't hard to see who was in charge.

"Mr. Connelly?" Savage extended his hand to the first man, whose eyes dropped to the star on his hip.

"Sheriff Savage, I presume." Connelly's grip was firm and authoritative.

"That's right."

"What the hell is going on here?" Connelly demanded. "My foreman has informed me a body's been found on my land."

My foreman. My land. This man liked to claim his ownership, all right.

"Sadly, yes. The medical examiner is on his way."

Connelly frowned. "How soon can you get him off my construction site? It's holding up our schedule."

No, 'who is he?' 'Was he one of my crew?' 'How did he die?'

That told Savage two things. One, Connelly already knew that the dead man wasn't one of his employees, and two, he was a narcissistic asshole only interested in keeping to his precious schedule.

"That I can't say," Savage said, unwilling to appease this guy. "As long as it takes."

Connelly ran a frustrated hand through his hair.

"You're going to have to shut down the site," Savage added. "This is now an active crime scene."

"What?" Connelly exploded. "That's impossible. We have deadlines. We can't shut down the site just because—" He stopped.

"Just because a young man has died here?" finished Savage, shooting him a black look.

The other suit put an effeminate hand on his boss's arm. "Let me handle this, Douglas."

The boss scowled at Savage, then gave a curt nod.

"Does it have to be the entire site?" Connelly's sidekick asked, in a clipped, east coast accent.

"Yes, it does." Savage was fast losing patience. Connelly might be able to boss people around in his own company, but the crime scene was Savage's turf. The same rules didn't apply. "I'm afraid it's the law."

"Of course, if that's what you have to do. Do we know how long it's going to take?"

"A day or two."

The thin man nodded and turned to Connelly. "A day's not going to hurt us much. Let's let the Sheriff do his job and hopefully we'll be up and running by tomorrow."

"Thank you." Savage studied the thinner man. At least someone had some sense. Sandy colored hair, intense pale blue eyes, and a hawk-like nose, he seemed intelligent. "You are?"

"Steven Bryant." He held out a manicured hand. "I'm the Chief Financial Officer on this project." That explained the fancy accent.

The hulk didn't introduce himself. He just stood there, scowling.

More crunching tires and a battered Ford Taurus station wagon that had to have been built in the late 80s wheezed to a stop. This time it was the medical examiner Ray and his wife Pearl, a forensic expert. Originally from Denver, they'd moved to Hawk's Landing earlier that year in search of a quieter life. So far, they hadn't had much luck.

"Morning Ray. Pearl." Savage had first worked with them earlier in the year when a member of the Crimson Angels motorcycle gang had turned up dead in a parking lot out on the Durango Road. "Sorry to bring you out here so early."

"It's our job." Ray shook hands with Thorpe and Sinclair, then his gaze turned to Connelly and Bryant.

"Douglas Connelly, Apex Holdings," the construction boss said, stepping forward. "I'm in charge of the building project. This is my Finance Officer, Steven Bryant." They briefly shook hands, while Pearl got her forensic kit out of the trunk. She was already dressed in protective coverings, including latex gloves, so didn't shake hands.

"Which way is the body?" she asked.

"Over there." Thorpe gestured to the other side of the cement foundation. "I'll take you around." They followed him, their white paper suits bright against the drab background of the building site.

"I'm going to need a list of everyone who works for you," Savage told Connelly, whose forthright gaze followed the forensic experts as they walked toward the body of Eddie Youngblood. "That includes permanent and temporary staff, contractors, and anyone who had access to this site."

"Why? The kid was a drug addict," Connelly said.

It seemed the foreman had taken a very good look at the body before he'd reported back to his boss. The needle mark wasn't obvious, although the vomit may have given it away.

"He wasn't," Savage corrected.

Connelly frowned. "What do you mean? I was told he'd OD'd."

"Who told you that?"

"Well, uh, my foreman found the body. He reported back to me."

"Is your foreman a medical professional?" Savage asked.

Another scowl. "No, of course not."

"Then perhaps you'd better let the ME decide the cause of death before you jump to conclusions."

Connelly made a frustrated sound at the back of his throat. "Okay, you've made your point. Can we go now?"

"Yes, you can go, but don't leave town."

The sharp gaze tightened. "You suspect foul play?"

"Like I said, we're waiting for the ME to report back. It's just a precaution."

"Well, rest assured, Sheriff, I'm not going anywhere. Not until this development is finished."

Good. At least he knew where to find him.

"We'll get that list of names to you as soon as possible," Bryant said.

Savage gave a curt nod. "In the meantime, send your men back to the barracks. This site is off limits."

THREE

"EDDIE YOUNGBLOOD WAS a passionate activist against the new development," Littleton said. The youngest member of the team, Littleton, was as green as they came, but he was learning. And what he lacked in experience, he made up for in enthusiasm. "He wrote a feature length article on it in *The Drum*, the tribal newspaper. In it, he said they wouldn't stop shouting until someone listened."

"Maybe someone decided to silence him?" suggested Sinclair, stretching her neck. She'd had a stressful morning controlling not only the laborers, but also the protesters. In the end, they'd had to threaten the angry group with arrest if they didn't disperse. Feelings were running high after Eddie's death. His friends and family were demanding to know what had happened to him. How had he died? But Savage couldn't give them any answers. Not yet.

"I made some coffee," Barbara announced, walking in with a tray of steaming mugs. "Thought you might need it." Barbara White was the Hawk's Landing Sheriff office's receptionist, but she treated them like her own children.

"Thanks Barbara." Savage reached for a cup.

"You're a star." Sinclair took a grateful sip.

Thorpe smiled his thanks.

"Our forensic expert thinks the drug was administered by someone else." Savage outlined his conversation with Pearl at the potential crime scene. "I agree with her. The needle missed his vein and hit muscle in his arm. Then the syringe was thrown into the woods, as if the user didn't want it to be found."

"Drug addicts will inject anywhere," Sinclair pointed out. "Maybe he missed it."

"Agreed, except according to those that knew him, Eddie Youngblood wasn't an addict."

"There's always a first time," Littleton said.

"True. If he were an amateur, he may have missed the vein." Thorpe gripped his coffee mug. "That could also explain the adverse reaction."

"It's possible," Savage agreed. "But why toss the syringe into the trees? Don't you think that's suspicious?"

There was silence as they all contemplated this.

"What was in the syringe?" Sinclair asked.

"Ray thinks it was crank," Savage said, "but he's going to get it analyzed."

She scrunched up her forehead. "Would that kill him?"

"It might, if it was a large enough dose and he wasn't used to it."

"Poor guy," she muttered.

"Tomahawk Winter found the syringe discarded in the woods behind the construction site," Savage told them, after a pause.

Barbara glanced up, her arms full of printer paper as she crossed the office. "Tomahawk from the reservation?"

"Yeah, he was on the scene before we were. He knew the victim well, apparently."

"Shouldn't we question him?" asked Littleton. "He might have seen something."

"Eddie was dead before Tomahawk got there," Savage informed him. "He heard about the body, so went looking."

"How do we know he was dead before Tomahawk got there?" Thorpe asked. "We only have Tomahawk's word for it."

"Tomahawk's a member of the tribal police," Savage said. "He wouldn't lie about this."

"Still, I think Littleton's right. We should question him."

Savage gave a brief nod. Even though he was sure Tomahawk wasn't involved, his team was right.

"I'll call him," Savage said. "See if we can stop by. Right now, we'd better notify Eddie's next of kin."

"Eddie lived with his grandparents." Littleton looked up from his screen. "I have no record of his biological parents."

"Then that's where we'll go. Got an address?"

Littleton nodded. "Sent it to your phone."

"Great." He glanced at Thorpe. "You ready?"

Thorpe got to his feet. "Yeah."

"Let's go."

————

EDDIE'S GRANDPARENTS lived on the reservation in a town called Ignacio, a forty-minute drive from Hawk's Landing. The unassuming yellow house sat behind a flimsy, chain-link fence that looked like it had fallen over a couple of times. The few trees in the front yard had turned a golden yellow and were already starting to lose their leaves.

"Fall is on the way," Savage muttered.

Thorpe pressed the buzzer next to the door. A woman in her sixties opened it, then turned away when she saw the two law enforcement officers standing there.

"Ma'am?" Savage said.

She kept walking. "If you've come to tell me about my grandson, I already know. My husband was at the building site this morning."

"I'm sorry for your loss," Savage said. "Do you mind if we come in?"

She got to the middle of the hall and turned around. "What happened to Eddie?"

Savage felt her pain. He hated these visits. It was the worst part of the job. But it was also important not to get caught up in the emotion of the moment and try to maintain a cool head. The majority of murders were committed by people who knew the victim, including friends and family, although Savage doubted that was the case here.

The elderly woman hovered in the doorway, almost ethereal with her long, white hair and pale dress. Her eyes were cloudy, like a mist had moved in front of them.

"We don't know yet, Mrs. Youngblood. That's what we're trying to find out."

Her shoulders slumped, and she teetered up the hallway. "Mrs. Youngblood, did you know Eddie wasn't here last night?"

She turned in the doorway, a hollow look in her eyes. "Yes, of course we knew. He went to meet that girl."

"Girl? Which girl?" Savage shot Thorpe an inquiring look, but his deputy just shrugged. Nobody had mentioned a girl. "A girlfriend?"

But Mrs. Youngblood carried on as if he hadn't spoken. "I always thought she was bad news... a father like that... what they're doing to the land. Eddie was determined to stop them. Oh, God—" she cried softly, tears running down her lined face.

Thorpe looked at Savage who held up a hand as if to say, let's give her a moment.

Finally, she sniffed and dabbed her eyes with a tissue from a pocket in her dress. "Is that how he died? Was it something to do with the protesting?"

"We're not sure," Savage said. "He was found on the construction site, but it might not be related."

Her eyes hardened. "Of course it's related. One of them killed him. They must have. Why else would he have died there?"

That was the question Savage was trying to find an answer to. "Mrs. Youngblood, I'm sorry to have to ask this, but did Eddie ever do drugs?"

"What?" She froze, stunned. "No. He hated them."

"You're sure about that?"

"I'm positive. His mother... Well, she had issues with drugs. There's no way he'd touch them." That's what Tomahawk had said too.

Savage steered the conversation back to the girl. "Who was he going to meet?"

"That property developer's daughter. Celeste—no, that's not it. Celine. She was always messaging him."

"Were they in a relationship?" Savage asked. He wondered if Douglas Connelly knew. Perhaps there were reasons other than the protest for the property developer to want Eddie gone.

"I don't know. Eddie said not, but it sure didn't seem like that to me."

"Would you mind if we took a look at his room?" he asked.

Sniffing, she gave a sad nod. "It's down the hall to the right."

Savage got up.

"He was such a good boy. So clever—" Eddie's grandmother started crying again.

"We're so sorry for your loss," Thorpe repeated, as he got to his feet to follow Savage.

All he got was a nod in response.

"I feel so bad for her," Thorpe murmured, as they opened the door to Eddie's bedroom.

"It's never easy." Savage focused on the room. If he kept thinking like a detective, he wouldn't have to think like a human being. Mrs. Young-blood's pain was palpable, and he seethed at the killer who'd brought this heartache on her family.

Eddie's room was indicative of a boy becoming a man. At nineteen, Eddie had finished school and just started his job at the newspaper. His bedroom was neat and uncluttered but contained a couple of throw-backs to his teens. A compact disc player sat on a shelf next to a leaning pile of CDs. Mostly rock from what Savage could make out. There was a lacrosse stick in the corner with a ball beside it, and several pairs of sneakers.

"Look at this." Thorpe pointed to the poster on the wall.

"Green Peace," read Savage, then his eyes dropped to the ancient computer on the desk. It was covered in eco-warrior stickers. *Save the planet. Zero waste. Save our land. Think green.*

"He was definitely an activist," Thorpe acknowledged.

Savage looked in the wardrobe but couldn't find anything unusual. "There's nothing here. Let's get back to Hawk's Landing."

"You want to swing by Tomahawk Winter's place?" Thorpe enquired. Savage was impressed he hadn't forgotten about that.

"Yeah, he'll be at the police department, but they won't like us rolling up unannounced."

Thorpe shot him a sideways glance. "Since when has that ever stopped you?"

"Relations aren't great between us and the tribal police," he told Thorpe. "They don't like us interfering in their affairs, and the death of one of their own will qualify."

"He was murdered in Hawk's Landing," Thorpe said.

"I know." Savage sighed. "That complicates matters. But you're right. Tomahawk might be able to tell us a little more about Eddie's relationship with Connelly's daughter."

FOUR

THE SOUTHERN UTE POLICE DEPARTMENT was a wide, flat brick building on the western side of Ignacio with a low, slate-gray roof that gleamed in the mid-afternoon sun. The grass sloping down to the street was brown and sparse, resulting from the combination of hot summers and icy winters. Not to mention, they had no money for landscaping. No trees, shrubs, or potted plants decorated the exterior, just a straight concrete path leading up to the front door.

"It's bigger than I thought," murmured Thorpe, assessing the squat structure as they pulled up in Savage's Chevy Suburban.

"Yeah, they rebuilt it after a fire a couple of years back. It's a sizable police force, but they cover over six hundred thousand acres of South-western Colorado. They need all the help they can get."

They got out of the SUV and headed up the path. Before they could get to the door, it swung open and a large man with long, flowing gray hair stepped out. He had a pockmarked, round face and arched eyebrows that gave him a stern expression. "What can I do for you, Sheriff?"

"Chief Ouray, this is my deputy, James Thorpe."

Thorpe nodded at the robust police chief who was barring them from entering his police station. The chief didn't nod back.

"We need to talk to Tomahawk about Eddie Youngblood."

"Why? He already spoke to you at the crime scene. You have no business here."

"We need an official statement."

The big man's mouth set into a straight line, and he looked like he might refuse. Beside him, Savage felt Thorpe bristle as Tomahawk appeared in the doorway.

"Sheriff Savage, what a surprise. Twice in one day."

"Thought we'd save you the trouble of having to come to us." Savage held his ground.

"What for?" asked Tomahawk politely.

"Your statement," Savage explained. "You were one of the first people at the crime scene and you found the syringe. I can't record that without an official statement." He hesitated. "You know that."

Tomahawk sighed. "Fair enough. Let's go inside." He turned on his heel and marched back into the building.

The chief scowled at them. "Tomahawk had nothing to do with Eddie Youngblood's death."

"We're not saying he did."

"My officer was good enough to hand over the syringe, even though Eddie was one of us."

"He wasn't murdered on Ute land," Savage pointed out.

The Chief grunted. "I know." He swiveled fast for such a large man and followed Tomahawk into the station.

"Come on," Savage said to Thorpe. "Let's get this over with before they change their minds."

Inside, the SUPD was similar to the outside. Functional but stark, containing a little more than the basics. The walls were bare, save for the community notices and a missing persons board. Haunted faces stared down at them from yellowing posters.

The chief's office was situated at one end, the reception at the other, and in between was a wide, open-plan squad room where several officers worked. There was a gentle hum of machines, the sound of fingers on keyboards, and the occasional cough of the printer spitting out a document.

"Take a seat." Tomahawk gestured to a worn, four-seater table. The chief shot them a disapproving look and went into his office.

Savage spoke first. "Tomahawk, how did you first find out about Eddie's body?"

"I did not know it was Eddie," he began, his forehead furrowed. "All I knew was that the body of a Native American had been found on the building site, so I thought I had better check it out."

"Were you surprised to find it was Eddie?"

"Yes, I was. I knew he had been there protesting, but it was nothing to get himself killed over." Savage saw a flash of pain register in the other man's eyes, indicating he'd been fond of the boy.

"How often did they protest?" Savage asked.

"Every day, pretty much. I have already told you that it is Ute land. When Eddie was not there, he was writing about it or lobbying the local government."

"Was it effective?" Savage asked.

"No. They didn't listen. That land has been sold off. Nothing we can do about it." The grief was replaced by a flash of anger.

"Who told you that a body had been found?" Savage asked.

"Word spreads fast around here."

"Very fast. You got there before us, and we arrived pretty soon after it was called in."

Tomahawk pursed his lips. "I got a call from a concerned parent. Her son told her that he and his friends had seen a dead body at the construction site."

"What time was this?"

"First thing this morning, but the kids were there last night."

Savage nodded. The ME had backed that up. Time of death had been the day before, between the hours of six and eight p.m.

"I have spoken to them," Tomahawk said. "They do not know any more than what I already told you."

"I'm sure you're right. We'd still like their names and addresses though. One of my deputies will have to speak to them to verify their story."

Tomahawk wrote the information down on a piece of paper and handed it over, although he wasn't happy about it.

Once that was out of the way, Savage asked him a couple of questions about Eddie's relationship with Connelly's daughter.

"Her name is Celine and I do not think they were dating," Tomahawk admitted. "I know he liked her, but I didn't think his feelings were reciprocated."

"His grandmother seemed to think they were."

Tomahawk shrugged. "She'd know better than me."

Savage doubted that. Tomahawk and Eddie were friends. Only a couple of years apart in age, they both lived on the res, not far from each other. If anyone knew about Eddie's love life, it would be Tomahawk, not his aging grandparents.

"How did they meet?" Savage asked.

A shrug. "Eddie didn't say."

"Where is Celine staying?" Savage asked, although he could guess.

"That fancy hotel outside Hawk's Landing. Apparently, the company has booked out a couple of suites."

Savage nodded. That didn't surprise him. Boulder's Creek was the best hotel in town. "Why is she here with her father and not with her mother or at school?"

"The mother is not around. I do not know why. The girl is doing online schooling. Eddie told me she is trying to get into some Ivy League college. That is all I know."

Savage glanced at Thorpe. "We need to speak to Celine."

"If that's all?"—Tomahawk placed his hands on the table as if to get up. "I've got work to do."

Savage took the hint and got to his feet. "Thanks for your time, Tomahawk. We'll see ourselves out."

. . .

25

SAVAGE'S PHONE rang as he got back into his car. It was Ray, the medical examiner.

"Hi Ray. What have you got for me?"

"I haven't done the autopsy yet," the ME said, "but I do have some information for you. Pearl ran the liquid in the syringe through her mass spectrometer and we can confirm it is crystal meth. She also ran it through the FDA's drug database and got a hit. It's a new drug, pretty potent. The street name is Pink Soda."

"I've heard of that," Savage said, wracking his brains. "Didn't they issue a health warning about it?"

"That's right. It's killing kids in the big cities. Lethal stuff."

"And now it's in Hawk's Landing."

"Seems that way."

"Thanks Ray. Appreciate it."

"What did he say?" asked Thorpe, getting in the passenger seat as Savage hung up the phone.

Savage repeated what Ray had said about the Pink Soda.

"How on earth did it end up here?" Thorpe asked.

Savage raised an eyebrow. "Know anyone from the big city who's come into town recently?"

"Connelly?"

"Bingo."

FIVE

"WHERE IS THIS PLACE?" Thorpe asked as they followed a winding mountain road out of town. On either side, the trees were shading to burnished orange and gold.

"Not far from here." Savage navigated the meanders with ease. In his over two years in Hawk's Landing, he'd gotten to know the roads around here pretty well. "Will you get ahold of Sinclair? Ask her to talk to those kids who told Tomahawk about the body. And ask her to check out the list of workers that the foreman sent through. We need to run them through the police database. See if any of them have priors."

"Littleton's got the names of the crew members," Thorpe said. "The foreman sent them through. He's checking them out now. Problem is, they're mostly from out of town."

"Run them through," Savage replied.

"This must be it," Thorpe said as they pulled up in front of a sprawling, rustic lodge. Set against the backdrop of the mountain, the hotel was secluded by state forest.

They pushed open the large oak door and went inside. The fresh-faced receptionist smiled up at them. "How may I help you, gentlemen?"

Savage flashed his badge and watched her smile falter. "Is something wrong, Sheriff?"

"No, but we'd like a word with Mr. Connelly, please. I believe he's staying here."

"Of course. If you'll wait in the Saloon Bar, I'll contact him for you."

"Where's that?"

She pointed across the lobby. "Behind you, through the glass doors."

Savage nodded but didn't move. He waited as the receptionist placed the call. "Yes, they're here now. Okay, I'll let them know."

She gave a watery smile. "He's on his way down."

"Thank you," he said as she put the phone down.

They crossed the lobby and walked through a pair of swing doors into an upmarket Wild West-themed saloon complete with wood paneling, high bar stools, and a baby grand piano in the corner.

"Nice," murmured Thorpe, gazing around.

They took a seat and waited for Connelly to arrive. When he did, it was with an air of annoyance. "Sheriff. Deputy." He gave them a brief nod. "I was in the middle of a meeting. Do you have any news?"

"Only that it was a drug-related death."

He exhaled. "See, what did I tell you? The kid's a junkie. Can we get back to work tomorrow? We're already behind schedule. I've got—"

"We're treating his death as suspicious," Savage interjected.

"What?" Connelly raked a hand through his thinning hair. "You've got to be kidding me." It was clear the man was stressed. Fine lines dented the sides of his eyes, and the muscles in his neck and shoulders were tense.

"I'm afraid not. So, I'm going to have to ask you a couple of questions, okay?"

Connelly huffed and puffed, then threw his hands in the air and sat down next to them. "If you must."

"Your foreman sent over a list of names," Savage said.

"Yeah, like you asked."

"I've seen that list," Savage continued. "There aren't many local boys on it."

Connelly shrugged. "Construction is a transient workforce. People come and go. We get all types. Drifters, foreigners, those down on their luck, you name it."

"What about illegals?" Savage asked. There was the possibility that some names weren't on that list because they weren't meant to be here. He wouldn't put it past someone like Connelly to hire men off the books and pay them cheap. It's not like they would ever go to the authorities and complain.

"Not when I hire them." Connelly scowled. "My staff are thoroughly vetted, Sheriff, and I don't like your insinuation. We run an honest business."

"Glad to hear it. Had any problems on site with drugs?"

"Drugs? Are you suggesting one of my crew was responsible for this boy's death?"

"The victim had an unusual drug in his system," Savage said carefully. "It's a new drug, just come on the party scene. We haven't had a case of it here before."

"Well, they all get around eventually, don't they?" Connelly stared at Savage, frustrated.

"I suppose so, but the kid turned up dead on your building site."

"Well, I ain't had any problems with my men. They arrive on time, they work hard, and they go back to the barracks. My foreman would have told me if there were any drug problems."

"Mr. Connelly, did you know Eddie Youngblood?"

"The victim?"

Savage nodded.

"Not personally. I mean, I've seen him on site protesting a couple times."

"And what were you doing yesterday afternoon, around six o'clock?"

"Hey, now wait a minute."

"We're asking everyone who works on that site," Savage cut in. "If we know where you were, we can rule you out of the investigation."

He grunted but gave a surly nod. "I was in a meeting."

"Can anyone vouch for you?"

"Sure, Mr. Bryant can. He was on the call too, along with a group of gentlemen from Denver."

"If you could give my deputy their names?"

"Is that really necessary? These gentlemen are not going to be impressed when I tell them we've had to stop construction."

"I'm sorry to have to put you in that situation." Savage wasn't, really. The CEO's alibi had to be verified by someone other than his right-hand man.

Connolly sighed. "Fine."

"That rules out Bryant and Connelly," Thorpe said, once they left the saloon.

"I still want you to follow up with those gentlemen in Denver. Find out who they are and run a check on them. I want to know who Mr. Connelly is afraid of."

"Will do."

They walked outside into the fresh night air and nearly bumped into a young girl coming the other way. She was wearing leggings and a T-shirt, her earphones on. The thin layer of perspiration on her skin told him she'd been out for a jog.

"Excuse me, ma'am." Thorpe stepped out of the way.

She shot him an apologetic smile.

"Celine Connelly?" Savage said. The young woman had the same intense look as her father.

She stopped, removed one earphone. Her eyes darted from Thorpe to Savage, then flickered. "Do I know you?"

"Not yet. I'm Sheriff Savage and I'm investigating the death of Eddie Youngblood. I believe you knew him?"

She flinched. "Who told you that?"

"His grandparents."

"Oh right. Yes, we were friends."

Savage smiled reassuringly. "Could you tell me the last time you saw Eddie?"

He saw her lip tremor and knew she was more affected by his death than she let on. She played with the earphone in her hand, twisting the cord around her finger. "Yesterday morning. We had coffee together before he went out to the site."

"Your father's site?"

"Yeah, he was attending a protest there."

"How did you feel about that?"

Her face dropped. "I liked Eddie, but he was idealistic. He thought by protesting he could stop the development. I told him it was too late, that there was nothing he could do, but he wouldn't give up."

"Does your father know about Eddie?"

She dropped her gaze. The cord around her finger tightened. "There's nothing to know. We were just friends." Her voice shook a little.

Even if they were just friends, Celine was still shaken by his death.

"Do you know anyone who might want to harm Eddie?" Savage asked.

Her eyes widened. "Why? I thought he died of a drug overdose."

"Who told you that?"

"It's what everyone is saying."

"We don't know that for sure yet," Savage said carefully.

She stared at him, then her forest-green eyes grew wide. "Are you saying he was murdered?"

"There is a possibility, yes."

Her hand flew to her mouth. "Oh, my God."

"Celine, do you know of anyone who would want to—?"

"No, of course not. It's just so shocking to think that this could be deliberate." Savage got the feeling there was something she wasn't saying.

"Celine, if you know anything—"

"I don't, okay. I've got to go." And she took off into the hotel.

Savage looked at Thorpe. He trusted his deputy's intuition. "What do you think?"

"She's holding back."

"We'll give her a day or two, then talk to her again," Thorpe said. "In the meantime, let's see if Sinclair's managed to back up Tomahawk's story and follow up on those names the foreman sent over. You never know, something might jump out."

SIX

SAVAGE DIDN'T GO STRAIGHT HOME after work. Instead, he swung by the Hidden Gem trailer park. If drugs were coming into the county, there's one man who would know about it.

Zebadiah Swift.

Once a corrupt Denver cop—although he'd deny it until his last breath—Zeb was now the proud owner of the Hidden Gem trailer park. He was also friendly with several members of the Crimson Angels, an outlaw motorcycle gang who used Mac's Roadhouse on the Durango Road as their headquarters.

The trailer park was quiet as Savage drove in. The waning crescent moon had almost disappeared into the inky blackness, so the only light source came from the streetlamps at the entrance to the park and the warm, orange glow from a few trailer windows.

A raccoon scurried across the dirt track in front of him, its eyes luminous in the Suburban's headlights. Savage crawled along until he reached Zeb's yellow mobile home with the Harley-Davidson out front. He pulled over and cut the engine. Around the back, he could hear the muffled throb of house music reverberating.

Sighing, he got out of the SUV. Zeb was known to operate an informal brothel out of the three campervans parked on his property. Ignoring that for now, Savage walked up to the front door and pushed the doorbell.

Heavy footsteps on the wooden floor, and then the door opened.

"Jesus, if it ain't Dalton Savage." Zeb stood there in cargo pants and a black T-shirt with a heavy metal emblem on it. His hair was longer than the last time Savage had seen it, his beard thicker. "What the hell are you doing here?"

"Came to see my old friend," Savage replied.

A loud snort. "Now I know you're lying."

"Can we talk?" Savage looked past him into the house, hearing voices and laughter coming from the living room.

"Now's not a good time." Zeb glanced over his shoulder.

"It's good for me," Savage retorted.

Zeb ushered him in. "Okay, but for God's sake, don't let anyone see you. My clients would get pretty antsy if they knew the Sheriff was on the premises."

"I won't compromise your business." Savage rolled his eyes. While he didn't approve of Zeb's little side hustle, he'd opted to turn a blind eye. For now.

The sheriff's department wasn't popular in this part of the world, but Zeb was. If Savage shut him down, another operator would rise up in his place, allowing him even less control. Rather the devil you know was his philosophy as far as Zeb was concerned. And he knew Zeb pretty well.

"This way." Zeb gestured to follow into a study off the main hallway. It wasn't a room Savage had ever been in before. Surprisingly neat for Zeb, it had a large wooden desk, a computer, and a filing cabinet under the window which looked out on his precious motorcycle.

"How are things?" Savage asked.

"Can't complain. How about you?"

"Same."

Zeb had carved out a very nice niche for himself here in Hawk's

Landing. He might have been a crooked cop, but he certainly had a good head for business.

The shrewd eyes turned on him. "What did you want to talk about?"

Savage faced him. "There's a new drug in town, street name is Pink Soda. Know anything about that?"

Zeb stroked his beard. "I've heard of it. Isn't that a big city problem?"

"It's now a Hawk's Landing problem. Kid OD'd on the construction site yesterday."

"Shit, really? That's bad." For all Zeb's faults, he was still an ex-cop, and he didn't like drugs.

"Yeah. Any idea who's supplying?"

A pause.

"Zeb?"

The trailer park owner sighed. "You didn't hear this from me, okay?"

Savage raised his hands.

"Rumor has it the boys from Denver are moving in. Big shot mobster types who take no prisoners, if you get my drift. We dealt with a couple of those guys back in the day."

Savage remembered it well.

"Do you know who?"

"Nah, but talk is they want to take over the drug trade in the county. It's turning out to be a pretty lucrative business model."

"You'd know this because of the Crimson Angels?"

"I didn't say that."

Yeah, you did.

"Okay," Savage said, "so where are these big shots? They here already?"

"From what I hear, yeah. I don't know who they are though. You'd have to ask around in town."

Savage already knew of a couple Denver big shots who'd come to town. Were they involved in the drug trade too?

"Ever heard of a guy called Douglas Connelly?"

"Nah, I don't get out much."

Savage thought about the head of the Crimson Angels MC. "I'll bet Rosalie's not happy."

Zeb shrugged, but he looked worried. "It's not good, Dalton. These guys want the gang's Mexican connections. They're looking to take over the supply and distribution network in the county. Things could get ugly."

"Violent?"

"Sure. You know how these guys are."

Yeah, he did. Most of them had priors, all of them carried weapons. If things kicked off, it could turn ugly, fast.

"What about the distribution network? Who's running that?" He didn't think Rosalie and her gang were dealers. They just transported the product.

"You should know. This is your town, Sheriff." Savage didn't miss the mocking tone.

"That guy Kevin Handsome still selling out of his convenience store?"

Zeb chuckled. "Why are you asking me if you already know?"

A shrug. "Things change."

"Things *are* changing. But as far as I know, Kev's still the go-to guy in these parts."

"Got it."

"My advice is to stay out of this one," Zeb warned. "It's a war you can't win. These guys mean business."

"So do I," Savage said through gritted teeth. "This is my town. No one's going to shoot it up if I can help it."

Zeb gave a weary nod. "I thought you'd say that. Dalton Savage, always the boy scout." The ex-cop showed Savage to the door, careful to keep him out of sight. "Don't say I didn't warn you."

SEVEN

BECCA WAS STILL awake when Savage got home. "There you are. We were getting worried."

Placing his hand on her rounded belly, he smiled. At eight and a half months, his fiancée was nearing the end of her pregnancy. "Sorry to keep you up. How are you two doing?"

"We're good, but I won't lie, I'll be glad to get this last part over with." She eased herself down onto a chair in the kitchen. Becca, a psychiatrist, ran a facility for challenged youth in Pagosa Springs, an hour's drive from Hawk's Landing. Uncomfortable most of the time, she'd stopped working and was trying to take it easy. Doctors' orders.

"Not long now." He joined her at the table. As much as he was eager to meet the new addition to their family, he had to admit, he was also terrified. A baby. *His* baby.

That was huge. What kind of dad would he be?

Becca reached for his hand over the table, probably seeing his thoughts mirrored on his face. "It's going to be fine." Her voice was soft. "We're in this together, right?"

He nodded.

"I'm nervous too."

Savage was exalted. "Are you? You seem so together." Becca always took everything in her stride.

"I'm not." She laughed softly. "I'm excited, but I'm also nervous. I've never done this before."

He was relieved she was having the same thoughts as him. He squeezed her hand. "We'll figure it out together, then."

She gave a little nod. "I know we will. But Dalton—"

He raised an eyebrow. "Yeah?"

"I can't do this alone."

"I know."

"If there's one thing I'm asking of you, it's to be present. I need you to help me raise this baby."

"I will," he said. "Don't worry about that."

"I mean it. No unnecessary risks, okay? This baby needs a father."

"I won't take any unnecessary risks."

"You promise?"

"I promise."

"Okay." She smiled. "I made some dinner. It's on the stove."

His stomach rumbled loudly at the suggestion of food. "Great, I'm starving. It's been a long day."

He got up to dish up a plate for himself.

"Want to tell me about it?"

"Only if you want to hear."

"Please," she said. "I'm so bored hanging around the house. I think I've read every book I own at least twice."

He grimaced sympathetically. Like him, Becca hated to be inactive. "We found the body of a teenager on that new building development this morning. He'd been injected with crystal meth, a new kind that's coming in from the city."

She took on a pained expression. "That's awful. The Apex Holdings development?"

"Yeah, that's the one. You know anything about it?" Something in her voice told him she did.

"A friend's husband's company was bidding for that property, and he got shouldered out by the guys from Denver. Apparently, the council wanted to sell it to a local company, but then Apex sweetened the deal."

"Really? How?" This was news to him.

"I'm not entirely sure. My friend seemed to think someone at the council took a payout."

"They bribed a local councilor?"

"That's what I heard. I don't know whether it's true or not."

Savage frowned. "Who is this friend of yours?"

"A woman from my prenatal class. Her name's Yvonne."

"I'd like to speak with her husband."

Becca tilted her head to the side. "Sure. I can get his number for you." Her normally smooth forehead wrinkled. "Do you think the company is responsible for what happened to that boy?"

"It's one avenue we're looking into."

She exhaled. "Dalton, be careful. These guys could be dangerous. They bribed an official to purchase the land, and now someone has died on it. I don't like the sound of that."

Neither did he. "I will be, don't worry. But something shady is going on, and I want to find out what it is."

"Who was he? The boy who died?"

"A kid from the res." His gaze told her how serious it was.

"Not the group that was protesting?"

He nodded.

"That's not good." Her voice was a whisper. "You'll have the Ute on your back now too. That land is supposed to be theirs."

"I know. It's a volatile situation."

Her eyes bore into his. "You will be careful, won't you?"

He put down his knife and fork. "You know I will."

DESPITE THE PREVIOUS day's tension, Savage left for work with a smile on his face. It was a beautiful summer day, the kind that made everything seem brighter. Aside from that, he and Becca had spent some quality time talking about the baby and planning for the future. Life was good.

"What have we got?" he asked, walking into the Sheriff's office, after saying good morning to Barbara.

Sinclair looked up. "I spoke to those kids yesterday. Tomahawk was telling the truth. They were hanging out at the construction site last night when they saw the body and ran away. One of the boys told his mother early yesterday morning, and she called Tomahawk. That's how he ended up at the crime scene."

"What were they doing there?" Savage asked.

"They said they were hanging out, but I think they were smoking pot. I could smell it on them."

"Did they touch the body?"

"They say not. Once they got closer, they realized he was dead and took off."

"Okay, thanks." He turned to Littleton. "What about the construction crew?"

Littleton turned away from his computer. "I've been going through them one by one," he said. "I've found nothing, apart from one guy who did two years for assault back in 2016. You think he's worth following up?"

"Six years ago," Savage muttered. "Who is he?"

"Matteo Verona. I could call his old parole officer and ask for details."

"You do that. It's probably not related, but worth checking anyway."

Littleton nodded and picked up his phone to make the call. Savage sat down at his desk, smiling at Barbara as she came over with a cup of coffee. "You're a star, Barb."

"How's Becca?" she asked.

"Hanging in there."

The motherly receptionist patted him on the shoulder, before walking back to her desk in the lobby.

Littleton was saying, "Really? Thanks for letting me know."

"What?" Savage asked once he'd hung up.

The deputy's cheeks were flushed. "Turns out Verona has a history of drug dealing. The person he beat to a pulp was a user who tried to fleece him."

Savage jumped up. "I think we'd better go have a talk with Matteo Verona. Good work, Littleton. Thorpe, you with me?"

Thorpe, who'd just sat down at his desk, stood up again. He hadn't even taken off his jacket. "I'm ready," he said. "Let's go."

EIGHT

THE BARRACKS WERE NESTLED at the foot of the mountains, overlooking the building site with its exposed earth, concrete foundations and dirty machinery. Beyond the building project, the countryside stretched uninterrupted for miles. Parts of it were sunken in shadow like mauve dimples in the landscape, while others were already drizzled in honey-colored sunshine.

Savage knocked on Matteo Verona's front door.

A half-dressed man came to the door. "Yeah?"

He scowled at them, bare chested. Six foot two inches, two hundred and twenty pounds and a chest of pure muscle.

"Mr. Verona, I'm Sheriff Savage." He pulled himself to his full height and opened his jacket to show his star. "This is Deputy Thorpe. Would you mind putting on a shirt so we can talk?"

The man's gaze fell to Savage's pocket, then he gave a gruff nod and grabbed a shirt lying over the back of the table. "This about that kid?"

"Yeah, did you know him?"

"Nope. I ain't from here."

Savage looked around the room. It was basic with not much more than a bed, a sink, and a countertop containing a kettle and microwave. "Where you from?"

"New York State." He rubbed one eye. Judging by the crumpled bed, he'd just woken up. His defenses were still down.

"What brings you to these parts?" Thorpe asked.

"Work." A slight hesitation. "And I needed a change of scene."

"Yeah?" The deputy raised an eyebrow. There was only a small table with two chairs, so they didn't sit down.

"Yeah." Verona didn't elaborate.

"That change have anything to do with your parole?" Savage prompted.

The man gave him a hard stare. "There's nothing wrong with wanting a fresh start."

"Didn't say there was."

There was a pause. Verona crossed his arms over his barrel chest. "I didn't have anything to do with that kid's death."

"Why do you say that?"

"That's why you're here, isn't it? Because the kid OD'd and I've got a record."

"For dealing," Savage clarified.

The man's lips morphed together in a straight line. "That was a while back. I don't do that anymore. As you can see, I've got gainful employment."

"Then you won't mind if my deputy has a quick look around?" Savage handed him the search warrant. It hadn't been hard to get, considering the guy was an ex-con on a building site where a kid had been killed.

Verona said nothing as Thorpe searched the room. It didn't take long, being so small.

"Did you sell drugs to Eddie Youngblood?" Savage watched the man's face.

He threw up his arms, his brow creased with frustration. "Hell, no. I didn't sell drugs to no one." Savage studied him. The guy had an open stance. He wasn't apprehensive, no anxiety on his face other than the indignant attitude of someone whose privacy had been interrupted.

Thorpe finished searching the room. "Nothing."

"I told you."

Savage gave a firm nod. "Sorry to have bothered you."

———————

SAVAGE LEFT the sheriff's office after lunch without telling anyone where he was going. This visit was off the books. He got into his Suburban and drove out to Mac's Roadhouse. The rowdy biker bar was the headquarters of the Crimson Angels motorcycle gang run by the inimitable Rosalie Weston.

There weren't many 'one-percenter' outlaw MC clubs—if any—run by a woman, but Rosalie was different from most. She'd used Savage to get rid of her ex-husband so she could take over the gang. Savage hadn't seen it coming. She was smart, that one, and he'd learned not to underestimate her.

Axle Weston was now serving time for murder, along with a range of other offenses, and wouldn't see the light of day for a very long time. Rosalie was to thank for that, not that her ex was even aware of her involvement. That was what was so brilliant about it. She'd gotten rid of the competition without the blame landing at her feet. A good thing, really, as Axle wouldn't take too kindly to her betrayal.

Savage took a deep breath of fresh, mountain air through the open car window. Out here, there was nothing but wilderness. The asphalt sliced through the landscape like a silver scar shimmering in the midday sun.

Eventually, he turned into the Roadhouse parking lot, his tires creating a dusty swirl. The Roadhouse was your typical roadside bar. He had it on good authority that the steaks were pretty good, even if the clientele left something to be desired. It didn't have live music. It did have a jukebox, however, and could get pretty raucous on a Saturday night. The sheriff's department had been called out several times over the last year to break up fights.

They'd only just opened for the day, and the parking lot was deserted other than Savage's vehicle, a food delivery van, and three gleaming Harley-Davidsons. He recognized Rosalie's, the low rider with the cream fenders.

He gave his weapon a quick 'press check'. There was one in the chamber. Satisfied, Savage holstered it, then walked up to the front door. Inside, he could hear folk music, a strange choice for the Roadhouse. Usually, it was rock or heavy metal.

He pushed open the door.

"Can I help you?" Hostile, but not unexpected words from the bartender. Over the long strip of mahogany, Savage saw a face he didn't recognize. A new recruit. That would explain the folk music.

"I'm here to see Rosalie."

"She's not here. Who can I say stopped by?" Standard response. Rosalie didn't talk to just anyone. This guy vetted them before they came anywhere near the MC club President.

Savage sized him up. Average height, roughly a hundred and eighty pounds, stocky build. The other man was in good shape and could probably handle himself in a fight. Still, Savage figured he could take the man if he had to.

"Dalton Savage." He looked up at a framed landscape painting above the bar. Behind it was a hidden camera. If the police asked, they didn't have surveillance. No one was going to get busted drinking at the Roadhouse. It was for their internal security, so they could vet whoever came in here. Being an outlaw motorcycle club, they had their fair share of enemies. It paid to be cautious.

The bartender hadn't, or pretended he hadn't, noticed Savage's badge. "I'll pass that on."

Savage pursed his lips and nodded. "You do that. In the meantime, I'll have a coffee."

The barman scowled at him. "We don't do coffee."

A door at the back opened and Rosalie Weston walked out. Biker boots, tight jeans, leather jacket. She looked good in a don't-mess-with-me kind of way. "Make the man a coffee, Burner."

The barman glanced at her, surprised, then turned his attention back to Savage. This time it was with open curiosity.

"I see you've got a new member," Savage remarked, ignoring the look Burner sent his way.

"Sheriff Savage meet Burner Wilson. He's from your neck of the woods."

The newcomer's eyebrows shot up at the mention of sheriff.

"Really?" Savage turned back to Burner. "Which part?"

"Congress Park."

"I know it. Welcome to Hawk's Landing."

Burner gave a stiff nod, then turned away to get the coffee.

"How are you keeping, Rosalie?" Savage asked, conversationally.

"Good. Now why don't you tell me what you're really doing here?" It was just like her to cut straight to the chase. She gestured for them to sit down.

"Just a friendly visit." He eased his lanky frame into one of the wooden chairs around a small circular table. Rosalie slotted in opposite him, crossing her long legs. In her mid-forties, she was a striking woman with long black hair, smooth skin only starting to crease at the sides of her jade green eyes. Her dark liner and lipstick made her appear harder than she was, or maybe it just emphasized the toughness that was already there.

"No such thing." She winked at him. "Burner, I'll have one too, and can you turn that down?"

"Coming right up," he called, his back still to them. A second later, the music volume decreased.

Rosalie studied him. "What do you want, Dalton?"

Burner chose that moment to come back with the coffee, so Savage waited until the barman had walked away. "I hear there are some new players in town."

Her expression turned wary. "Really?"

"Yeah, rumor has it they're muscling in on the drug trade."

"I wouldn't know anything about that."

Savage nearly spluttered his coffee out at the blatant lie. He managed to keep it together, although it scalded his tongue. "I'm sure. Anyway, I don't know if it's related, but a kid OD'd a couple of nights back on a new type of meth. Pink Soda. You heard of that?"

"I've heard of it," she said, after a beat. "Never seen it."

"It's here." He tapped the table. "And it's dangerous. I want it gone."

She leaned forward, her eyes boring into his. "Like I said, Sheriff, I've never seen it." That was her way of saying they didn't import that particular narcotic.

"I didn't say you had."

"I don't want to either. I heard it's a kid killer."

"You heard right."

She sat back again. "Then I'm not sure how I can help you, Sheriff."

"You don't want these guys here anymore than I do. We both know they're encroaching on your turf. I was thinking maybe we could help each other out."

Rosalie's hands tightened around her coffee cup. The green eyes narrowed. "How so?"

"You tell me what you know about the new boys in town, and I'll see what I can do to get rid of them." It was a similar game plan to what they'd done before, but this time, it was his idea.

She paused for a moment, sipping her brew. He knew her lightening quick mind was going through the various scenarios, weighing up the benefits versus the risks. Eventually, she put her mug down. "I haven't seen any newcomers myself, but I'll tell my boys to keep their eyes open."

It wasn't a yes, but it wasn't a no, either.

Savage nodded, then drained the rest of his coffee. "You know where to find me."

NINE

SAVAGE RAN a check on Burner Wilson—obviously not his first name—the moment he got back to the office. It took some digging before he found an arrest report for a Max Wilson, from Congress Park, Denver. The arresting officer was Detective Clinton Manning. Savage's lips curled back in a grin. He remembered Clint. Middle-aged, mostly office-bound due to a shooting that had messed up his leg. He was a good guy.

Savage picked up the phone.

"Clint, it's Dalton Savage. How the hell are you?" The sputtering and colorful expletive on the end of the line made him chuckle. Manning hadn't changed.

"I'm in Hawk's Landing now," Savage continued. "Yeah, I'm the sheriff, that's right. Listen, I need a favor. I'm investigating a guy called Max Wilson. I see you busted him for GBH back in 2018."

"Burner Wilson?" Manning asked.

"Yeah, that's the guy." Savage listened while Manning filled him in.

Member of the Destroyers MC. Previous convictions included drug possession, car theft and failing to appear in court. All in all, not a nice guy.

"What kind of drugs?" Savage asked.

"Low grade stuff. Cannabis, pills, meth."

"Okay, thanks."

They shot the breeze for a while longer, then Savage said goodbye and hung up. He sat at his desk, thinking. He was still trying to figure out whether Burner Wilson was a person of interest when Sinclair burst into his office.

"There's been a shooting out near Chimney Rock. The woman said she heard multiple gunshots from a convenience store."

Savage grabbed his jacket. "Where?"

"Little Creek Mart."

He frowned. "That's Kevin Handsome's place."

They sped out to the convenience store in the small town outside of Hawk's Landing. There wasn't much out there other than a hunting and fishing store, a mechanic, and Handsome's place. The town catered to the surrounding farming community and regular hikers who frequented the trails.

The roads weren't much more than dirt tracks, so it wouldn't be hard to see them coming. The plume of dust the Suburban kicked up would be seen for miles

A crowd had gathered outside the convenience store by the time they pulled up, sirens blazing. Heads turned, but no one got out of the way. A Harley-Davidson gleamed in the sunshine.

"Coming through," yelled Savage, as he and Sinclair marched across the wide sidewalk to the front of the shop. Glass covered the exterior, a result of the windows having been shot out. Glistening shards covered the fresh produce, all of which would have to be thrown away.

"Jeez," Sinclair muttered, as they drew their weapons. "What a mess."

Savage went in first, followed by his deputy. The place was littered with items that had been blown off the shelves, including glass, plaster from the ceiling, and anything else that had found its way into the line of fire.

"This was more than your run-of-the-mill hold-up." Savage surveyed the damage. Sinclair moved past him, down one of the aisles.

"Shit! Over here."

He saw the blood before the bodies. It seeped under the shelving units and oozed over the floor in one ever-growing puddle. He sucked in a breath. "Jesus."

"There are two victims," Sinclair whispered.

He reached the end of the aisle and froze. Two men lay opposite each other, both punctured with bullet holes. He counted five in one and three in the other. A Glock 44 lay on the floor between them.

"The other weapon is over there." Sinclair pointed underneath a wall-mounted shelving unit. The gun was too far back to see clearly.

"Do you think they shot each other?" Sinclair stared at the two men. The first dead guy was skinny and pale, the other stocky and rough.

"It sure looks that way."

"Who are they?" Sinclair whispered. "I don't recognize either of them."

"Neither is the owner." Savage tilted his head to get a better look at the skinny guy's face. He couldn't move any further forward because of the blood pooling around the bodies.

"You know Kevin Handsome?" Sinclair asked.

"Yeah, he's easy to recognize 'cos he's probably the ugliest bastard you'll ever meet. Street smart, though. His parents owned this place before he took over."

"Maybe these guys were customers?" she suggested.

"This one looks like a junkie." Gaunt, malnourished, bad skin, and that yellowish pallor of a longtime user. "I'm guessing he's a user or a street dealer. Maybe both."

"What about the other guy?" Sinclair nodded to the heavyset man in a black leather jacket.

Savage eyed out the patch on the pocket. "He belongs to Rosalie Weston. That's a Crimson Angels patch and I'm guessing that's his motorcycle outside."

Sinclair's eyebrows shot up. "Was he buying drugs?"

"Selling, more like. I think the Angels are bringing drugs in from Mexico and selling them to guys like Kevin who run distribution hubs out of mom-and-pop stores like this one." He nodded to himself. "This was about drugs."

Sinclair shook her head. "Well, whatever it was, it didn't go down too well."

Savage took out his phone and snapped some photographs of the victims. The CSI team would take more, but he didn't want to wait for them to filter down to him.

"We need to find Kevin," he said.

On cue, a man with a noticeable overbite and uneven, pockmarked skin rushed in. "Holy shit, what happened here?"

Savage looked at him. "Hello Kevin. I was hoping you'd be able to tell us."

It took a moment for the store owner to register the carnage. "I—I don't know." Savage had never seen the drug dealer speechless before. For that reason alone, he was inclined to believe him.

"This your man?" Savage nodded to the skinny guy.

"Aaron." Kevin took several steps forward, but Sinclair put out her arm. "Careful."

Kevin stopped. "Is he dead?"

"Uh, yeah." The guy was riddled with bullets.

"Sorry, stupid question." The store owner exhaled shakily. "Aaron works for me."

"What about the other guy?"

"Never seen him before," he said too quickly. He also didn't look at the biker's face.

"Right." Savage turned to Sinclair. "Call the State Troopers. We're going to need their help on this one." It was too big a job for Ray and Pearl. They needed a full-scale CSI team down here to do a proper sweep.

While Sinclair was on the phone and Kevin was pulling himself together, Savage studied the crime scene, trying to make sense of what happened. Multiple bullet casings lay scattered on the floor, the majority halfway down the aisle, not at the end where the victims lay.

That was strange. He bent down to take a closer look. Those definitely weren't .40 caliber shell casings from the Glock. They were bigger.

Taking a knee, Savage lowered himself to floor level and looked at the back of the casing. Just as he'd thought, they were .45s. He peered at the second gun under the shelves. Didn't look like a match. He'd wait until the crime scene was properly tagged and photographed to be sure, but at first glance it would appear the guns present were unlikely to have been used in the shooting. This could be a real problem. It might mean they had another shooter on their hands.

"I only left him for an hour," Handsome mumbled.

"Lucky you weren't here," Savage remarked.

Kevin swallowed. "Do you think this was meant for me?"

"I don't know, Kevin. You tell us?"

Sinclair came back. "They're on their way. Said to contain the scene."

Savage frowned. Something about the bodies and the way they were lying. "Does anything about the way they fell strike you as odd?" he asked.

Sinclair hesitated.

"If they'd shot each other, they'd have fallen backwards," Handsome said, catching on.

"Exactly, but they both fell sideways, against the back unit."

Sinclair frowned as she looked from one victim to the other. "What are you saying?"

"I'm saying they didn't shoot each other." Both Sinclair and Handsome stared at him. He raised a finger. "Hear me out. What if somebody else walked into the store and opened fire? What if that person stood right here and unleashed eight gunshots from a .45? Five hitting your man, Aaron, and three hitting the biker."

"You think that's possible?" gasped Sinclair.

Handsome frowned, which made his eyes appear closer together. "That would mean neither of these two fired their weapon."

"Or they did, and they missed." Savage scanned the floor where he stood. "Check the store for any signs of impact."

"Already did. Nada. Guess we'll have an answer once we process the guns," Sinclair said.

Savage shrugged. "There's a faster way to determine if either man fired a shot."

He went out to his vehicle and returned a moment later with two small packets. He slipped on a pair of latex gloves and unsealed one of the packs. Sinclair leaned over his shoulder as he wiped a sterile Q-tip over the webbing of the dead man's right hand. He took the sample and applied it to the gunshot residue test zone for a five second count. The indicator circle turned white. "Negative for GSR."

He then went over to the other victim and repeated the process. He looked back at Sinclair and shook his head. "Well, that's a problem."

"What're you thinking?" Sinclair asked as Savage stood.

"Someone else did this."

"But who would do that?" Handsome's hands clenched into fists. "Who would come into my store and open fire?"

"That," Savage said, "is what we have to find out."

TEN

"THE SURVEILLANCE CAMERA has been shot out." Savage looked up at the shattered remains above the shop door. "The assailant must have known it was there."

"Who'd want to do this, Kevin?" Savage asked as Sinclair got a roll of police tape out of the trunk and cordoned off the store.

"I told you, man. I don't know. Aaron's harmless to everyone else but himself, and I don't know the other guy. Maybe this is all because of him."

Savage glanced at the Harley-Davidson outside. "What was the biker doing here? Negotiating a deal? Offloading merchandise?"

"What?" Handsome whipped a hand through his messy hair. "I ain't never seen that guy before."

Savage didn't believe that for a moment. He went back into the store and took another look at the bodies. Bending down, he peered under the shelves. No backpack. If the biker was delivering merchandise, where was it? Had the shooter taken it? Something had been going down here, when it had been violently interrupted.

Then he heard the thunder.

It started off as a low rumble, growing louder with each passing second.

"Hey boss. You're going to want to see this," called Sinclair.

Savage already knew what it was. The Crimson Angels were coming.

Shit.

Where the hell were the State Police?

"This could get ugly," he muttered, under his breath. Handsome was already backing away from the door, his face a wide-eyed mask of fear.

"I'll be in my office." He turned, ready to bolt. Savage grabbed his arm.

"No, you don't. You'll be safer with us." He took out his cuffs.

"What you doin'? I ain't done nothing."

"That remains to be seen. You need to come down to the Sheriff's office and give a statement."

"But I didn't have anything to do with this," he yelled, trying to twist out of Savage's grasp. "I was meeting a supplier in Durango."

The dust cloud bellowed closer as the rumbling became deafening. Savage guessed twenty to thirty bikes, all steaming up the dirt road toward them.

"I can arrest you," Savage said, an urgency in his voice. "Or you can come voluntarily. I don't like your chances if you stay here." People began backing away from the store, dispersing as the thunderous cavalcade came up the road.

"Okay. Okay. I'll come in," he said.

Savage turned to Sinclair. "Secure him in the SUV and lock the doors."

She nodded, but her eyes were fixed on the approaching swarm of bikers. They were a mesmerizing sight.

"Now!" Savage barked.

He stood at the entrance to the store, his legs spread, hand on his holster. At least two dozen motorcycles pulled up outside, the smell of gasoline pungent in the warm afternoon air.

Rosalie headed the pack, flanked by Scooter and another guy Savage hadn't seen before.

"Sheriff," Rosalie called, "you have one of ours in there."

Savage stood his ground. "It looks that way, Rosalie, but there's nothing you can do for him now."

She glanced around. "Where's Kevin?"

"Kevin's not responsible for this. He wasn't even here when it happened."

"I'd like to ask him myself, if you don't mind."

"I do mind. Now, if you want, I'll show you the body so you can make a positive ID. I'm sure you'll want to notify his next of kin, but only you. This is an active crime scene."

She looked over at Scooter. "Wait here, I'm going in."

"Want me to come with you?" the VP asked.

She hesitated, but Savage's gaze bore into hers. His hand twitched on his Glock.

"No. I'll be right back." She got off the motorcycle.

Savage exhaled slow and quiet under his breath. "Follow me." He turned and walked into the store. Rosalie ducked under the sheriff's tape and followed him.

"Holy shit," she muttered when she got to the end of the aisle.

"Yeah." That about summed it up.

"That's Gav." He heard her suck in a breath. "Gavin Stacey."

"What was he doing here, Rosalie?"

"Beats me." She didn't meet his gaze.

"Come on. I know you guys are bringing in product from Mexico. Is Kevin your buyer? Does he distribute the drugs for you, or is it a clean sale? You wash your hands of it once you hand it over?"

"I don't know what you mean, Sheriff." Her green eyes blazed. "But I do know that whoever is responsible for this is going to pay. That's Kevin's man. I know him. Weasel drug dealer called Aaron Pritchard."

"Yeah, he was manning the store when it happened."

She frowned, as she took in the body of her man, the blood that had now stopped flowing, the gun beside him. "You saying they didn't shoot each other?"

"Look at it," Savage prompted. Rosalie was a smart woman. She'd figure it out just like he had. Hopefully, it would dissuade her from exacting her revenge on Kevin Handsome.

Her head turned as she looked at the bullet casings, the bodies, the damage to the store. "The shooter was someone else," she hissed.

He nodded. "It looks that way."

Her expression hardened.

"You know who?" he asked, reading the signs. She knew who'd done this, or she suspected someone, but she wasn't saying. "Rosalie?"

She shook her head. "No."

"No, you don't know, or no you won't say?"

"I don't know who did this." But she spun around on her boot heel and stalked back up the aisle and out of the store.

Savage clenched his jaw. "Like hell you don't."

A moment later the thunder started up again, and as he walked out of the store, the motorcycle brigade turned around and took off down the road. "How'd you get rid of them?" Sinclair asked, emerging from the car. Behind her, through the tinted glass window, he glimpsed the pale face of Kevin Handsome.

"They left on their own accord." His eyes followed the swarm as it disappeared out of sight. The dust cloud took a lot longer to dissipate, like an ominous warning hanging over the town. Silence returned. A few onlookers scurried back, drawn by the tape, the sheriff's presence, and the drama.

"You stay here and wait for the State Police," Savage said. "I'm going to get this guy back to the office and take his statement."

Sinclair nodded. "Sure thing. Anything you want me to tell them? You know, about the shooter?"

"Nope, let them figure it out. We'll need a copy of the forensic report once they're done." They'd collaborated with the State Police before, and relations were good. He didn't envisage a problem. Sinclair could handle it.

"Am I under arrest?" Kevin asked.

"Not yet," Savage responded as he climbed into the driver's seat. "Let's get out of here."

"They're gonna come for me," Handsome warned, sitting back against the leather. Sinclair had cuffed him, as was standard protocol. "The bikers. You know that, right?"

Savage didn't reply. He hoped not, but you could never tell with Rosalie.

"Who did this, Kevin?" Savage asked, as they drove back to Hawk's Landing. "And don't tell me you don't know."

"I don't."

"Think. Who would want to send a warning to both you and Rosalie Weston?"

Savage watched him shake his head in the rearview mirror.

"Come on. I know there are some new people in town."

Kevin briefly met his gaze in the mirror before Savage looked back at the road.

"Was it them? Are they muscling in on your turf? Is that what this is about?"

"I don't know." His reply was muffled as he looked away, out of the side window.

"Give me a name, Kevin. I want to get rid of these guys as much as you do." It was the same line he'd fed Rosalie, but while the MC President would use it to her advantage, Kevin was a different animal. His inbuilt mistrust of the law meant he wouldn't give up any information, even if it benefited him. He remained silent.

Sighing, Savage drove the drug dealer back to the sheriff's office. He had a bad feeling about this. Very bad.

ELEVEN

"WHO CALLED IT IN?" Savage asked Barbara. Kevin Handsome was giving his statement to Littleton. His alibi checked out. He had indeed been in Durango that morning. His truck had been picked up on the traffic camera on the US-550 leading into town.

Barbara looked up from the filing cabinet she was rifling through. "The lady who lives across the road from the store. She heard gunshots and dialed 911."

"Did she see anything?" he asked.

"I don't know." Barbara bit her lip. "I didn't ask, it was an emergency. Do you want me to call her back?"

"Don't worry. I'll go and see her myself."

"You just got back," Sinclair said.

"I know, but we need to interview any potential witnesses."

"I can go," Thorpe offered.

Savage wavered. It had been a long morning and he could do with a coffee and a sandwich. Besides, Becca had sent him a message with her prenatal friend's husband's number, and he wanted to follow up on that.

"Okay but call me on the way back with an update. If she saw anything, I want to know straight away."

"Will do."

Harvey Makepeace sounded like a decent man—for a property developer. Savage introduced himself and found that Makepeace was only too happy to tell his side of the story. "We were about to close the deal," he said, "when the guy we were dealing with at the county clerk's office did a full-on U-turn."

"What did he say?" asked Savage.

"That we hadn't submitted the right documentation, which was bullshit. Everything was in order, I made sure of that myself. It was just an excuse to get out of the deal so they could award the contract to Apex Holdings." He spat out the words.

"Why do you think they did that?" Savage enquired.

"Money, I guess. Apex is run by Douglas Connelly, a cut-throat developer who's got more than a few officials in his back pocket."

"Do you have proof of this?"

A pause.

"Not exactly, although I saw Connelly coming out of the county courthouse the day I went in to complain. He gave me such a smug look that I just knew."

It did sound suspicious. "Did you know Connelly prior to this?"

"Only by reputation. In the industry, he's known as a shark, but he gets the job done." Harvey shrugged. "He's got friends in high places."

"Like who?"

"The Governor for one. They're always playing golf together." He hesitated. "I looked into it. I was so mad at losing that contract. We needed that."

He had a kid on the way too.

"Did you file a complaint?" Savage asked.

"Yeah, but nothing was done about it. There wasn't even an investigation. The work went ahead, and now it's too late to do anything. That's obviously what they were banking on."

"That's rough," Savage said, and meant it. "Thank you for talking to me. I appreciate it."

"It's good to tell somebody," Harvey admitted. "Even though I know there's nothing you can do to put things right."

Put things right.

The words resonated with Savage. Wasn't that why he'd become a cop in the first place? To catch the bad guys, to bring justice to the victims and their families, to put things right?

Unfortunately, he couldn't do that here.

"Douglas Connelly is a person of interest in an investigation, so your account has given me more of a handle on the man."

"He's a ruthless bastard, Sheriff," Harvey warned. "I wouldn't trust him as far as I could throw him."

"Don't worry," Savage said. "I won't."

No sooner had he hung up when Thorpe called. "What you got for me, Thorpe?"

"I just interviewed the witness." Savage could hear by the hollow echo that he was driving. "She's about ninety years old and blind as a bat."

Savage's heart sank. "Thanks for trying anyway. Sorry you had to drive out there."

"As soon as she heard the gunshots, she called 911," Thorpe continued, as if he hadn't heard Savage. "And she took a picture out of the window, just in case."

"A picture?"

"Yeah, with her phone. She used to live in Colorado Springs and was part of her neighborhood watch team, so she knows the importance of gathering evidence. Even though she can't see more than a few yards in front of her, she took some pretty decent photographs."

"And?" Savage's pulse ticked up a notch.

"I've got a picture of the killer's vehicle, parked outside the convenience store at the time the gunshots were fired. You can clearly make out the license plate."

Yes! He fist-pumped the air.

"Send it to me. I'll run it through the DVLA database."

"On its way. And the State Police are there in full force. They've shut down the entire street."

"Did you speak to the officer in charge?"

"Yeah, Brent Radley. He said he'd send us the forensic report once it's finalized. They've called a team in from Colorado Springs."

"Good work, Thorpe."

"Thanks, see you soon." Thorpe cut the call.

A few seconds later, Savage's phone buzzed. As promised, Thorpe had sent a couple of photographs of the outside of the convenience store. A dirty pickup truck was parked outside, door open, motor running.

The 90-year-old witness's house was diagonally across the road. From the angle of her window, the plates were just about readable. Savage zoomed in and wrote down the number on his notepad, then he logged into the system and ran the plates through the DVLA database.

Holding his breath, he waited for a hit.

There it was. The plates were registered to a Mr. Ronnie Jameson. 1023 Red Rock Road. Hermosa.

TWELVE

RONNIE JAMESON LIVED in a neat white house with a wooden porch and a mowed front yard where a child's tricycle lay. Sinclair raised an eyebrow. They got out of the car and proceeded to the front door. Savage rang the buzzer, and they waited.

From inside, a child could be heard laughing, and a short while later, a smiling woman answered the door. "Hello?"

"Mrs. Jameson?"

She looked the two officers up and down. "Yes?"

"I'm Sheriff Savage and this is Deputy Sinclair from Hawk's Landing sheriff's office. We'd like to ask your husband a few questions. Is he home?"

"Ronnie's still at work," she said. "What's this about?"

"Your pickup truck," Savage said. "It was recently involved in a shooting."

"Oh my God." Her hand flew to her mouth.

"Do you know where it is now?"

"No, it was stolen a couple of days ago." She shook her head. "Ronnie took my car into work today."

"Where does he work?" Savage asked.

"Alpine Bank, in Durango."

Savage nodded. It was as he'd feared. The car wasn't registered to the man involved in the shooting. That would be too easy. "Was it stolen from here?"

"Yeah, last weekend. We came out on Sunday morning and it was gone. They must have taken it overnight. We didn't hear a thing."

"Did you report it stolen?"

"We did, yes. My husband reported it on Monday." Savage nodded. It probably hadn't filtered through the system yet.

"Okay, sorry to bother you Mrs. Jameson."

"I hope you find whoever took it."

"We'll certainly try."

"Well, that was a dead end," Sinclair said, dejected.

"I thought as much." Savage glanced up at the streetlights. "No CCTV either. This is a peaceful residential area. It's doubtful anyone has private security cameras on the front of their properties."

"I can't see any." Sinclair strained her neck to look up and down the street.

"Let's make a quick stop in Durango," Savage said. "There's someone I want to see."

A short time later, they pulled up in front of the Durango Sheriff's office. Shelby came out to meet them.

"Hey Savage. Long time, no see." Shelby had been instrumental in helping them apprehend Axle Weston earlier that year. "To what do I owe the honor?"

"Mind if we pick your brain?"

"You know I'll help you if I can." He led them up the steps into the Durango Sheriff's station. It was bigger than Hawk's Landing, but they covered a larger jurisdiction.

They followed him up a flight of stairs to the first-floor office. The Durango deputies looked up and nodded. "Come this way."

Shelby opened the door to his office and waited for them to go inside.

Then he closed it behind them, walked around the big wooden desk, and took a seat. "Now, what do you need?"

"I'm looking for some new kids on the block," Savage began. "City types from Denver. You see anyone like that around?"

Shelby frowned. "No offense, but we're a bit bigger than Hawk's Landing. It's hard to know everyone who's coming and going."

"Thought you might have noticed something, that's all."

Shelby stared at Savage for a long moment. "You know, there was a report of a disturbance at a restaurant downtown the other night. The caller reported a large group of people from out of town. I don't know if they're still around, though."

"When was that?" Sinclair asked.

"Couple of days back. Friday, I think."

"Could be our guys," Savage muttered. "Which restaurant?"

"The Old West Grill. It's—"

"I know it. Do you mind if we check it out?" He looked at Shelby.

"Sure, go ahead. We sent a deputy, but the party had broken up by then." Shelby narrowed his gaze. "What are these new guys up to?"

"We think they might be involved in the meth game," Savage said. "The locals have reported some city types trying to muscle in on the action."

Shelby snorted. "I can't imagine that went down well."

"We had a shooting this morning out near Chimney Rock. Two men gunned down in broad daylight."

Shelby tutted. "That's not good."

"No. It could get out of hand."

"Hope you find 'em," Shelby said. "Let me know if I can be of any assistance."

"Will do."

"YEAH, THEY WERE HERE," said Magna, the well-dressed middle-aged restaurant manager. "Rowdy bunch. Almost got into a fight with one of our locals."

"That why you called the Sheriff?" Savage asked.

She looked sheepish. "Actually, that was more of a precaution. Sheriff Shelby comes in some nights for dinner, so I thought if he was here, things might settle down." She tossed her rich mane of auburn hair over her shoulder.

"Makes sense," Sinclair said. "Did he come?"

"No, he was busy. He sent one of his deputies, but things had quieted down by then."

"Did you know the men who caused the disturbance?" Savage asked.

"Not really, but they're staying across the road at the Dorchester. They're in here a lot. I think they're from Denver."

"What makes you think that?"

"The one guy complained about the slow service. He said this would never happen back in Denver." She shrugged. "We were busy that night, and short-staffed."

"Thank you, Magna. You've been a great help." Savage shot her a grin.

She smiled back. "You're welcome. Come back soon." As they left, Sinclair said, "She's sweet on Shelby."

Savage did a double take. "How did you figure?"

"The way she talked about him. I wonder if Shelby knows."

Savage looked doubtful.

"He's not married, is he?" They didn't know much about the Durango Sheriff except he'd worked for the government before settling in Durango and running for office.

"I don't know. He's never mentioned it."

"He doesn't wear a ring."

Savage arched an eyebrow. "Let's leave the matchmaking for now and go pay these out-of-towners a visit, shall we?"

———

"THEY'VE RESERVED THREE ROOMS," the motel receptionist told them. "Two twins and a standard double."

"What name are they booked under?" Savage asked.

"Onyx Marketing Solutions," she said. "It's a corporate account. They've reserved all three rooms on an ongoing basis."

Savage scratched his chin. They could be here for weeks, or months. As long as it took to take over the drug trade in La Plata County. "Can you give me a name?" he asked.

She shook her head. "I'm sorry, I don't know the guests' individual names as the rooms were all booked under the company."

"Do you know where I can find them?"

"The gentleman staying in the double room is in the bar right now. I'm not sure about the others." She hesitated. "Is there a problem, Sheriff?"

"No, no problem." He was quick to reassure her. "It's just standard protocol."

She exhaled. "Good. This is my first job. I don't want anything to go wrong."

Sinclair smiled at her. "You're doing great."

The young woman grinned back.

Savage surveyed the man in the bar. He was lounging in an armchair reading the paper, his cellphone on the table in front of him. Judging by his fancy suit and shoes, he had to be high up in the organization. There was an empty chair beside him.

"Excuse me, is this seat taken?" Savage slid into it. Sinclair was waiting at the bar, keeping a beady eye on the exchange. They had no idea how the man was going to react to the impromptu questioning.

The suit looked up, surprised. "Actually, no." Beady eyes took in Savage's attire, lingering on his badge.

Savage leaned forward and held out his hand. "Sheriff Savage, and you are?"

"Jonny Star." The man gave it a reluctant shake. "You the Sheriff of this town?"

"I'm from Hawk's Landing, next town over. This is just a social call. I hear you're from Denver too?" It was more of a question than a statement.

A raised eyebrow. "Did you?"

"Yeah. Some folks in the Old West Grill happened to overhear you the other night."

He cocked his head. "News travels fast."

"Always does in small towns. What's your business here, Mr. Star?"

"Scouting mission. I'm thinking about investing out here."

Savage nodded and leaned back in his chair. "I used to be a cop in Denver. Gave it up to come down here a couple years back."

"And now you're Sheriff?"

"Yeah, funny how things work out."

"I guess once a lawman, always a lawman." The beady eyes gleamed, although he didn't laugh.

"Guess so."

"What do you want with me, Sheriff?" The man was direct. Savage liked that.

"I believe there are a group of you staying here at the hotel."

"Is that a problem?"

"No problem. I was just wondering if any of your boys were in Hawk's Landing this morning?"

He frowned. "I don't think so, although I'm not accountable for my men."

"Aren't you?"

A hard look. "No, Sheriff. They come and go as they please. I'm here to investigate some business opportunities."

"Do you need four others to do that?"

"They're my sales team," he huffed.

"What business are you in exactly, Mr. Star?"

"Logistics. We're thinking about extending our network into La Plata County."

"I see." Savage paused. "I think this county is pretty much covered already."

Star crossed his arms over his chest. "No offense, Sheriff, but that's what me and my team are here to find out."

Savage raised his arms. "Don't say I didn't warn you."

"Is that a threat?"

"Call it some friendly advice." Savage got to his feet. "Have a good evening, Mr. Star."

THIRTEEN

"JONNY STAR," Savage told his team first thing the next morning. "He's from Denver, as are his 'sales team'. They're holed up at the Dorchester Hotel in Durango."

"Sales team?" Sinclair handed Savage a coffee in a takeout cup. She'd stopped by the Bouncing Bean on the way to work and got one for everyone. "More like a mini army."

Savage clenched his jaw. "Yeah, it's not good."

"What are they doing here?" Thorpe asked.

"They're a logistics firm." Savage took the lid off his coffee. "Appropriate, don't you think?"

Thorpe smirked. "There's five of them in Durango. Do you think one of them was responsible for the shooting this morning?"

"Could be, although we have no evidence. No names. No descriptions. Nothing."

"We could watch the hotel?" Sinclair suggested. "See where they go."

"All five of them?" Savage scratched his head. "We don't have the manpower."

"Does Shelby?"

"Maybe. He could watch Jonny Star, at least. I'll give him a call." He walked outside with his coffee and his phone.

Barbara poked her head out after him. "The CSI team working at the Eddie Youngblood crime scene just called. That boot print they found in the concrete was Eddie's."

"Thanks."

The sun warmed his face as he took a sip of coffee and closed his eyes. Becca had been up a lot in the night, unable to get comfortable. Any day now, the doctor had said. He hoped there wasn't going to be trouble in Hawk's Landing. Once the baby was born, he'd promised Becca he'd take some time off. He couldn't leave his station in the middle of a turf war.

Sighing, he called Shelby, who said he'd put a man on Jonny Star.

"Let me know if he meets up with anyone," Savage said. Shelby promised he would.

"Eddie was found on the south side of the site," Savage said once he was back inside. "And yet his footprint was in the concrete on the north side. What was he doing way over there?"

"He must have tried to cross it," Thorpe pointed out. "Then realized it was wet and went around."

"Which means he had seen something on the other side." Savage frowned. "Or was he being chased and trying to make it to the cover of the trees?"

Littleton, who hadn't said much, was staring at his computer screen.

"What about Connelly?" Savage asked. "Did his alibi check out?"

Thorpe consulted his notes. "Yeah, he was on a Zoom call with Bryant and two other directors of Apex Holdings. They vouched for him."

Savage gave a slow nod. "What about that Kushner guy? Did we get his alibi? Eddie was a thorn in his side. The protests were disrupting their schedule. Costing them money."

"Kushner said the foreman had shut down the site for the day. He was back at the hotel. I have his statement here." Thorpe had taken down their alibis at the crime scene.

"Any CCTV to back it up?"

"There aren't any cameras at the barracks, and the ones at the site entrance are aimed at the gate. They don't cover the interior, which as you know is pretty big."

"Nothing near the crime scene?"

Thorpe shook his head.

"Kushner could be lying," said Sinclair.

Littleton cleared his throat. "I think I know who Eddie was meeting at the site."

They all turned to him.

"I've been going through his phone records, and he received a text message from Celine Connelly that afternoon asking to meet."

"Celine?" Savage frowned. "Let's see."

Littleton turned his screen toward Savage. They all crowded round.

Can you meet today? Same place. 6:30pm.

"She told us she hadn't seen him since early that morning," Thorpe pointed out.

Savage clenched his jaw. "She lied."

THEY FOUND Celine Connelly by the hotel swimming pool, reading a book underneath an umbrella.

"Morning." Savage stood in front of her so she was looking up at him. Thorpe hovered in the background.

"Sheriff." She sat up, her book falling to the side. "What are you doing here?"

"We just need to ask you some questions about the evening Eddie died."

Her face clouded over. "I already told you everything I know."

Savage pulled up a chair to make it easier for her. Thorpe continued to hover.

"Celine, we've been through Eddie's text messages on the day he died. There's one from you asking to meet up later that afternoon at the construction site."

"What?" She frowned. "That's impossible."

"Not according to Eddie's phone records." Savage shot her a hard stare. "Did you meet him the afternoon he died?"

"No. The last time I saw him was that morning, I swear." Her slender arms flexed as she gripped the sides of the sun-lounger.

"You said there was something you wanted to tell him."

She averted her gaze. "That was when we met for coffee. I didn't text him again after that." She seemed upset, but Savage didn't know whether to believe her or not.

"Do you mind showing me your phone?"

She hesitated, then gave a little nod.

"Would you open it for me and show me your outgoing messages?"

She did as he asked, then handed the mobile device to him. He browsed through it and found the message sent earlier in the day. According to the phone log, she hadn't called or messaged Eddie again. Of course, she could have deleted the text. Without a warrant, he had no way of checking, and no judge was going to allow him to access a seventeen-year-old girl's phone records. Not without a damn good reason.

He handed the phone back. "What did you want to tell him?"

"Excuse me?"

"Your message, you mentioned there was something you wanted to tell him. What was it?"

"Nothing."

"Didn't sound like nothing." He watched her fidget on the lounger.

"I wanted to tell him how I felt," she said, flushing. "He'd been asking me out for weeks, but I always said no. I didn't want to get involved with a boy I'd never see again."

"Never see again?"

"Yeah, I'm starting college in the fall."

Savage frowned. "You were going to end it?"

"No, the opposite. I was going to say I liked him, and that I would date him. I know it's silly, but I just thought, what the hell. Life is short, right?"

Savage gave a confused nod. Something about her story didn't add up, but he couldn't put his finger on it. If what she said was true, and she hadn't sent that second message, then who had?

"Celine, does anyone else have access to your phone?"

"No." She flinched at the thought. A teenager's phone was sacred, he knew this from the stories Becca had told him about kids at the clinic.

"Not your father, nor any of his colleagues?"

She pulled a face. "Definitely not."

Savage glanced at Thorpe. It was time to go before Connelly descended on them again and accused them of harassing his daughter. "Thanks for talking to us. Enjoy the rest of your day."

She didn't respond.

———

"SHE MUST BE LYING," Thorpe insisted as they drove back to the sheriff's station. "That second text definitely came from her phone."

"Then she deleted it," Savage said, his brow creased. "Which means she met him and she's trying to hide the fact. Now why would she do that?"

"You don't think she could have done this?" His deputy cast him a sideways look.

Savage shrugged as he drove. "I don't know. Given the size of her, I wouldn't have thought so. Someone of Eddie Youngblood's stature would easily be able to fight her off. I can't see her plunging that needle into his arm and killing him, can you?"

Thorpe massaged his forehead. "Unless he let her do it."

The radio crackled. Thorpe answered it. "Hi Barbara, what's up?"

Savage listened to Barbara's urgent tone. "I've just had a call from Zebadiah Swift out at the Hidden Gem trailer park. There's a party going on and a kid looks to be OD'ing on the premises. He said to send an ambulance."

Shit.

Savage spun the car around. "Have you done that?"

"Yep, it's on its way."

"We're heading out there now."

FOURTEEN

THEY HEARD the music as soon as they got out of the car. The insistent, recurring beat of rap music was so loud it almost made the trees shake. Savage could feel it beneath his feet as he walked around the back of the mobile home to where an inflatable swimming pool stood filled with half-naked teenagers.

There were at least twenty kids frolicking in the water, most of them holding beer cans.

"You can tell school's out for the summer," Thorpe muttered.

Nobody seemed to notice the curled-up figure of the young woman underneath the trees or the two teenagers standing worriedly beside her. The boy stared down, while the girl stroked her friend's hair. From where they were standing, she appeared unconscious.

They rushed over. Savage dropped to his knees and felt for a pulse. It was faint, but she was alive. "What happened?" he asked the teenagers.

The boy's eyes dropped to the sheriff's badge, and he backed away. Before Thorpe could grab him, he turned and darted inside. Thorpe glanced at Savage who shook his head. The kid could wait.

"Alice was partying," the girl said. She couldn't have been older than sixteen, seventeen. Like the others, she was wearing a bikini and her hair was wet. "The next minute she collapsed in the pool."

"Did she take anything?"

"She smoked a joint. I think it was laced with something."

"Do you know what?"

"No, I don't." She stifled a sob. "Is she going to be okay?"

"Hopefully. The ambulance is on its way." Alice was breathing, at least. He felt her forehead. It was clammy and cold to the touch.

"You call it in?" Savage asked her.

She nodded. "Everybody else is either stoned or drunk. I didn't know what to do."

"You did the right thing," he told her. "What's your name?"

"Penny Vincent."

"Do you live in the trailer park, Penny?" He kept her talking, while he monitored the girl on the ground. Her pulse was fluttering erratically.

"No, nearby."

"Whose party is this?"

"Peter's."

"He a friend of yours?"

She shrugged. "Kind of. My friends and I heard this was going to be a good party, so we came along. It was supposed to be fun." She sniffed and rubbed her eyes, smearing make-up down her face. She looked absurdly young, despite the mascara smudges.

"Do you have someone you can call to pick you up, Penny?"

Her eyes widened. "No, I'll make my own way home."

"You sure? We can give you a lift, if you like?"

"I'm sure. Thanks."

He got it. She didn't want her parents to know where she'd been. They wouldn't approve. Maybe she'd snuck out or told them she was going to a friend's house.

An ambulance pulled up, and a paramedic jumped out carrying a satchel. He ran over and nodded at Savage. "Unresponsive?"

"Yeah." Savage got up and gently moved a tearful Penny out of the way, handing her to Thorpe. The paramedic crouched down beside the unconscious teenager and took her pulse, eyes on his watch.

"Her name is Alice. She may have smoked something."

The paramedic responded with a grim nod.

Penny sobbed into Thorpe's shoulder as an oxygen mask was fitted over her friend's nose and mouth. Another man brought over a stretcher, and they carefully lifted the unconscious girl onto it.

Penny reached for her friend's hand, but Savage stopped her. "Let them do their job." They watched as Alice was loaded into the ambulance.

Once it had driven away, Penny sniveled and swiped at her eyes. "I guess I'll go home now."

"You can go see your friend tomorrow."

She tried a weak smile but failed. "Okay."

The rest of the kids were still partying, oblivious to the drama unfolding only yards away. The single-mindedness of youth, Savage thought to himself as he walked into the mobile home and pulled the plug on the music system.

"Party's over!" Savage held up his badge. "Go home." There was a chorus of complaints, but the kids inside began drifting out.

"Hey dude!" exclaimed an incensed youth.

"You Peter?" he asked. The kid shook his head, his gaze darting to a boy standing by the makeshift bar. "Thanks."

Savage moved across the room, homing in on the guy. "Peter?"

Peter turned ashen when he saw the sheriff's badge, and he spun around, about to take off. Unfortunately for him, he barged straight into Thorpe, who grabbed him by the arm. "Not so fast, buddy."

The kid's shoulders slumped. "What's the matter?"

"What was in that joint you gave Alice?" Savage glared down at him.

He looked bewildered. "Just some dope."

"No, not just some dope. She OD'd on the grass out there and is now on her way to hospital."

Peter swayed as he stared at them. A hand flew to his forehead. "Oh, crap. She okay?"

"No, she's not okay. What was in the joint?"

"I laced it with new shit, man. Everyone's taking it."

Savage scowled. "What's it called?"

"Pink Shoda, but it was jusht a dusting. A little buzz." His words were becoming slurred.

"That buzz has put her in the hospital. You got any more of this stuff?"

He glanced away. "No, man."

Liar.

Thorpe read Savage's mind and pulled the kid's hands behind his back.

"Whoa! What you doing?"

"Arresting you for possession with intent to distribute. That's a five-year sentence, Peter, unless you tell us where you got the drugs."

Peter sighed. "Fine. Don't get all Dirty Harry on my ass. I bought them off this guy I know."

"Does this guy have a name?"

"Yeah." The kid shifted from foot to foot, but Savage couldn't work out if it was because he was teetering, or he just didn't want to say.

"Peter?"

"Kevin Handsome. But don't tell him I tol' you. He's no' the kind of guy you wan' on your bad shide, if you get my drift." His words rolled into each other in a kind of drunken slur.

Kevin Handsome. The guy whose store had been shot to pieces.

Peter's eyes rolled back in his head. He wasn't looking too good.

"You smoke any of that joint, Peter?" Savage asked, worriedly.

"Only a little." His legs buckled and Thorpe fought to hold him up.

"Dammit." Savage pulled out his phone and called 911. They were going to need another ambulance.

———

KEVIN HANDSOME LIVED in an old farmhouse on the outskirts of Chimney Rock. Behind him, the mountains stabbed at the cornflower blue sky, while in front, the wilderness stretched for miles, unin-terrupted.

"What a view!" Thorpe gazed at the expansive vista as they drove up to the front of the property. "Does he own all this?"

"Family money," Savage confirmed. "Kevin took over his father's business when he died, and that included the distribution network. Kevin is not as dumb as he looks."

Thorpe raised an eyebrow.

Behind them, the dust cloud billowed in the early morning air, and by the time they got to the house, Handsome was waiting on the porch with a shotgun. He put it away once he saw who it was.

"Afternoon, Sheriff," he drawled, as Savage and Thorpe got out of the SUV. "You got news of who shot up my store?"

"Not yet." Savage strode toward him, hand on holster. "We're working on it, though." Thorpe stayed by the car, sunglasses on, ready for action.

The drug dealer's gaze faltered. "Then what you doin' here?"

Savage climbed the steps to the porch. Up close, Handsome's skin had an almost cheese grater appearance. Years of teenage acne and poor nutrition had contributed to that. Drug use wouldn't have helped. "Kevin Handsome, you are under arrest." Savage grabbed the man's wrist and slung on the handcuffs.

At first, Handsome was too shocked to react, then he went for his gun, but it was too late. Savage had him cuffed.

Handsome strained at the constraints. "What? Why? This is bullshit. I haven't done anything."

"There are two kids in the hospital who would disagree with you," Savage said.

Kevin fell silent, but his guarded expression told Savage he knew exactly what he meant.

"You've been supplying a nasty brand of meth, and now kids are getting sick."

"I want a lawyer," he grumbled.

Savage gave a stiff nod. "Wise move. You're gonna need one."

FIFTEEN

"MY CLIENT WANTS TO MAKE A DEAL," the lawyer said. They stood outside the interview room, in the drafty corridor. Above them, the fluorescent light flickered.

Savage nodded. He'd figured as much. The weasel was trying to wriggle out of the charges by giving up where he'd gotten the Pink Soda.

"I'm listening."

They hashed out the details for a while longer, then Littleton put it in writing. Once they'd both signed, the lawyer handed the contract back to Savage. "Go ahead."

Kevin Handsome leaned back in his chair. If it wasn't bolted to the ground, he'd be rocking back and forth in it. The fingers of his right hand drummed on the metal table.

Savage sat down. "Right, Kevin. What can you tell me?"

"These guys came to see me," Kevin began. The drumming stopped. He was afraid, Savage realized. "They told me they had this new product they wanted to offload and if I didn't comply, they'd go to my competitor."

By the shifty gaze, Savage thought they'd probably said more than that.

"So you bought it?"

Kevin shrugged. "Yeah, I said I'd give it a try."

Savage gave him a hard look. "Was this before or after they shot up your store?"

The drug dealer swallowed. "You don't know that was them."

"Don't lie to me, Kevin. You're no good at it." In the short time Savage had known the drug dealer, he'd figured out the man's tell. Every time he lied, his eyes shifted off center, an involuntary reaction.

"Shit Sheriff. You saw what they did to my store. If I rat them out, hell's gonna rain down on me."

Some would say he deserved it.

"We'll make sure that doesn't happen."

Kevin scoffed. "You can't protect me. These guys mean business."

"Is that where you were yesterday? In Durango talking to your new friends?"

Kevin shifted in his chair. "Yeah."

"But they shot up your store anyway?"

"That was a warning. I didn't know it was gonna happen, I swear. Else I would have told Aaron to get outa there."

A thought struck Savage. "You sell any of this Pink Soda to anyone from the Apex Holding development?"

"Nah, I don't deal."

"You don't remember seeing anyone from the building site in your store?"

"No, I don't think I ever seen any of them. What's that got to do with the shooting?"

"Nothing." The drug dealer was sweating, dark patches of sweat spreading under his arms. Savage sighed. "Give me a name, Kevin. Who threatened you?"

"They're from Denver."

"A name."

Kevin bit his lip. "If this gets back to them, I'm a dead man."

Savage fixed his gaze on him, waiting.

Kevin's voice was a strangled whisper. "Jonny Star."

————

"THERE'S no way Kevin will testify," Savage told his team after they'd let Handsome go. "He's too shit scared of them."

Sinclair shook her head. "How are those two kids doing?"

"Okay, I think. Thank goodness they smoked the stuff, else it could have been much worse."

"We need to get that stuff off the streets before more kids get hurt."

"I told Kevin if he heard from them again to give me a call."

"You think he will?"

"Nah," Savage said. "But it was worth a shot."

"Should we put him under surveillance?" Thorpe asked.

"No point. We're short of manpower and Shelby's got a guy watching Jonny Star anyway, so hopefully we're covered."

————

SAVAGE HAD JUST FINISHED HAVING supper with Becca, when his cellphone rang. There was no caller ID, so he answered it with a short, "Savage."

A pause.

"It's me. Kevin."

Savage's pulse beat a little faster. "Yeah?"

The dealer's voice was low, cautious. "There's a shipment coming in tonight. The Crimson Angels are bringing it in. I think Jonny Star is going to intercept it."

"What makes you think that?"

"He asked me for the details. I had no choice but to tell them."

"Does Rosalie know her men are compromised?"

Kevin's voice went up an octave. "Jesus? Do you think I'm crazy? If she thought I was selling her out, I'd have the whole freakin' club on my tail." He wasn't wrong there.

"Which route do they use to come in?"

"I don't know, man."

"Time?"

"Don't know that either."

"But you're sure it's tonight?"

"I'm sure. Rosalie told me I could expect more supplies tomorrow."

"Thanks for the heads up." He hung up and stared at his empty plate. The shipment was coming in via the Angels, already making their way up from New Mexico. He wondered if they could get a chopper up. That way, they'd know which route the bikers were taking and could lie in wait.

"What's going on?" Becca asked. "I know that look."

He grimaced. "There's a shipment of drugs coming in tonight, and a Denver gang waiting to hijack it. I'm sorry. I have to go to work."

Her forehead crinkled with concern. "Be careful, Dalton."

He kissed her on the cheek. "I will. Don't wait up. It could be a long one."

––––––––

"THEY'RE ON THE MOVE," Shelby confirmed on the speaker phone.

Savage had mobilized the team on his way in. Not even Shelby, who had more sway with the State Police, could get a chopper up at such short notice, so they'd congregated at the station and were waiting for updates. "Star and his gang left the hotel ten minutes ago."

"Let me know where they hole up," Savage said.

"Will do."

Savage spread a large map of the area over his desk, and they all crowded around it.

"I wish we knew where they were," Sinclair muttered.

"If Jonny Star and his men are on the move, they can't be too far away," Savage pointed out.

"They'll probably set up an ambush somewhere along one of the approach roads," Thorpe said, his head tilted sideways. A born statistician, he loved using technology to work with maps and data.

They didn't need a helicopter, they just had to follow Jonny Star and his group of thugs. "Yeah, we'll have to cover all the inbound roads."

Thorpe's finger traced a yellow line from New Mexico up to Colorado. "This is the most obvious route. Straight up from Albuquerque. If we wait at the Cedar Hill junction, we'll spot them."

"They could go around the reservation." Littleton pointed to the dotted line that demarcated the Southern Ute land.

"Agreed, you take the 140." Savage said. "But don't take any action, just report back if you see them. We'll intercept them before the ambush site, once we know where that is."

Littleton gave an anxious nod. Fieldwork wasn't his forte, but tonight, it was necessary. Savage needed all hands on deck.

"What about me?" Sinclair asked.

"You and I will wait there." Savage pointed to a squiggly white line on the map. "This is the least obvious route and the one I think they'll take."

"Through the mountains?"

"Yeah, less chance of being seen or heard."

"You'd think they'd be more under the radar about bringing in the merchandise," Thorpe said. "Not in one go like this."

"Too risky," Savage said. "There's safety in numbers, and these guys ride as a pack. It's normal to see them in a group, even at night. One member alone on a deserted track would be more unusual."

"Do you think we'll be able to stop them?" Sinclair asked. "I mean, we have no idea how many of them there are."

Savage rubbed the stubble on his jaw. "We're going to have to try. It's the only shot we've got." He didn't want to think what would happen otherwise. It could potentially be a massacre.

Thorpe and Littleton set off, while Sinclair and Savage drove out to the third location, the quietest and most secluded of the roads leading into Hawk's Landing. For that reason alone, he figured it was the likeliest entrance point. The mountain road snaked around the forested foothills and was only really used by locals who lived out that way. You could get to it from the highway, though, which made it a viable option. It was also a natural valley with dips and rises, the perfect territory for an ambush.

Once in position, Savage engaged the four-wheel-drive mode and turned off the mountain pass onto the verge. The SUV bumped along the uneven terrain until it was hidden behind a clump of trees. Savage killed the engine, and they sat in near total silence, listening to it tick down.

When the dust had settled, he picked up the radio. "Sit rep?" All communication was to be kept short with minimal details. You never knew who was listening in to the police frequencies.

"Nothing here," Thorpe reported, his voice rising above the static.

"Clear," Littleton answered.

"Same," Savage said, although his gut was telling him it wouldn't be long.

Sinclair's cellphone rang. "It's Shelby."

Savage waited, his thumb hovering over the transmitter button.

"Where are they?" she asked. After hearing his reply, she nodded. "Gotcha."

Savage arched his eyebrows.

"The Denver crew have turned off toward the mountain pass," she whispered.

"They're headed this way," Savage said into the radio. "They're taking route three. I repeat, route three. Proceed to our location for backup."

"Copy that." Thorpe hung up.

"Okay." Littleton's voice wobbled at the thought of confronting the drug smuggling bikers.

A short while later, Shelby sent another text message. "Denver is driving past now." Almost immediately, the yellow smudge of headlights could be seen snaking up the dark, mountain pass. It illuminated the vegetation ahead, outlining trees and shrubs, but the dark Suburban was too well hidden to be seen.

Two SUVs drove past, one after the other. They reminded Savage of great black birds waiting to swoop down on their unsuspecting prey. Savage and Sinclair stayed put, their eyes following the vehicles until they disappeared around the bend up ahead.

"They're going to lie in wait, and I bet I know where."

"Where?" Sinclair studied a smaller version of the map on her phone.

"There's a dip in the road about a mile ahead," Savage said. "I think they'll wait there." He would, if he was planning an ambush. They'd park their vehicles across the road, forcing the motorcyclists to stop, and then open fire. It would be violent, he had no doubt about that. "You wearing your vest?"

Sinclair gave an anxious nod.

Savage contacted Shelby on the radio. The Durango Sheriff and his men had pulled over a mile back. "Anything?"

"Not yet. Wait. Hang on—" Savage's heart thumped in his ears as he waited for Shelby's response. "Yeah, here they come. Get ready."

Then they heard it. The dull rumble of several Harley-Davidson engines riding in convoy. It wasn't as loud as outside Kevin Handsome's place, but there weren't as many of them this time.

Savage rammed the Suburban into gear, flew over the dry earth and shrubs, and bumped back down onto the road. Turning side on, he screeched to a halt.

No sirens, but the SUV's blue lights pulsed through the night air. The first two motorcycles came into view. They had no time to get the spike belt out and lay it across the road.

Savage flashed his headlights, while Sinclair stood in the road and waved at them to stop. It didn't work. The two lead Harleys simply swerved around both Sinclair and the Suburban and kept on going.

"Shit," Savage muttered.

Sinclair raced around to the trunk and pulled out the spike belt. It was the only way to stop them.

More lights came around the bend.

"Get back," Savage yelled.

Sinclair stepped off the road just as the next two bikers came into view. "I need help," she yelled, struggling with the heavy belt.

Savage grabbed the end, spreading the strip over the asphalt. The pointed spikes gleamed in the Suburban's headlights.

There was a yell as the two bikers hit the spikes and went skidding across the road into the dusty verge. They were both wearing helmets and hadn't been going so fast as to cause an injury. When they looked up, groaning, they saw two guns pointed at them.

Savage gestured for them to stand up. "Get up slowly and keep your hands where I can see them."

Both bikers complied. "What's the problem, Sheriff?" asked the taller of the two. Savage recognized him from Mac's Roadhouse.

"There's an ambush up ahead," he said.

"What?" The taller one glanced at the shorter one, lowering his hands. "Shit, we've got to warn them."

"It's too late." Savage shook his head. "They should've stopped. Keep 'em up." The biker glared at Savage but lifted up his hands again.

"What are you doing way out here, anyway?" Savage kept his tone casual, even though he knew that in under a minute, the lead bikers would be in real trouble.

"We're just out for a night ride," the taller man said innocently.

Sure you are.

Another police vehicle approached, and Shelby pulled up beside them. "I'll go after the others."

Savage gave a quick nod. "Right behind ya."

Sinclair removed the spike belt and Shelby roared off into the night. No sooner than he left had Littleton arrived to take his place. The young deputy pulled over onto the verge and got out. "Am I too late?"

"Nope. Let's get these two settled in the back, then we'll head up the road. The shit's about to hit the fan."

Together, he and Littleton patted the bikers down while Sinclair kept her weapon trained on them. They weren't carrying any concealed arms that Savage could see. The drugs were probably hidden in their motorcycles. Fuel tank, seat, battery pack, or even behind the headlamps. They'd have to impound them to conduct a proper search.

Savage was about to cuff the two men when the booming echo of gunshots ricocheted off the mountain peaks.

Sinclair turned to him in alarm. "It's started."

SIXTEEN

AS THEY DROVE over the rise, they saw Shelby's vehicle, abandoned on the shoulder. Behind it, in the pulsing neon-blue light, crouched the Durango Sheriff, along with his two colleagues. They were trading shots with the gangsters.

The two SUVs blocked the road in an arrow formation right where Savage had said they'd be. From behind them, multiple shooters rained bullets down on the four hapless bikers, cowering behind a makeshift wall of chrome and steel. One biker lay on the road clutching his thigh while the other three were trying to stanch the bleeding while still returning fire. One direct shot and those fuel tanks would explode.

The night sky fizzed with flying bullets.

Savage heard the metallic ping as gunshots peppered the side of the Suburban.

"Get down!" he shouted. The cuffed bikers in the back ducked out of sight. With a growl of tires, Savage pulled in beside Shelby. The pinging halted now that they were out of the firing line.

"Let us out, man," one of the bikers yelled. "Can't you see they need help?"

Savage ignored him. The last thing he wanted to do was add fuel to the fire. "Go!" he ordered.

Sinclair pushed open the door and slid out, keeping low. Glock in hand, Savage climbed out behind her.

"Boy, am I glad to see you!" Shelby let off a shot in the direction of the aggressors. "These guys have got some serious firepower." Savage could tell by the burst of rounds as they arrived that the Denver thugs were using semi-automatics.

Littleton slotted his cruiser in behind theirs. Ducking, he joined them behind the Suburban.

"Cover them," Savage shouted.

The law enforcement officers opened fire on the thugs behind the SUVs, buying enough time for the trapped bikers to drag their friend out of the lethal onslaught behind a boulder.

A bullet hit the back window of Shelby's cruiser. Glass shattered, spilling out like diamonds over the asphalt. One of the bikers took a hit to the shoulder and cried out. The yelling from the back of Savage's SUV got louder.

"Stay down!" He thumped on the hood of the Suburban.

"I've called for backup," Littleton shouted. "State Patrol are on their way."

"It'll take them a while to get here." Savage emptied his magazine and paused to reload. Even though the Durango field office wasn't that far away, there would only be a handful of officers available this time of night.

Another vehicle screeched in behind Littleton.

Thorpe.

Savage took stock of the players. Four police vehicles, seven officers, four bikers in the firing line and eight Denver thugs, as far as he could tell. Four in each SUV. All heavily loaded. The thugs were unleashing the full power of their semi-automatics on the bikers and the law enforcement officers.

Savage heard a new sound. Distant and low, getting louder with every terrifying second.

Thunder.

His heart sank as around the bend came an army of Harley-Davidsons. The Crimson Angels had arrived. This was going to get ugly.

The bedlam of bikers pulled over a quarter of a mile behind the thugs. Savage watched as dark shadows leaped off their machines and raced along the sides of the road, keeping to the shrubs and trees while firing manically at the gangsters.

The initial assault on the four bikers still hunkering down behind the boulder stopped as the Denver thugs were distracted by the oncoming bikers. They spun around, took cover and returned fire, but not before there were several screams of pain as the outlaws' bullets found their marks.

With the change in the dynamic of the gunfight, Savage and one of Shelby's deputies darted from behind the Suburban to assist the injured bikers.

"We got two down," a bearded biker shouted to Savage. He looked a lot like ZZ Top.

"Come on!" The two uninjured took cover behind Shelby's vehicle, while Savage and the deputy helped the two injured ones. The guy who'd been shot in the shoulder would be fine, but the same couldn't be said for the guy with the thigh wound. It looked like the bullet had nicked an artery. Blood stained his pants a dark red. Too much blood. The guy was barely conscious.

More screams cut through the darkness. The Denver thugs were taking a beating. Through the eerie glow of their headlights, Savage saw Jonny Star and a sidekick scuttle into one of the SUVs. The vehicle shrieked into reverse and a moment later, blasted off, leaving a patch of scorched tarmac behind it, skirting the bikes lying on the road.

So much for loyalty.

The rest of the thugs were either injured, dying, or surrendering. Savage made out several pairs of hands in the air. Surrounded, with no backup, it was game over.

Yet the frenzy continued. Savage realized with a shock that the bikers were going to slaughter the remaining thugs despite their attempt at surrender. No mercy. Anyone who was still alive would not be in the very near future.

Savage made to run out there, but Shelby held him back.

"It's too hot."

Shelby was right. The Angels wouldn't listen to him, not now that their blood was up. And he'd promised Becca he wouldn't take any unnecessary risks.

Gritting his teeth, Savage sat tight until he heard approaching sirens and the headlights of the State Police vehicles appeared like some godly vision over the rise.

Sinclair heaved a sigh of relief.

On hearing the sirens, the attacking bikers scattered. Those who weren't injured jumped onto their motorcycles and took off in a cloud of gas fumes and burning rubber. Some weren't so lucky, now cornered by the State Patrol vehicles.

Soon, the place was crawling with law enforcement officers. There were sharp cries of, "Drop your weapons" and "get your hands up". The few remaining bikers and Denver thugs who weren't bleeding out on the tarmac complied. They were outnumbered and outgunned.

The two bikers who'd taken cover behind Shelby's car glanced at each other, then turned, as if to make a quick getaway into the hills.

"Oh no you don't." Thorpe blocked their way, his pistol leveled at them. "Put your guns down."

The two men didn't resist. They dropped their weapons and put their hands in the air. Nobody felt like more bloodshed.

"Is Lennie gonna be okay?" ZZ Top glanced at his friend who was in and out of consciousness. It didn't look good.

"We need to call an ambulance," Thorpe said, cuffing the uninjured bikers.

"Already have." Littleton was learning fast. A couple of months back, he wouldn't have done anything on his own initiative, now he was making decisions on the battlefield. Savage grunted his approval.

The other injured biker had a shoulder wound, and while the bullet was still inside, it didn't look too bad. Not life threatening. Sinclair gathered up all the weapons and locked them in the trunk of the Suburban.

Shelby put the two cuffed bikers in the back of his vehicle, and then he, Savage, and the Durango deputies went to meet the Troopers, rounding up the remaining participants of the gun fight.

"Sheriffs Savage and Shelby." Savage shook hands with a no-nonsense man in uniform who looked to be in charge.

"Brent Radley," he said with a curt nod. "What happened here?"

Savage raked a hand through his hair. Where to begin? "Turf war."

Shelby backed him up with a bob of his head.

Radley accepted that. His team busied themselves cuffing everyone, both injured and survivors, taking no chances. They'd sort out what happened later.

"We've got three fatalities by the SUVs," Radley said somberly. "And numerous gunshot victims. I've called for multiple ambulances."

"We've got two injured on our side, one critically," Savage said.

"Hell of a gunfight." Radley shook his head. "I'd love to know what kicked it off."

"It's related to that shootout at the convenience store earlier in the week," Savage told him.

"Ah," Radley nodded. "These things escalate quickly."

"Especially when you have twenty outlaw bikers rocking up, guns blazing."

Radley shook his head. "It's a miracle there weren't more casualties."

"Savage, freeze." Shelby's voice was low and urgent.

"What?" Savage turned toward him.

"Don't move," the Durango Sheriff hissed, staring at his torso.

"Oh, jeez." Radley took a step backwards.

Savage glanced down and saw a red dot on his chest. Unmoving. Right over his heart. The shooter had steady hands.

He let out a slow breath, willing himself not to move when every instinct was screaming, run! The activity at the crime scene slowed to a halt as everyone's eyes were fixed on Savage's chest. Time seemed to slow down. All he could hear was his own hollow breathing as he braced for the shot that would end his life.

Then it came.

A deafening crack from a rifle.

SEVENTEEN

EVERYONE WHIRLED around as the shot echoed through the quiet recesses of the mountain.

Savage checked himself for bullet holes. He was intact.

How?

Had the gunman missed? In a dreamlike state, he looked up. Shelby and the State Trooper Radley charged toward the hills, accompanied by Thorpe and one of Shelby's deputies. He could see their flashlights bobbing around like fireflies. They spread out, scrambling through the wilderness to the rocky ledge where the shot appeared to have come from.

Still, he couldn't move. His legs seemed glued to the ground.

Sinclair raced over. "Are you okay?" She looked him over, checking for blood. There was none.

He patted himself down. "I think so."

"What the hell is going on?"

"A sniper. From that ledge." He nodded in the direction of the officers who'd nearly reached the spot. There was a shout, followed by a call for a medic. A flashlight waved back and forth.

"Let's go." Savage shook off the paralyzing shock and spurred into action. Someone had taken a shot at him, and he wanted to know who.

He and Sinclair scrambled up to the rocky ledge. The other officers stood around the prostrate form of a body.

"Here's your shooter." Shelby nodded toward the dark figure of the man. Face down, he'd collapsed on top of his long bolt-action rifle. Shot through the back.

"Who is he?" Sinclair shone her flashlight on what little they could see of his face. Short black hair, swarthy skin, at least two-day's worth of stubble.

"He's not one of Rosalie's guys." Savage would have recognized him.

"Could be one of Denver's." Sinclair tilted her head to the side. The dead man wore black jeans, a dark long-sleeved shirt, and military-style boots. Inconspicuous. Dressed to blend into the shadows.

Then there was the rifle.

"No. This guy's a mercenary," Savage muttered. "A hired gun."

There was a pause as his words sunk in.

"But why?" Radley frowned. "Why you?"

"I don't know."

"You don't recognize him?" Shelby asked.

"Never seen him before." Savage shook his head, confused. The man was a complete stranger. "Who shot him?"

They all looked at each other.

"I could've sworn the shot came from up here," Radley said. Shelby nodded.

Thorpe felt the barrel of the gun with the back of his hand. "Cold. This rifle hasn't been fired."

Shelby looked at Savage. "Someone took him out before he could get a shot off."

Sinclair shivered. "And it wasn't one of us."

"Somebody else is in these hills." Radley glanced up, the beam from his flashlight roaming over the hillside. They followed it like a spotlight. Twisted branches and dark leaves jumped out at them.

Savage inspected the man's bullet wound in the middle of his back.

Center mass. A safe shot, hard to miss. "The shooter was behind him." He stood up and peered into the darkness. "Maybe behind those trees."

Shelby's deputy nodded. "It looks like the shot came from that elevation over there."

"Let's check it out." They set off in the direction of the trees. Savage didn't hold out much hope. The second shooter would be long gone, and impossible to trace in the all-encompassing darkness. There were no lights up here. The only source was the moon, and even that had given up and slunk behind a bank of clouds.

"We need to call the ME," Savage said as he watched the three flashlights dance through the trees. "Let's get Ray on the phone."

"On it." Sinclair pulled out her cell. "I've got one bar. Should be enough."

"You sure get a lot of action around here," Radley said, coming back. "First you had that serial killer maniac running around in the mountains, and now mercenaries. Remind me to never settle in Hawk's Landing."

"Tell me about it," Savage snorted. "I thought it would be a lot quieter than Denver."

Shelby broke into a wry grin. "It's not normally like this."

"Glad to hear it." Radley put his hands on his hips. "We'll tape off this spot and cover the body, just in case. We don't want the wild animals getting to him before your medical examiner does." Savage appreciated him taking control of the situation. He wanted to get back to the station and call Becca, let her know he was okay. The close call had left him shaken.

"Ray said he'll be here at sunrise." Sinclair pocketed her phone.

"I'll post a couple men to guard the body," Radley offered.

Savage nodded his thanks. "We'll take the uninjured bikers back to the station for processing."

By the time they got back to the road, emergency services had arrived. The kaleidoscope of flashing red and blue lights lit up the valley. Medics were tending to the injured, while the worst had been taken to the nearest hospital. Five body bags lay in a respectful row beside one of the ambulances.

"I did what I could, but I don't think Lennie's going to make it." Littleton looked like he was about to burst into tears. His hands were covered in blood, and there was a red smudge on his cheek.

"Lennie?"

"The thigh wound."

"What about the guy with the bullet in his shoulder?"

"They've both been taken to hospital."

Savage glanced behind Littleton to the Suburban. "How are our prisoners?"

He pulled a face. "Mad as hell."

A grim nod. It was to be expected. Savage would be mad too if a bunch of big city mobsters had shot up his team. "Let's get them back to the station."

Radley came over. "I've got two more Crimson Angels, if you want 'em. My men apprehended them when we moved in. I haven't got any Denver thugs for you. They're all dead or on their way to the hospital."

"I'll take 'em." Shelby came over with a deputy. "Probably better to split them up."

Savage nodded his agreement. Four Angels in his cells were enough. "Jonny Star got away," he said. "I saw him leave with one of his men before you arrived."

"You sure it was him?" Radley asked. "It's dark, they're all wearing masks. Hard to see who's who."

The State Trooper was right. Without a positive ID, they wouldn't be able to pin anything on him. Body language and stature weren't enough. "I know it was him."

"Not enough for an arrest warrant." Radley patted Savage on the shoulder.

"How badly injured are his men?" Savage asked, as Shelby and his deputy led the two sullen bikers away.

"One's critical, probably not going to make it," Radley said, his expression neutral. "The other took a bullet in the chest. Think it punctured a lung 'cos he's coughing up blood. Still, he might be okay if they operate soon."

Savage gave a curt nod. At least he could question the survivor in the hospital when he came to. He had to find out who wanted him dead and why. His gut told him it wasn't Rosalie. They were working toward a common goal. She needed him to get rid of the competition—unless she'd figured an all-out massacre was more effective. Except this wasn't her style. Way too messy. Sure, she'd respond to the threat, lead her men into battle, but she wouldn't instigate something like this.

The President of the Crimson Angels was usually easy to spot, but today she'd flown under the radar. They'd parked too far away for him to recognize her motorcycle. They'd also worn black facemasks under their helmets, which made it difficult to identify anyone.

He kicked a stone in frustration. They had nothing that would hold up in court, and he already knew the six bikers they had in custody weren't going to talk.

"See you back at the station," Thorpe said.

Savage nodded. Even though the sky was turning yellow in the distance, he couldn't go home yet.

EIGHTEEN

"RADLEY CALLED. THE MOTORCYCLES WERE CLEAN," Thorpe reported later the next day. The State Police had collected all the abandoned Harleys in the back of several large pickup trucks and taken them away for processing.

"How could they be clean?" Savage frowned, standing beside his deputy's desk. Then he knew.

Rosalie.

She'd made sure that no evidence would be found on her guys. In the chaos, the Angels had swapped the drug-laden motorcycles with clean ones. No one would have noticed the exchange amidst the carnage that had ensued. It was a brilliant ploy.

"Did Radley get photographs of the confiscated motorcycles?" Savage asked.

"I'll ask him," Thorpe replied.

Savage went into his office. Becca had been fast asleep when he'd crawled into bed last night, so he hadn't woken her. As he'd looked across at her belly lifting the covers, he'd felt a frisson of excitement. That was his child in there, waiting to come into the world.

Except what a world it was. He thought of the melee he'd been involved in only hours before and winced. He had to clear this up before Becca gave birth.

I need you to be present, she'd said. He intended to honor that promise, even take some time off, but he had to solve Eddie Youngblood's murder first.

Was last night linked to the teenager's death at the building site? Indirectly, maybe. It was connected to the shootout at the convenience store. That much he did know.

"Sending those photos to you now," Thorpe called.

Savage opened the file and stared at the entry-level Harleys. His theory was correct. These bikes weren't worth more than four or five thousand dollars, secondhand. They probably had a bunch leftover from members who'd upgraded over the years. Sacrificial lambs, in effect. Bring the drugs in on the real bikes, then substitute them for the drug-free, cheap versions.

Once again, he'd underestimated her.

"Sheriff?" Littleton stood beside the door. "What's going on? I thought these guys were shipping drugs from Mexico. Where'd they go?"

"They did a switch," he explained. Thorpe stood beside Littleton, listening, while Sinclair sat at her desk sliding bullets into two separate magazines. One for her duty issued Glock 22, the other for her backup, a Glock 26 9mm, which she kept in an ankle holster. Both had been emptied in last night's shootout. Savage continued. "Those bikes Radley impounded were old and cheap, not the ones they used to ride up from Mexico."

"They switched the bikes last night?" Sinclair stopped what she was doing and stared at him.

"Yeah, we missed it in the mayhem. The drugs aren't in these." He nodded at the photograph. "They never were."

"Jeez." Thorpe pushed his glasses up his nose. "That was smart." Littleton shook his head.

Savage nodded. "Yeah."

"What about the first two?" Sinclair asked. "The guys we stopped with the spike belt? Those motorcycles were the real deal, weren't they?"

"Bikers ride in formation in case they get pulled over," Savage explained. "The President and Vice President are at the front, followed by the muscle in the middle of the pack. They're usually heavily armed. The last few riders are clean. No records, no guns, no drugs."

Littleton's eyes widened. "So if the cops pull them over, only the last ones stop?"

"That's right. If they're searched, they're clean. Much like the situation we've got here." Savage nodded to the door leading to the cells where the four bikers were locked up. They could only hold them for forty-eight hours before they had to let them go.

"Well, that sucks." Thorpe turned back to his screen in disgust.

"You going to question them?" Sinclair asked, seating the fully loaded magazine back in place. She then chambered a round, putting the weapon in battery. After which she ejected the mag and topped it off. She did the same with her backup weapon before tucking it back in her ankle holster.

"Yep, right now." Savage got up and went to look at the live camera footage of the men in the cells. Because they only had three cells, they'd had to put the two guys they'd picked up first together. Right now, they spoke softly to one another. The video feed contained no sound, so Savage couldn't hear what was being said.

It didn't really matter. They'd ridden up from Mexico together and had plenty of time to get their story straight.

ZZ Top was fast asleep, while the guy who'd tried to stop his buddy from bleeding out looked ragged and upset.

"Littleton, bring me the one covered in blood." Savage knew something ZZ Top didn't, and it would play to his advantage.

A short while later, he faced the bloodied biker in an interview room. Bloodshot eyes, thick stubble, and a weary expression. The man was also shaking a little, probably from shock.

"What's your name?" Savage asked.

A stony silence.

"Listen, I know you've been told not to speak to me, and I can't make you, but this will go better for you if you do.

The man said nothing.

"I'm sorry about your friend."

The guy looked up.

"He died an hour ago," Savage told him.

The biker dropped his head into his hands.

Savage gave him a minute. "Were you close?"

No reply.

"It's hard when you lose a friend." He leaned back, studying the suspect. "Even harder when you lose a brother."

The man looked up. "You don't know shit."

"Lennie was your younger brother, wasn't he?"

The doctor had called Barbara with an ID earlier that morning. After looking him up on the database, Savage had discovered the victim had an older brother, Patrick, also a member of the Crimson Angels. There were even some physical similarities, although it was hard to compare when you only had an "after" photograph to go by. Death altered a person's appearance so much that sometimes their own relatives couldn't identify them.

The burly biker's eyes glistened, and he swiped at them. Savage could feel the anger radiating off him.

"Dangerous business, drug smuggling."

"Shut up," growled Patrick.

Savage shrugged. "You wanna tell me about it?"

"Nothing to tell." At least he was talking now.

"Did you know there'd be an ambush?"

Patrick shot him a scornful look. "What do you think?"

That was a no, then. "Did you know the guys who ambushed you?"

"No idea who they were," Patrick seethed. "We were out for a night ride like we do sometimes, and we came over the rise and there they were, waiting for us."

"Did they say anything before they opened fire?"

"Nah. We slid off our bikes and used them for cover. We were sitting ducks." His meaty hand clenched into a fist. "Lennie took a bullet to the thigh. I knew it was bad. There was so much blood." The man's eyes were haunted.

"If you need to speak to a trauma counselor, we can provide one."

Patrick scoffed. "What I need is to get the hell out of here."

"So you can hunt down the men who killed your brother?"

No reply.

"You'd be wasting your time. Most of them are dead," Savage told him. "The rest of your gang took them out last night." He didn't mention that Jonny Star and one other had escaped, and two more were in critical condition. Rosalie would know, though. She'd find out. Shelby had stationed an armed guard at the hospital, just in case.

Patrick gave a snort. "Good."

Savage studied him. A night ride. No drugs. No record. The man was as clean as a whistle. It wasn't his fault they'd been ambushed on the way home. That's what his lawyer would say, if he had one. With four guys locked up, Savage was surprised they hadn't seen one already. Perhaps Rosalie didn't think it necessary, given the glaring lack of evidence. Still, there was one more thing he had to check.

"Do you recognize this man?" Savage slid a photograph of the dead sniper across the table.

Patrick looked at it. "No. Who is he?"

"It's not important." He shoved it back into his pocket and walked out of the interrogation room. "You can let him go," he told Littleton.

"Seriously?"

"Yeah. He's not going to tell us anything, and he's grieving his dead brother." Sinclair nodded.

"What about the others?" Thorpe asked after a beat.

"Leave them to stew for a while." Savage scratched his stubbly chin. He'd woken up late and hadn't had time to shave this morning.

"Sheriff, I've got Shelby on the line for you." Barbara's voice called through the door.

"Okay, put him through."

"Morning," the Durango Sheriff said once Savage was on the line. "Got some news for you."

"Yeah?"

"The Denver thug died on the way to hospital last night."

Savage sighed. "What about the other guy?"

"He's in surgery. It's not looking good."

Hell. He needed to speak to them. "Thanks for letting me know, Shelby. Any sign of Jonny Star?"

"Nope, looks like he ran home with his tail between his legs."

"I damn well hope so."

"I think we can relax on that front for a while, at least."

"With any luck, they'll take their business elsewhere. Any ID on the sniper?"

"Not yet. Your mom-and-pop team is still up there. I'll let you know if they find anything." Shelby paused. "Hey, did you get anything from those bikers?"

"Nothing yet." Savage told Shelby about the motorcycle switch. The sheriff gave a dry laugh. "Even with all my years in law enforcement, I never saw that coming."

"Me neither. Wasn't even looking for it."

"Well, they got away with it this time," Shelby said. "But we'll know for next time."

"I hope there isn't going to be a next time," Savage said sourly.

"Amen to that."

NINETEEN

THERE WERE three hotels and seven motels in Hawk's Landing, and Savage visited them all. Nobody knew the dead sniper. He even left photocopies in the hopes that someone might recognize the man. So far, nothing.

Taking a break, he grabbed a sandwich and coffee at a roadside diner on the outskirts of town, not far from Kevin Handsome's farm.

He glanced out of the window at the rolling countryside, marveling at the expanse of space, the impossibly blue sky, and the lush, velvety mountains. Across the road, an enormous oak tree was turning copper.

His phone rang. It was Becca.

"Hi," he answered. "Everything alright?"

"I can feel him kicking." She sounded breathless.

"Him?"

She chuckled. "With a kick this strong, it's got to be a boy."

"You okay?"

"Yes, just uncomfortable."

"Hang in there. It won't be long now." That's what the doc had told them. "Do you need anything?"

"No, I'm good. Just checking in."

Savage started as a familiar figure walked past the diner window.

No way.

Jonny Star.

What the hell was he still doing here? "Er, honey, I have to go."

"Okay, see you later."

"I'll be home as soon as I can."

He hung up, his gaze on the retreating figure. No one could actually prove that the Denver businessman had been at the shootout last night. He'd worn a mask, and the SUVs had fake Colorado plates, having been reported stolen a week ago. Not even the Crimson Angels knew him, although Rosalie would be asking questions. It wouldn't be long before she found out who'd ambushed them. Savage didn't like Star's chances when she did.

The suspect strode along the sidewalk into the park. Throwing money on the table, Savage leaped up and followed him. The park rambled through wilderness and overgrown shrubs. It was pretty but needed some maintenance. Regardless, it provided enough coverage for Savage to keep himself hidden.

Star left the footpath and ducked under some leafy branches into a cluster of trees. Savage stalled. Following him in was too risky. Instead, he circled around and tried to sneak up from the other side. As he got closer, he heard voices. Star had met someone behind the trees.

What were they saying? He couldn't work it out, there was too much peripheral noise. A dog barked nearby, while a gaggle of teenage girls sashayed past, screeching at each other in high pitched voices.

Sneaking closer, he tried to get a visual, but there was too much foliage in the way. Straining his ears, he tried to hear what they were saying, but their voices were too low.

Dammit.

Who was that? The voice sounded familiar.

Ducking, he crept through the foliage until he could peek between the trees.

What the—?

Talking to Star was the guy running the construction project for Apex Holdings. Kushner. Savage rubbed his forehead. What was *he* doing here?

Easing away from the trees, Savage walked back to the path. Why was the Denver gangster talking to Douglas Connelly's man? And why here, in the park, out of the way of prying eyes? They clearly didn't want to be seen together.

Savage strode back to his SUV, deep in thought. Questions swirled through his head. Was Kushner the one bringing the lethal new meth into the county, or in cahoots with the Denver mobsters? Was Connelly involved? Could Kushner be the person who'd murdered Eddie Young-blood? Perhaps the youngster had discovered Kushner's part in the drug smuggling operation and threatened to go to the police.

He sighed. He didn't know anything for a fact. All he had was questions. Endless questions—and no answers.

Perhaps it was time to get some.

On the way back to Hawk's Landing, Savage pulled in at Mac's Roadhouse. It was time to shake the tree and see what fell out. He was tired of fumbling around in the dark. Rosalie might be able to give him some answers after what had happened last night.

Burner looked up as Savage walked into the bar. The bartender's hood-eyed expression said it all. The jukebox was silent. Only the sound of clinking glasses could be heard as Burner stacked them above the bar.

Scooter, the MC club's Vice President, sat at a table going over some paperwork. "What do you want?" he snarled. "We're not open yet."

Savage spotted a nasty graze on VP's cheek. "What happened to your face?" Savage asked, keeping his voice even.

"Came off my bike," Scooter gritted.

"Looks fresh."

"Yesterday. Right here in the parking lot."

Sure it was.

Savage walked over to him. "Rosalie here?"

"Sheriff, this really isn't a good time," came a gruff feminine voice behind him. He turned to find Rosalie standing at the door. Scooter scowled, then went back to his paperwork.

Physically, she seemed well. No scratches or bruises. No apparent injuries. The only sign that she was suffering was her drawn face and hollow eyes. "I don't know if you heard, but there was an ambush last night. Lost one of our brothers."

"I know." Savage fixed his gaze on her. "I was there."

Rosalie's eyes darted over Savage's shoulder. To Scooter.

Shared grief. A warning. A silent agreement. Say nothing.

He knew the game.

Rosalie walked past him to the bar. "Give me a coffee, Burner?"

The bartender nodded and turned away. She sat down on one of the stools and stared at her reflection in the mirror behind the bar. Gaunt face. Heavily kohled eyes. Perhaps she thought they'd mask her feelings. They didn't.

"Mind if I join you?" Savage asked. "That coffee smells good."

She looked like she might refuse, but when he sat down beside her, she relented. "No offense, Sheriff, but you look like hell."

He scoffed. "It's been a long twenty-four hours."

She turned away.

"I'm sorry for your loss," he said. He meant it. Even criminals had feelings.

"Thank you."

There was a scrape of a chair and Scooter got up, collected his file of papers, and disappeared into the back office.

"What happened?"

She raised an eyebrow. "I thought you were there?"

"I want to hear your version."

Burner put two cups of coffee down in front of them, then went out the back, leaving them alone. Rosalie reached for hers, black and hot. She took a scalding sip, her eyes narrowed against the steam.

Savage waited.

"A couple of the guys were out for a night ride when they were ambushed," she began. Sounded like the biker gang agreed on their stories before the event. "I don't know what the murdering scumbags were after, but two of my gang were shot. One died, the other is in the hospital."

"I believe he's going to be okay," Savage said.

She perked up at this information.

He gave a wry smile. "I spoke to the doc this morning."

Rosalie exhaled, a soft hiss like air escaping from a tire. "Thank God."

"Where were you last night?" Savage asked.

Her vivid green stare fixed on him. "You think I was there?"

He met her gaze. "Were you?"

She went very still. He imagined what was going through her mind. Could she trust him?

No.

What would he do with the information? Would he be duty bound to act on it?

Yes.

"No," she said.

Liar.

"So where were you?"

"At home, obviously."

"Can anyone vouch for you?"

"No. I live alone, as you well know."

He nodded. "I'm afraid that doesn't leave you with much of an alibi."

"Only guilty people need alibis."

He smiled at the truth in that statement.

"Anyway, why would I need one?"

"For the murder of the men who ambushed your guys. I was there, remember? I saw the Crimson Angels coming over the rise."

Angels of death.

"I'm not responsible for what happened." She kept her voice even. "I can't help it if a couple of bikers went to my guy's assistance. I'm glad they did, otherwise we'd have more casualties."

"A couple? It was more like a swarm."

She shrugged, but he didn't miss the angry light in her eyes. It was only a flicker, but it was there.

"Is that the story you're sticking to?" He shook his head.

Her eyes widened now. "Isn't that what happened?"

He sighed. "Those dead thugs are having multiple slugs taken out of them as we speak, and sooner or later, they're going to lead back to you." He had to give her credit.

Her poker face gave nothing away.

"You think this problem is solved?" he said, angry now. "It isn't. The Denver mob isn't done yet. They're regrouping and are going to come back stronger. If you want to finish this, you're going to have to work with me."

For the first time, he saw a flash of alarm in her eyes. That would give her something to think about. Still, she didn't budge. "Sheriff, if there's nothing else, I've got work to do."

He downed his coffee and stood. "Before I go, we found this guy in the hills with a sniper rifle. Do you know him?"

He showed her the crime scene photograph.

"A sniper rifle?" Puzzled, she took the photo and studied it, then shook her head. "No. Who is he?"

"That's what I'm trying to find out."

"Nobody I know."

"How about you?" Savage showed it to Burner who'd just come back into the bar, a crate in his arms.

He shook his head.

Savage turned back to Rosalie. "Not one of your Mexican connections?"

That blank stare again. "I don't know anyone in Mexico."

He gave a resolute nod. "Thanks for the chat." He nodded to Burner who was watching the exchange, then turned his back on them and stalked out of the bar.

———

THAT WOMAN.

Irritating didn't begin to cover it.

Feisty. Stubborn. Resolute.

All the characteristics he admired in a cop but hated in an adversary.

Savage sighed and held his face up to the sun, hoping the warmth would calm him. It didn't. A breeze had kicked up, bringing with it a hint of winter. He exhaled. It was time to put some heads together.

He dialed Shelby's number and waited for the Durango Sheriff to pick up, when he saw the folded piece of paper tucked under his windshield.

A quick glance back at the bar. Nobody was watching. The parking lot was empty, save for Rosalie's van, Scooter's black beast of a motorcycle, and Burner's low rider. Grabbing the note, he climbed into the SUV.

It wasn't until he was on the road back to Hawk's Landing that he pulled over and opened it.

WE NEED TO TALK.

MEET ME TONIGHT. 9PM.

CRAZY DOG RANCH.

COME ALONE.

TWENTY

"WHO'S IT FROM?" Sinclair asked.

"Scooter or Burner. It must be. They were the only two there, apart from Rosalie, and I was with her the whole time." Savage rubbed his forehead.

"Burner?" Thorpe asked.

"He's the new guy. Only been there a couple months. Took over as bartender when Scooter was promoted to VP."

Thorpe arched his eyebrow. "That's quite a promotion."

"I think it had something to do with his role in Axle's downfall. He's always been close to Rosalie. Internal politics." Savage shrugged.

"Are you going to go?" Thorpe asked.

Savage gave a brief nod. "It could be important."

"It could be a setup," Sinclair reminded him. "Someone's already tried to kill you once. Maybe they want to try again."

He grimaced, remembering the red dot on his chest. The cold fear that had engulfed him in that moment. The thought of never seeing Becca again or meeting his unborn child. He took a steadying breath, pushing the thought aside. "It could be legit. Someone might know something, and we need a lead."

"Crazy Dog Ranch is deserted," Barbara told them, coming into the main office. "The bank foreclosed on the property last year and it's been standing empty ever since."

"You can't go alone," Thorpe said. "I'll come along for backup,"

"The note said to come alone."

Thorpe squared his shoulders. "They won't know I'm there."

"He's right," Sinclair said. "It would be foolish to go by yourself."

I won't take any unnecessary risks.

"Fine." Savage relented. He wasn't sure this qualified for keeping his promise, but it would be better if Thorpe was there, lurking in the shadows. Just in case.

―――――

THEY SET OUT AFTER DUSK. The sky had turned slate gray and mist unfurled around the jagged mountain peaks. Savage loved its wild beauty. He remembered when he'd first arrived in Hawk's Landing, he'd been blown away by the untamed wilderness, the huge skies, the endless prairie. So much space. So much air. So unlike the city.

"Looks like rain." Thorpe glanced out of the window.

"Let's hope it holds off for a few hours."

Savage drove until they reached the ranch perimeter. The fence had long since fallen down, as had the wooden gate. The only thing left standing was a rusty signpost that read Crazy Dog Ranch. It shrieked in the wind.

"It's getting colder." Thorpe climbed out of the Suburban, pulling up the zipper on his jacket. He'd approach the house on foot, keeping to the shadows. Once he had a clear vantage point, he'd hunker down and wait. When whoever it was turned up, they'd have a rifle trained on him the whole time. A sensible precaution, since they had no idea who the mystery note-leaver was.

"See you later," Savage said.

Thorpe gave a firm nod and strode into the brush, the rifle slung over his arm. Savage watched him until he was absorbed by the shadows.

"Here we go," Savage muttered as he drove up the meandering drive to the derelict ranch house.

This better not be a setup.

He strained his eyes but couldn't see any lights up ahead. The windows were in darkness, as was the porch. There were no vehicles that he could see, nor motorcycles, although they could be hidden behind the house, or in the various small outbuildings scattered over the property. Could Sinclair be right? Was he heading into a trap?

He took a deep breath to settle his nerves. If this was a setup, Thorpe would call and warn him.

His phone stayed silent.

Savage checked his Glock, then opened the car door. He'd taken a couple of steps toward the house when a sound to the left made him swing around. "It is you."

Burner, the Roadhouse bartender, stood there, hand on hip as if he was going for a quick draw.

Savage drew his weapon. "If this is some kind of joke—"

"No joke." Burner raised his hands in a gesture of surrender.

Savage glanced around, expecting a troop of outlaw bikers to appear and give him a beating for arresting their friends. He hoped Thorpe was watching this through his night vision binoculars.

"It's just me," Burner said.

Savage shook his head. "Why do you want to talk to me?"

"Firstly, my name isn't Burner. And secondly, I'm not part of the club."

What the hell?

Savage stared at him. "Who are you then?"

"My name is Special Agent Grayson Carter. I'm an undercover DEA operative from Denver. I infiltrated the Crimson Angels in the hopes of getting the name of their Mexican supplier. We've been watching them for some time now."

Savage took in the long hair, the tats on his hands, the stubble you could light a match on. "*You're* a DEA agent?"

"I know I don't look it, but that's the point, really."

Savage had known a few DEA agents in his time. He frowned, not sure he believed him. "How'd you sell it to Rosalie? She's not easily fooled." She'd have vetted him thoroughly before hiring him.

"I assumed someone else's identity," he explained. "The real Max Wilson was shot and killed in a drug-related incident three months ago. He had no immediate family, so instead of letting word of his death get out, we made it look like he'd disappeared."

"How?"

"Spread a rumor around the biker bars. Burner bolted because it was getting too hot. According to rumor, he was last seen waiting at a bus station downtown."

"Nice." Savage was impressed.

"It's worked well up until now. Max Wilson's life is now mine. I even look a bit like him. All it took were a few tattoos and growing my hair."

Savage narrowed his eyes. "How do I know you're telling the truth?"

"You don't. I brought this to show you." The agent handed Savage an ID card. He inspected it in the light of the headlamps, the wind whipping his hair against his face. It looked legit.

"You had me fooled." Savage handed it back.

"That's why I wanted to meet. After last night..."

"You were at the shootout?"

"Yeah, crazy stuff. We only just made it out of there before the troopers arrived. Shame about Lennie. Rosalie's pretty upset. He was one of her loyal followers."

"Aren't they all?"

He shrugged. "There are those who don't think a woman should be in charge."

Savage gave a slow nod. There would be members who were still loyal to Axle, Rosalie's predecessor. "Trouble in the ranks?"

"Something's brewing, but I don't know what. I'm not privy to the workings of the inner sanctum. I just bartend and do odd jobs. Still earning my stripes."

"What do you know about the Denver thugs?" Savage asked.

Burner hesitated. "If I tell you what I know, are you going to reciprocate?"

"You know I can't talk about an active investigation."

Burner stared at him for a long moment, his gaze hardening. "Then we're done here." He turned around.

"Hang on." Savage hesitated. The guy had come clean about being an agent, and he appreciated that. It would be good to have someone on the inside. There wasn't time to check his story, but all things considered, he decided to give Burner the benefit of the doubt. "I'll fill in the gaps if I can."

Burner hesitated, then nodded. "The Denver connection is cause for concern. Mafia types, run by a bigshot businessman called Guy Hollander. You won't see him down here in La Plata County."

"Jonny Star one of his?"

"He's Hollander's point man."

"Know a guy called Kushner?" Savage asked.

The DEA agent gave a wry grin. "Yeah. Paul Kushner, or Crusher as he's known in the industry. I heard he once crushed a man to death with his bare hands. He's Hollander's henchman-slash-enforcer. He oversees things."

"Like the takeover of Rosalie's drug smuggling network?"

"Exactly like that."

"Then what is he doing on the Apex Holdings development?" Savage tried but failed to join the dots.

"That's where it gets complicated. Douglas Connelly borrowed money from Hollander to get this project off the ground, so now the Denver mafia owns them. Kushner is there to protect their investment."

"While at the same time keep an eye on Jonny Star and his thugs."

"Now you're getting the picture."

Savage exhaled. Things had just gotten a whole lot more complicated. For one, Kushner and Connelly had just moved to the top of his suspect list. "What about Steve Bryant? You know him?"

Burner thought for a moment. "Can't say I've heard of him. Who is he?"

"Works for Connelly. Chief Finance Officer or some such thing."

"Don't know him. He been with the company long?"

"No idea. I'll ask Connelly to see his personnel file."

"You'll need a warrant. Connelly isn't going to cough up that kind of information without a judge's say-so."

"You're probably right." The wind escalated from a whistle to a howl. Savage pulled his jacket tighter.

"Now my turn," Burner said.

"What do you want to know?"

"Was that kid's death drug-related?"

Savage frowned. "Yeah. How'd you know?"

"There's this lethal new party drug on the market, Pink Soda. We think Hollander's guys are bringing it in."

"From Denver?"

"And other places. We've got a growing list of kids who died after taking it. If it's here, I gotta report back."

"It's here," Savage confirmed. "The kid overdosed on it." He paused. "But it might not have been an accident."

Burner's eyes widened. "Seriously?"

"We found the syringe discarded in the nearby forest, and the injection site wasn't where you'd expect. Also, the kid didn't have a history of drugs."

"That doesn't mean it wasn't his first time," Burner reasoned.

"Trust me, I have several witnesses who swear he never touched the stuff."

"You think someone murdered him?" Burner ignored the buffeting wind.

"Looks that way."

"Who?" His eyes bore into Savage's.

"That's what I'm trying to find out."

"Any leads?"

"Nothing concrete."

"Shit." He turned away.

Savage couldn't make him out. He seemed frustrated, more so than what he would expect from an agent. Unless he had personal involvement in the case. "Did you know Eddie?"

"The kid? No." He shook his head. "But I've known many like him. What a waste of a life. That's why I became an agent, so I could stop this type of thing from happening."

Somewhere a barn door banged in the wind. Savage felt a speckle of rain. It was time to wind this up.

"Before you go, you didn't see anyone up on the ledge yesterday, did you?"

"Where, at the shootout?"

"Yeah, in the hills."

There was a pause. "You looking for the sniper who tried to take you out?"

Savage caught his breath. "You saw that?"

"Yeah, I was hiding in the bushes. I saw it."

"Did you shoot him?" Savage asked.

Burner gave him a long, hard stare. "I think it's time I headed back." He turned and walked in the direction of the house. Savage went after him.

Burner got to his motorcycle, then turned to face him. "Don't ask me questions I can't answer."

"Who was he?" Savage asked.

Burner got on his bike and kicked in the stand. "I don't know."

———

"YOU'RE VERY QUIET," Becca said as Savage got into bed. "Everything okay?"

"Complicated case." He hadn't told her about the sniper. The last thing she needed to hear was that an attempt had been made on his life. A hit, at that.

"Want to talk about it?"

He leaned over and kissed her. "No, it's late and you need your sleep."

She put a hand on her belly. "I can't wait to meet him."

A chill shot unbidden down his spine. He was bringing a child into the world while a target was still on his back. That sniper had been a pro, and if it wasn't Rosalie, and it wasn't the Denver thugs, then who had hired a hitman to take him out?

"You're okay with this, aren't you?" Becca asked, picking up on his mood.

"Yes, of course I am. I'm just worried I won't get this investigation tied up before the baby makes an appearance."

"The others can handle it. Can't they?"

No. As capable as they were, they couldn't do this without him. *He* had the connection to Rosalie, and he had a feeling he was going to need her help to get rid of the Denver thugs. *He* was the only one who knew Burner was an undercover agent. The sniper had set his sight on *him*, not any of the others.

"Sure, they can," he lied. "It'll be fine."

He only hoped it was a promise he could keep.

TWENTY-ONE

"HE'S A DEA AGENT?" Thorpe nearly spilled his morning coffee. Sinclair, Littleton, and Barbara all stared at Savage in disbelief.

"I saw his ID." Savage told them how Grayson Carter had assumed Burner's identity. "I called a friend at Denver PD this morning. Everything Carter said checked out. Max 'Burner' Wilson disappeared after a shootout between two rival drug gangs three months ago. My friend was interested to hear he'd turned up in Hawk's Landing."

Sinclair frowned. "Hang on. Don't Denver PD know he's dead?"

"Apparently not. The DEA didn't disclose that information just in case the Destroyers—the gang he used to ride with—had a man on the inside, I guess. I wasn't going to be the one to tell him."

"Wow." She pursed her lips. "Now *we* have a man on the inside."

"Inside the Crimson Angels, yeah."

"That's good, right?" Littleton glanced around at the others. "He can feed us information on their drug network."

"Exactly, and the Denver thugs. It's only a matter of time before Rosalie finds out Jonny Star is still around."

"Do you think she'll go after him?" asked Sinclair.

"I'd bet good money on it."

Thorpe sighed. "That's all we need. Another gunfight."

"Right now, our priority is finding out who killed Eddie Youngblood," Savage said.

"Did Burner know anything about that?" Littleton asked.

"No. He was interested in how the boy died, though. He mentioned Pink Soda, which we already knew was dangerous stuff. He said he thought it was coming in via the Denver crew."

"Jonny Star and his thugs?" Littleton asked.

"Yeah, although the big boss is a man called Guy Hollander. Apparently, he's some bigshot businessman in Denver."

"Never heard of him," Thorpe said.

Sinclair shook her head. "I don't recall the name either."

Thorpe shrugged. "I'll do some digging and see what I can come up with."

Savage told them about Guy Hollander investing in the construction project.

"Could be he's using it to launder his drug money," Thorpe said wryly.

"That's what I'm thinking." Savage gave a slow nod. "It would explain why Kushner is here. He's keeping an eye on the mob's investment. I saw him meet with Jonny Star."

"Jonny Star's still in town?" Thorpe asked.

"You didn't mention that," Sinclair said, a touch defensively.

"I got distracted by Burner. I should have told you guys earlier."

Thorpe frowned. "Jonny Star is bringing the dirty meth into the county, thanks to this mob boss, Guy Hollander, and Kushner is overseeing it?"

Savage nodded.

"But at the same time, Kushner is working for Connelly as a type of project manager on the construction site."

Littleton scratched his head.

"Do you think that finance guy Bryant is involved?" Sinclair asked. "If dirty money's flowing through the company, he'd know about it."

"That's true. But even if he is involved, it doesn't mean he killed

Eddie. Connelly and Bryant were in a meeting that afternoon. They weren't anywhere near the construction site."

"But Kushner was," Sinclair said softly.

"Yeah." Savage looked at them. "He was."

Littleton cleared his throat. "Do you think Eddie was somehow involved?"

Thorpe was quick to catch on. "You think he saw something?"

Littleton flushed. "I don't know. Maybe."

"It's a good theory." Savage nodded at Littleton. "Then there's that text message. Someone lured Eddie out to the site that night, and if it wasn't Celine, then who was it?"

"Could Kushner get ahold of her phone?" asked Sinclair.

"I doubt it." Savage let out a long, slow breath. "Her father would have more opportunity, but even then, it would be password protected."

"Pity we can't look at Celine's phone records," Thorpe muttered. "See if that text really came from her phone."

"It's out of the question," Savage said. "Unless we think she's implicit in the murder."

"Do we?" whispered Sinclair.

He hesitated, wishing he could say yes, but the truth was, he didn't believe she was. And he wasn't about to ruin her future by involving her in a police investigation. She was desperate to go to college. He didn't want to destroy that.

Savage had just gotten back to his desk when Barbara burst into his office.

"Sheriff, Tomahawk is on Line 1."

Savage picked up his desk phone. "What's up?"

He listened, his face grave, then nodded, and hung up.

Walking back into the squad room, he said, "That was Tomahawk. A teenager from the res has gone missing."

"Why's he calling us?" Thorpe asked. "Isn't that the Ute Police's jurisdiction?"

"She was last seen protesting at the construction site."

TWENTY-TWO

A CROWD of angry Ute residents had assembled at the entrance to the development. Tomahawk was trying to keep them back without much luck. Savage recognized some of the youths from the protest group.

A man at the front yelled at an armed security guard demanding to be let inside, while another banged on a new steel gate with a stick. It remained closed.

"That's new," Sinclair said, as they fought their way to the front. "They must have installed it because of Eddie's case."

"Won't do much good with that flimsy fence." Savage elbowed a beefy middle-aged man out of the way. "Excuse me," he shouted. "Let us through."

Finally, they got to the gate. Lightweight steel, it gleamed in the mid-morning sun. A more effective barrier was the security crew standing in a line behind the guard, hands on guns, stoic expressions on their faces. They were new, too, and primed for trouble.

"He hired a security company?" Savage said to Tomahawk, still doing his best to placate the crowd.

"Looks like it."

Savage looked around. "Where are the rest of your men?"

"The chief won't let them come out," Tomahawk replied. "Not our turf."

"Didn't stop you, though."

"Someone's got to control this crowd. It's a res girl who has gone missing. We have a responsibility."

Savage admired Tomahawk's nerve. He beckoned to his team, who were still forcing their way through the impatient mob. "Let's contain this crowd. If anyone gets out of hand, arrest them."

"Are you sure that's wise?" Littleton asked, his voice wobbling. There were some very angry people in the group.

"Yes, we can't let this turn violent. People will get hurt." Savage nodded to the armed guards inside the gate.

"Sheriff, we demand to be let in." The man who'd been banging on the gate grabbed at his arm.

Savage turned. "And you are—?"

"Henry Morning Song. Crystal is my daughter."

Sinclair, Thorpe, and Littleton attempted to move the surging crowd back, but the group wouldn't budge.

"Sir, if you'll come this way, we can talk." Savage couldn't hear a damn thing with all the shouting.

Mr. Morning Song reluctantly followed him away from the throng. It was still loud, but at least he could make out what the man was saying. "When did you last see your daughter?" Savage asked.

"Early this morning. She left the house for the protest and hasn't come back."

"You're very quick to pronounce her missing." It wasn't even midday yet.

"The other protesters came back. She wasn't with them."

"Could she have met someone? A friend. Her boyfriend?"

"No, she's sixteen years old. We told her to come straight home after the protest."

Savage nodded. He understood the man's concern, but it had only been a few hours. "Sir, why are you here?"

"This is where she went missing," he said. "She could be somewhere in there. Hurt, or worse." Crystal's father choked up. "We want to search the site."

Now Savage understood. The crowd surged again. "Okay, tell your friends to keep calm. Let me see what I can do."

He approached the gate and held up his badge.

"Excuse me," he called to the guard standing there, looking increasingly twitchy. "I want to speak to Kushner, or whoever is in charge."

"One moment, sir." The guard pulled out a walkie-talkie and spoke in a low voice. Shortly after, he gave a curt nod and opened the gate. Savage and Tomahawk slipped through, leaving the rest of the team outside to fend off the growing mob.

Tensions were rising. The people wanted answers. The protesters were worried about their friend. Nobody liked the development to begin with, and it wouldn't take much to push them over the edge.

"Calm down!" he heard Sinclair yell. "Sir, get back please."

The guard gestured to a prefab structure a hundred yards inside the gate. "He's in the site office."

Savage and Tomahawk walked past the line of security. All the men were heavily armed. Tomahawk met Savage's gaze. Open firing on the protesters would be carnage. They had to make sure that didn't happen.

"Sheriff Savage." Kushner got to his feet. He was an enormous man. Well over six feet and almost half as wide. His hands alone were the size of small turkeys. It wasn't hard to understand how he'd got the nickname Crusher. "How can I help you?"

Savage noticed he didn't greet Tomahawk.

"You have a volatile situation outside," Savage said.

"You think I don't know that? These damn protesters don't leave us alone. It's very disruptive, as I'm sure you can appreciate." He shot Tomahawk an annoyed look, as if the unruly behavior was his fault.

"They're concerned about a missing teenager," Tomahawk said, his voice flat.

"I heard. We haven't seen her."

"Have you looked for her?" asked Savage.

"Yeah, we did a recon this morning. She's not here, Sheriff."

"Then you won't mind if me and my team have a look around."

His expression hardened. "I suppose not, but *he* doesn't have any jurisdiction here. This isn't res land."

"It used to be," Tomahawk bit back.

Savage raised a hand. Now wasn't the time to get political. "Officer Winter is working with me. We've joined forces on this one."

Kushner turned back to his paperwork. "I'd appreciate it if you got this over with quickly, so my men can get back to work."

"We'll do our best."

He went out and signaled to the others to come inside. Thorpe, Littleton, and Sinclair squeezed through the gate, which was shut quickly after them despite more angry voices.

"We're going to look for her," Savage told Mr. Morning Song. "We'll let you know if we find anything."

There was a loud murmur of discontent. The shiny new gate was sturdy enough, but the flimsy fence would buckle in an instant if the angry protesters decided that was the best way to get in. Savage hoped it wouldn't come to that.

"Let's split up and spread out," Savage said. "We'll cover more ground that way." Last night's rains made the stark landscape seem even more drab. With the giant cranes silent and the excavation machines standing idle, the building site had an eerie, apocalyptic feel to it.

Savage headed toward the northern perimeter, closest to the reservation. He figured if the girl had somehow been locked in, she'd have tried to get out that way.

This part of the site was less developed. Structures had been demarcated, holes had been half dug, dirt and gravel lay scattered in forgotten pyramids. Beyond the fence, the desolate terrain stretched out toward the Southern Ute Reservation.

Maybe she'd tried to get out and injured herself. Maybe she was lying with a sprained ankle somewhere along the perimeter. In some places, there was no fence at all, just dusty service roads leading to the development. Crystal could have tried to walk home and gotten lost on the res. But why wouldn't she have called for help?

According to her friends, her phone was off. Was that because she had no signal, or for some more sinister reason? He checked his own phone. Two bars.

From what he could see, there was nobody on the other side of the fence. He walked along it, just to be sure. He walked along the open area too, but there wasn't so much as a dusty footprint. Looking up, he saw Tomahawk walking toward him.

"She did not climb over the fence," the Ute officer said. "I cannot see any track marks."

"None on my side either," Savage reported.

Tomahawk frowned, concerned. "If she did not leave with the group this morning, and she did not climb over the fence, where did she go?"

Savage wasn't sure he wanted to know the answer to that question.

They walked back together. When they were about halfway there, Tomahawk stopped.

Savage turned to him. "What is it?"

Tomahawk's eyes were on the ground. "There, can you see it?"

All he could see was a mishmash of shallow striations. "Not really."

"There was an altercation here." Tomahawk bent down. "Someone fell to their knees. See those two dents?"

Savage thought he could make out two minor indents in the hard ground.

"Then they were hauled up and dragged in that direction." The Native American tracker pointed to where the striations faded out.

Savage felt his heart sink. "Do you think it was her?"

Tomahawk met Savage's gaze, his own somber. "The knee prints are the right size. Small and bony. I cannot tell from the drag marks because they have been made by the toes of her shoes." He headed off in the direction of said drag marks, head down, face furrowed in concentration.

Savage followed, his heart thumping against his rib cage. Tomahawk traced the drag marks all the way to the edge of a pit.

Please no.

They stared into the shallow hole, roughly the size of a swimming pool and almost as deep. Loose dirt covered the bottom. Beside the pit was a cement mixer, its oversized belly still. No churning today, or at least not while the search was still on.

"You don't think—?" Savage glanced at Tomahawk.

"We've got to get down there." The urgency in his tone made Savage's stomach sink. He took off his jacket and slid down the side. Tomahawk followed, creating a mini rockfall. At the bottom, they split up. Savage went left, Tomahawk went right. Slowly, precisely, they explored the base of the pit.

A short while later, filthy and covered in mud, Tomahawk stood up. "She is not here."

Savage stretched his back. He was relieved, but also annoyed. This had been a waste of time. They clambered out of the pit.

Tomahawk stared at the drag marks again.

"You sure you're right about those?" Savage wiped dirty sweat from his brow.

"I am sure." The tribal officer walked around the hole, scrutinizing the perimeter. "There is one other possibility."

"Which is?"

"She was put into a car. There are multiple tire tracks on this side of the excavation."

Savage came around to take a look. Tomahawk was right. There were multiple tread marks in the ground. Several vehicles had used this as a loading zone.

"If those are Crystal's knee marks, and she was dragged to this spot, she didn't go any further. And if she's not in the pit..."

Savage stared at the imprints in the dirt. "She's been kidnapped."

TWENTY-THREE

"IT LOOKS like she might have been taken," Savage told the others when they reassembled at the site office.

"How do you figure?" Sinclair asked in a tight voice.

Savage told them what they'd discovered. "Tomahawk thinks she was put into a vehicle at the excavation site."

"Can we identify the tracks?" asked Thorpe.

"No, there are too many."

Sinclair took a shaky breath, got up, and began to pace. Beyond the gate, the protesters, including Crystal's father, were waiting for news. "What are we going to tell them?" she asked.

"The truth."

"I'll ping her phone when we get back to the station," Thorpe said.

"Good idea." Savage gave a nod.

"Should we get the CSI team in?" Sinclair's voice was tight. "They might find proof that she was there."

"Yeah, call Pearl and have her come down." The female deputy nodded and took out her phone. Her hands were trembling. "You okay?"

Swallowing, she gave a little nod. "I'm not looking forward to telling the parents, that's all."

"I'll do that. It's my responsibility."

Tomahawk got up. "It is mine, too."

The pair walked toward the gate. A security guard let them out.

"Did you find anything?" Crystal's father asked, as Savage knew he would. Worry etched into the lines around his eyes and the taut pull of his mouth.

"We searched the entire site. She isn't there." Savage struggled to meet his gaze. It was pointless telling the missing girl's father that she may have been abducted from the building site. They had no evidence of that yet, just some dents in the ground and accompanying drag marks, which could have been made by anyone.

The man colored. "You have nothing? My daughter is missing, and you have nothing?"

"We've called in a forensic expert to the site, just to be sure." He was glad for Sinclair's suggestion. "If we find any evidence she was there, we'll let you know straight away. In the meantime, it would be best if you stayed at home in case she finds her way back."

Mr. Morning Song raked a hand through his hair. "The one place I know she isn't, is at home."

"Do you have a recent photograph of your daughter?" Savage asked.

"Only on my phone." He brought up a picture of a smiling dark-haired girl in a yellow dress and a beaded necklace around her neck. She looked happy.

"Send it to me," Savage said. "It might help our people recognize her." He gave the man his number.

"She may have tried to walk back to the res," Tomahawk said. "There is no fence on the south side. She could easily have got out that way."

Mr. Morning Song hesitated. "You think she's lost?"

"Could be. I will organize a search of the res." Tomahawk raised his voice. "We could use some volunteers. If you want to be involved, follow me over here." He walked over to his police vehicle, hand in the air.

Savage was grateful for Tomahawk's intervention. He watched as the largely Native American crowd shot him angry looks before going over to where Tomahawk was standing to sign up for the search. If

Crystal was wandering around the reservation lost or hurt, they would find her.

"Pearl can be here in a couple hours," Sinclair said, as they walked back to the SUV. "She's got something to finish up first."

"Hey, you told us we could go back to work once you'd gone." The foreman shouted after them. He'd just been speaking to Thorpe. "Now you're saying we can't."

Savage turned around. "Sorry, this is important. You'll have to keep it closed for the rest of the day."

"This is a waste of man hours," he grumbled. "What am I going to tell the boss?"

"Tell him to contact the Sheriff's office."

———

ONCE THEY WERE BACK at the station, Savage held the blown-up photograph Crystal's father had sent him. "We'll put an APB out on her, but it's too soon to file a missing person's report." Twenty-four hours had to pass before someone could be declared missing.

"Even in this circumstance?" Sinclair said.

"We don't know she was taken yet," Savage said. "Tomahawk found some drag marks, but they could belong to anyone."

She huffed. "If she *has* been taken, every moment counts. You know that, right?"

"I'm aware, but we don't have the evidence yet."

"She didn't have a boyfriend," Thorpe confirmed. "I checked with her father before I left. They broke up a few weeks back. I also pinged her phone. It's either off or out of range. I'm not getting a signal."

"Have you spoken to the ex?" Savage asked. "Maybe they got back together?"

"Leaving now." He grabbed his keys. "I'll keep in touch."

Savage turned to Littleton. "Run the boyfriend through the system just to be sure. Actually, run the rest of the family too." Most people were abducted by someone they knew.

"If she was taken from the building site," Sinclair said slowly, "surely it must be by someone who works there?"

There was an awkward pause.

"Sinclair, can I talk to you in my office?"

She got up and followed him in, closing the door behind her.

"You seem to be taking this very personally," Savage began. "Is there something wrong?"

She sank into the chair opposite his desk. A full minute passed, then she said, "My older sister was kidnapped when I was a kid."

Savage stared at her. "I'm sorry. I didn't know."

There was a pause.

He cleared his throat. "Do you mind if I ask what happened?"

She took a shaky breath. "I was ten, she was fourteen. She was taken while she was walking home from school. I had track training, so I wasn't with her." Her head dropped. "If I had, she may not have been targeted."

Savage sat down. "Or you could have been taken too." Or instead of. But he didn't say that aloud.

Sinclair shrugged. It was clear she'd thought about it many times. "Anyway, when she didn't come home, my parents were beside themselves. I'd never seen them so desperate. They called the police, but it was twenty-four hours before she was found."

He raised his eyebrows. "Was she okay?"

"Far from it. That monster kept her prisoner all night, and she had to endure hours of..." Her voice faltered.

Savage got the picture. "I'm sorry," he murmured.

Sinclair gave a sad little nod. "Somehow, she managed to escape. She climbed out of a window and ran away. That's when the police found her."

"Brave girl," he said.

Sinclair nodded. "She was. It took years of therapy before we truly got her back, and even then, she wasn't the same person she used to be."

"I'm sure." The aftereffects of a crime were often as bad as the crime itself. He'd seen victims who'd struggled to get their lives back, who'd lost everything because they'd failed to regain their mental health. Jobs, spouses, friends. They'd alienated themselves, succumbed to depression, battled with PTSD, even contemplated suicide.

Sinclair leaned forward and placed her hands on his desk. "When something like this happens, the effects last a lifetime. And it affects more than just the victim. Entire families are destroyed. If she's been taken, Sheriff, we have to find her, and we need to start looking now." Her voice had risen a few notches and the seriousness in her eyes was a look Savage did not take lightly.

He didn't need his deputy to tell him how bad the effects of a crime could be, particularly one of this nature. And the victim was only sixteen.

"Deputy, I'm not disagreeing with you."

Sinclair sighed. "I know, I'm sorry. It just hits close to home, that's all."

"I'm sorry about what happened to your sister."

"Thank you."

He had to admit, it was beginning to look like the teenager had been kidnapped. Still, if he launched a full-scale search too soon, they'd have a lot to answer for.

"Okay, let's put out an APB on Crystal Morning Song. If Pearl finds any evidence that she was there, at that excavation site, we'll issue an AMBER Alert."

Sinclair broke into a relieved smile. "Thank you, Sheriff. Thank you."

TWENTY-FOUR

SINCLAIR MET Pearl at the construction site. The protesters had disappeared thanks to Tomahawk's quick thinking and were now searching the reservation.

"Thanks for coming out." She shook the forensic expert's hand.

"I hear you have a missing girl?"

"That's right. Tomahawk found evidence of a scuffle at one of the excavation points."

The forensic expert gave an efficient nod. "Lead the way."

Sinclair had cordoned off the area where Tomahawk had found the drag marks. Police tape flapped in the breeze. The sun had dried out the upturned earth and hardened the soil in the pit. It wouldn't be easy looking for evidence that Crystal had been there.

Pearl eyed out the shallow hole. Sinclair knew what she was thinking. She'd thought the same the first time she'd seen it. "She's not in there. It's been thoroughly searched."

A relieved breath. "Right, I'll get to work."

Setting her metal case on the ground, Pearl pulled on protective footwear, gloves, and a mask. Her dark hair, fading to gray at the temples, was already tied back in a tight bun.

"How about I start here?" She pointed to the knee-dents in the ground, where Tomahawk thought Crystal might have fallen. Had the teen been trying to get away from her attacker?

"Please," Sinclair said.

As she watched Pearl work, Sinclair ran through the possibilities in her head. Crystal had been locked in after the early morning protest. Unwilling to approach the surly guards, she'd looked for an alternative way out. She'd made it this far, to the southern perimeter, when her attacker approached. He'd asked her what she was doing on the building site. It was private property. Maybe he threatened to report her to the police. She'd panicked and ran away.

Then the knee marks. Falling, she'd put her hands out, sliding over the gravel to protect herself. Her assailant had caught her, picked her up, and dragged her the last few yards to his car.

"It certainly looks like someone fell here," Pearl said, on her hands and knees. She inspected the area, then took out a sheet of adhesive and laid it on the ground. It would pick up the top layer of dust and dirt, but also any hair, fibers, or skin that had fallen to the ground. She repeated the process all the way to the pit.

"Do you think we'll find anything?" Sinclair asked.

"Every contact leaves a trace. If your missing girl is the one who made these markings, we'll know soon enough." Pearl got to her feet and dusted herself off. "I'll analyze them as soon as I get back to the lab."

"Thanks, Pearl," Sinclair said.

"Saves going through the usual channels, eh?"

"Exactly. If the girl has been kidnapped, it would be good to know sooner rather than later."

Pearl squeezed her hand. "I'll be as fast as I can." Then she got back into her ancient station wagon and drove off. Sinclair watched as she bumped over the uneven ground back to the gate.

———

KUSHNER STORMED into the Sheriff station. "How long do you propose to shut us down for?"

"Let's talk in my office," Savage said, as everybody stopped working and looked up. He'd been debating issuing an AMBER Alert for Crystal Morning Song. In the end, he'd decided to wait a while longer. The tribal police were still searching the reservation, and he hadn't heard anything from the lab.

Kushner followed him in. "How many times are you going to shut us down? It's costing a fortune."

"We have reason to believe one of the protesters may have been abducted from the site this morning."

"What?" He shook his head. "That's impossible."

"Is it? She didn't return home after the protest."

"We have new security, as you might have noticed. As well as preventing unauthorized persons coming onto the site, they also prevent anyone leaving without being noticed."

"Only if they use the main gate. There are other ways on and off the site, unsupervised."

Kushner grunted. "We're replacing the existing fence. In a few days, the perimeter will be secure."

"Good to know," Savage said. "But that doesn't help us now."

"How do you know she was abducted?"

"I can't tell you that, but our forensic expert is on site and once she's done, your men can get back to work."

That mollified Kushner somewhat. "Who is it this time?"

"A young woman named Crystal Morning Song. She was last seen protesting with the group this morning." He placed a photograph of Crystal down on the desk.

"Damn protesters," Kushner grumbled, glancing briefly at it. "They're nothing but trouble."

"You recognize her?" Savage nodded at the photograph.

"No."

"Where were you at eight o'clock this morning?"

"What? Am I a suspect now?" His dark eyes burned into Savage's.

"Everyone is a suspect until I've cleared them."

"At my hotel. The foreman is always first on site 'cos he stays in the barracks. I usually get there around nine."

"Can anyone vouch for you?"

Kushner shrugged. "I had breakfast at the hotel. Steve Bryant was there. He'll back me up."

Savage's desk phone rang. "Excuse me for a moment."

Tomahawk reported in. "We did not find anything on the res, but one of Crystal's friends thought she had been seeing someone. Not her ex. An older man."

"Why does she think that?" Savage studied Kushner.

Late thirties, two hundred and twenty pounds, built like a wrestler. The beefy giant stood with his massive hands on his hips, staring moodily out of the window. Was he the older man Crystal's friend was talking about?

"Crystal told her friend that her parents would not approve. That she had to keep their relationship secret."

"Does the friend have any idea who it is?" Savage asked.

"No, but she once saw Crystal get into a black SUV. She could not supply a make or model."

That didn't narrow it down much.

"Okay." Savage hung up. Crystal smiled up at him from the photograph. The amber necklace brought out the yellow flecks in her wide mahogany eyes.

He turned back to the project manager. "Are you sure you don't know this girl?"

Kushner tensed. "No, goddammit! How many times do I have to say it?"

Savage gave him a moment to calm down.

"That it?" Kushner turned toward the door.

"Actually, since you're here, I have one more question?"

The hulk turned, scowling. "What?"

"Jonny Star. Do you know him?"

There was an electric pause. "Why do you ask?"

"Could you just answer the question?"

"Yeah, I know Jonny. We met in Denver."

"What's the nature of your relationship?"

"We don't have a relationship. I know the guy. That's it."

"Then what were you talking about in Whitefield Park?" Savage asked.

Kushner took a step closer, hands clenched. "You following me now?"

Savage rested his hand on his holster. An unspoken threat. Watch your step. "Nope, I was in a diner, grabbing a bite when I saw you cross the road. I was curious, so I followed you into the park. I saw you meet Jonny Star. Looked like you were discussing something important."

"We do business from time to time," Kushner said, but he was holding back. His body language had changed. Less threatening, more defensive. This was not something he was comfortable talking about.

Savage pushed on. "What kind of businesses?"

"The kind that has nothing to do with you," Kushner snapped.

"If it involves drugs being brought into my county, it has everything to do with me."

Kushner laughed, a hoarse sound. "You think I'm bringing drugs into the county?"

"Are you?"

"No. I work for Apex Holdings."

"I heard you worked for Guy Hollander," said Savage. "As does Jonny Star."

Kushner blinked. "How do you know that?"

"It's called police work."

Kushner took a deep breath, but the veins bulged in his neck. "I think I'm done answering your questions."

Savage shot him a hard look. "Are you denying that you work for Hollander?"

"I'm leaving." Kushner threw open the door, stomped through the open office, and out the front. Sinclair and Littleton glanced up at the surprise exit.

"Is there a problem?" Barbara asked, twisting around in her chair.

Savage went to the window and watched the hulk stride across the street, getting into the driver's seat of a black SUV.

TWENTY-FIVE

"I WANT to find out everything we can about that man," Savage told Littleton. "I like him for Eddie Youngblood's murder."

The young deputy gave a hurried nod. "What about Crystal? Do you think he took her too?"

"He has an alibi for this morning. Says he was having breakfast at his hotel. I'm about to go over there and check it out."

Sinclair jumped up. "I'll come with you."

Thorpe chose that moment to walk in. "Just spoke to Crystal's ex. He hasn't seen her since the breakup."

"Right." Savage thought for a moment. "Let's look into Guy Hollander. He's a mob boss from Denver. I think he's the one trying to muscle in on the Crimson Angel's turf. Kushner works for him."

Thorpe's eyebrows shot up. "I thought Kushner worked for Connelly?"

"Nope, he's there to keep an eye on Hollander's investment."

"What about the drugs?" Thorpe asked.

"I'm not a hundred percent sure he's involved in that, but he knows Jonny Star. I saw them talking together in the park."

Thorpe didn't question when or which park. He merely nodded and sat down at his computer. "I'll get right on it."

Savage and Sinclair had just stepped outside when Barbara called after them. "Sheriff, there's a call from Pearl."

Sinclair glanced up.

"Patch it through to my cell, won't you, Barbara?"

She gave him a thumbs up. A moment later, his cellphone buzzed. "Pearl, what have you got?"

"I took those samples straight back to the lab," the forensic analyst said. "It's a positive. Your missing girl was there. I found skin and hair particles at the excavation site. Ray ran them through the database and got a match."

His heart skipped a beat, and he glanced over at Sinclair.

"What?" she mouthed.

He listened, then nodded.

"Did she find anything?" Sinclair asked the second he hung up.

"Crystal was there. Pearl found her skin and hair samples on the ground."

Sinclair gripped his arm. "That means she has been taken, doesn't it?"

Savage's voice was grim. "Looks like it."

He called Barbara back. "We need to raise an AMBER alert for Crystal Morning Song."

―――――

SINCLAIR WAS quiet as they set off.

"Your instinct was right," he said, looking across at her. "We should have moved on this sooner."

"You put out an APB. You did all you could under the circumstances."

He gave a grunt. Sinclair knew as well as he did that every minute a person was missing decreased their likelihood of being found alive.

Savage fixed his eyes on the road. "We'll put everything we've got into finding her."

"I know." She turned away. "When my sister went missing, we feared the worst. If she hadn't managed to escape..."

"How did she get away?"

"She escaped through a window, but that's all I know." She clutched her hands together in her lap. "She never spoke about what happened. Not to me, not to my parents, not to the police."

"Did they ever find the guy?" he asked.

"They think so. A couple of months later, another young teenager went missing, but she had a cellphone on her. The police managed to track her to some guy's house, and he was arrested. He had her tied to the bed."

Savage grimaced. "Didn't your sister ID him?"

"No, she didn't even go to the trial. I think she just wanted to put it behind her. Going to court would have reopened those wounds."

He could understand that.

"That's why we have to find Crystal," she continued. "There's no telling what she's going through right now."

Savage didn't want to think about it. "We will."

———

THE BOULDER CREEK HOTEL was teeming with beautifully dressed people. "We're having a private function tonight," the receptionist told them with a smile. "It's a wedding reception."

Savage didn't care about the reception. "Is Steve Bryant in?"

Her smile faltered. "I believe Mr. Bryant is in the dining room." She pointed to a short corridor. "It's the first door on the left."

"Thanks."

Savage and Sinclair entered a rustic lounge filled with wooden tables and chairs. Various spotlights in the ceiling cast a champagne glow over the diners. Waiters scampered from table to table, delivering food and collecting empties.

"There he is." Savage spotted Bryant sitting by the window. He had finished eating and was nursing a brandy, apparently lost in thought.

In the background, they could hear the tinkling of the piano from the bar.

"Mr. Bryant." Savage approached the table. A couple of the other diners looked up.

"Sheriff, how nice to see you." There was an edge to his voice. Savage imagined he didn't appreciate the interruption of his post-dinner tipple.

"Mr. Bryant, do you mind if we have a word?"

Bryant gestured for them to sit down.

Savage shook his head. "This won't take long. We've just got one question to ask you."

Bryant tilted his head back. "I'm listening."

"Paul Kushner says he was with you this morning at eight o'clock. Can you confirm that?"

One eyebrow raised. "Why do you want to know?"

"A young girl is missing. She was last seen at the construction site."

Bryant's forehead creased. "And you think Kushner is involved?"

"We're questioning everyone who could potentially have been on the site this morning."

"Ah. Well, you can forget about him. We had breakfast together."

"What time was that?" Sinclair asked.

Bryant thought for a moment. "I came down around seven thirty and Kushner was already here."

She frowned. "What time did he leave?"

"Probably around eight thirty. He needs to be on-site by nine."

"What about you?" Savage asked. "What time did you leave?"

"Sometime after that. I work from the hotel. Douglas and I usually have meetings in his suite in the morning, and I spend the rest of the day working in mine."

"Do you know a man called Guy Hollander?"

Bryant froze. "There aren't many people from Denver who haven't heard of Hollander."

"Did you know Kushner works for him?"

Bryant cleared his throat. "Mr. Hollander is an investor in Apex Holdings. A silent partner, if you like."

"If he's a silent partner, why did he send his watchdog to keep an eye on Connelly?"

"It's not just Connelly, it's the company. This development will create hundreds of jobs for the community, it will generate millions of dollars in revenue. It makes sense that he'd want to protect his interests."

"Especially if those interests are a way for him to launder his drug money."

Bryant's gaze narrowed. "I don't know anything about that."

"You're Chief Finance Officer."

"I don't launder drug money, Sheriff, and I don't appreciate the accusation."

"I'm not accusing you of anything. I'm asking."

"And I've answered your questions." Bryant got up. "Now, if you'll excuse me, I still have some work to do."

TWENTY-SIX

"YOU SURE YOU'RE OKAY?" Savage asked Becca when he got home. She was sitting on the sofa watching TV, her feet up on a stool in front of her. She looked tired, with faint purple shadows beneath her eyes.

"Yes. The doctor says I'm fine."

He felt a pang as he sat down beside her. "I'm sorry I haven't been around much. This case gets more and more complicated as the days go on."

"What's going on?" she asked.

He told her about the missing girl. Just talking about it seemed to add another level of weariness, as if it drove home how far they were from finding her. "Our prime suspect has an alibi. All we know is that she was probably taken from the construction site."

"That must narrow it down?"

"Not really. The site is spread out over such a large area that it's impossible to contain. There are several service roads leading to it. Anyone could have gained access without being seen. There is one camera at the main entrance. They're installing more, but they're not operational yet."

"The site's near the Ute reservation?" Becca asked.

He nodded. "That's the other thing. We have no way of knowing whether her kidnapper took her onto the res, and even if he did, we have no jurisdiction there."

"What does your gut tell you?"

He sighed. "Nothing, right now. Tomahawk talked to one of her friends. She thinks Crystal was seeing an older man. A white man, she said. But we don't know who."

She absent-mindedly rubbed her baby bump. "You've checked her phone?"

"No signal."

Becca frowned. "That's not good."

He shook his head dismally. "I know. Thorpe even checked her phone records. We convinced the judge it might give us a clue as to who took her."

"Did it?"

"No. They either found another way to communicate or she had a burner."

Becca gave a slow nod. "Her kidnapper could have given her one so he could contact her privately. That's what men who groom young girls do. Have you searched her bedroom?"

"No, it's not for me to do that. She lives on the res."

"Someone should," she said. "Girls usually keep a photograph or some sort of memento of the man they're dating, especially if it's a secret. If there's nothing on her phone, there might be something in her room. A photograph, a letter, a note. Maybe a diary."

"I'll call Tomahawk." Savage got out his phone, but before he could place the call, it rang. "It's Barbara."

Becca raised an eyebrow.

"Hi Barbara, everything okay?" She took calls from her home after hours.

"Sheriff Shelby just called. He's at the Dorchester. Someone shot at Jonny Star."

"I can't say I'm surprised. Did they get him?"

"No, missed, but he's shaken up."

Savage snorted. It would take more than that to shake up Jonny Star. "Any idea who?"

"No, no suspects, no witnesses either. He just told me to pass it on."

"Thanks Barbara."

He hung up and stood in the kitchen, thinking. Had Rosalie figured out who was responsible for the ambush? Had she traced the Denver thugs to the Dorchester?

"Is Barbara alright?" Becca called from the living room.

"Yeah, a shooting in Durango. One of our suspects."

"You gotta go?" He heard the weariness in her voice.

"No, Shelby can handle it."

"Good."

"I'm just going to give Tomahawk a call. He's the tribal police officer on the case."

"Okay."

Tomahawk answered on the second ring. "Good evening, Sheriff. Do you have news?"

"If the guy was grooming her, Becca thinks she'd have a keepsake in her bedroom."

"I have spoken to her parents. They do not know of any boyfriend."

"They wouldn't. This was a secret affair. Young girl. Older man. Typical pedophilia behavior. Have you searched her room?"

There was a pause.

"Tomahawk, you have to search her bedroom. We might find a clue as to who this guy is. I can come with you, if you like."

"I will head over there now." His voice was abrupt. Savage suspected Crystal's parents wouldn't want him rifling through their daughter's stuff, whereas they'd trust Tomahawk.

"Keep me posted. Becca says to look under her mattress, her pillow, behind her mirror, places teenage girls hide things."

Tomahawk sighed. "I will do so."

Savage went back into the living room. "He's heading over to her house now."

Becca gave a firm nod. "I hope he finds something."

"So do I." If they could get an idea who this man was, they might be able to find Crystal and bring her home tonight.

"He's kicking." Becca looked down at her hand, still on her belly. "Do you want to feel?"

Savage nodded, and she took his hand and placed it on her stomach. He felt the butterfly kicks of the tiny baby inside, and a rush of emotion washed over him.

"Can you feel that?"

He nodded, not trusting himself to speak. It was crazy to think that was his son or daughter in there. He wanted to be done with this case, to be free to look after his baby, to be a father. He felt sullied by the investigation, as if he'd taken on the evils of the world and couldn't shake them. He wouldn't shake them until the case was solved, he knew that. But he was running out of time.

Becca squeezed his hand. "It's going to be okay."

"I know. I just wish I didn't have to do this right now. The timing couldn't be worse."

"It can't be helped." She was as pragmatic as ever. "There's a girl out there who needs your help."

And a boy who needs justice.

And two dead men in a convenience store.

The victims needed answers. The crimes against them couldn't go unpunished. He rubbed his eyes. "I hope Tomahawk finds something. We have no other leads."

"Who's your prime suspect?"

"An enforcer from Denver. He works for a bigshot mob boss called Guy Hollander."

Becca gasped.

"What? Is he kicking again?"

She'd gone white.

"Becca?"

"No, I—I'm fine. It was just a hard one, that's all." She struggled to her feet. He jumped up to help her.

"Is everything okay? You don't look so good."

"Honestly, Dalton, I'm fine. Don't fuss." She rubbed her belly. "I think I'm going to turn in."

"I'll come with you."

"No."

It came out too sharply. He frowned.

"Sorry. It's really okay. You wait to see if that officer finds anything. I'll see you when you come up."

He sensed she wanted to be alone. Was it something he'd said? Or was it really just the baby kicking? "Okay, if you're sure you're alright."

A smile. It didn't reach her eyes. Becca turned and left the room.

SAVAGE WAS WOKEN up by his buzzing phone. Groggily, he reached for it. What time was it? He stared at the screen.

Two in the morning. He'd fallen asleep on the couch.

Tomahawk.

"Your fiancé was right," Tomahawk said, once Savage had picked up. "I did find something in her room. A diary."

His heart leaped. "You did? Anything in it?"

"She mentions meeting someone. He approached her in a coffee shop, and they got talking. From what I can gather, she has met him three times. Each time was in secret, and she does not mention his name."

"Damn," he muttered. "Is there anything that will give us a clue as to who he is? Anything at all?"

"She meets him at 'their place'. I do not know where that is."

Savage scratched his head. "It might be the coffee shop where they first met."

"Maybe."

In the morning, he'd go around all the coffee shops in Hawk's

Landing and show them a photograph of Crystal. It was a long shot, but maybe someone would recognize her.

"How does she refer to him?" Savage asked. "A nickname?"

"She just calls him He, with a capital H."

"No names?"

"Nothing."

Savage ground his teeth in annoyance. "Get some sleep and we'll follow up in the morning. There's nothing more we can do tonight."

TWENTY-SEVEN

THE SUN WAS JUST POKING its head over the mountain peaks when Savage walked into the Bouncing Bean, a photo of Crystal Morning Song in his pocket. He figured he'd start at one end of town and work his way across to the other. There weren't many coffee shops in Hawk's Landing, so he didn't envision it taking long.

"No, I haven't seen her." Neither had the two bleary-eyed trainee baristas.

He tried further up the road. Another shake of the head, another apology.

"Can't help you, Sheriff. Sorry."

At the third one, he got lucky. "Yeah, I recognize her," the barista said, a grungy kid in his early twenties. He wore jeans with holes in them and his long hair fell over one eye. "Skinny latte with chocolate sprinkles."

Savage blinked. "Huh?"

"That was her order."

"Gotcha. You ever see her with anyone?"

Please say yes.

He shook his head. "I don't see what they do after they order their coffee. I'm too busy for that."

"You didn't see her with an older man?"

"Like I said, I don't keep tabs. I just serve 'em."

Savage looked around. The coffee shop was small, with only a few tables and chairs. It looked more like a takeout joint. A queue was forming behind him. "You always this busy?"

"This is the morning rush, so no. But your girl always comes in on the weekend. We're always busy then." It was feasible the kid hadn't noticed her meet her kidnapper. Then there were the large windows. Anyone from the street could see inside. This wasn't a place two secret lovers would meet. Too visible.

"You got a security camera?" Savage hadn't spotted any inside the store.

"Nah. Nothing used to happen here, so there was no point. But Fred, the owner, said he would get one, what with all the shootings lately. This town's really going to hell in a handbasket."

Savage cringed. Even if the kid hadn't meant it to, it hit hard. A lot of people here were probably thinking the same. First a kid overdoses on meth, then there's a shootout at the convenience store, followed by a gunfight on the mountain pass just outside of town. Now a young woman had gone missing and every law enforcement agency in the state was on the lookout. They'd think he was losing control of his county.

Not good for the election next year, although he couldn't think about that now.

"Probably a good idea."

"Hey man, I've got customers. You done asking questions?"

Onto the next one. Two more coffee shops later and Savage hit paydirt. The Native American woman behind the counter nodded at the photograph. "Yes, I know Crystal. She's a lovely girl."

"Does she come here often?"

"She likes to come by after school with her friends. They always sit in that corner over there." She pointed to a table at the back.

"Have you ever seen her with anyone other than her friends? A man, for example?"

"Oh, no. Crystal's not like that. She used to date that boy, what's his name? Bobby Someone. But they broke up."

"Bobby Thornton. Yes, we know about him."

She frowned. "Has something happened to Crystal?"

"She went missing yesterday morning." Twenty-four hours since she'd disappeared.

"Oh, my goodness." The woman's hand flew to her mouth. "I hope she's alright."

"You never saw her with a man? An older man, perhaps?"

"No, but—" She paused, frowning.

"What?"

"A few days ago, I thought it was strange."

"What was strange?" He leaned forward over the counter to hear her as she lowered her voice.

"I ran across the road to pick up something from the drug store, and I was on my way back when I saw Crystal get into a black car. One of those big four-by-four things."

Savage caught his breath. "Did you see who was driving?"

"I couldn't see who was inside, but she jumped in, and they sped off. I thought it odd because her father doesn't have a car, and none of her friends are old enough to drive."

"When was this?" he asked.

"Last week. Thursday, I think."

It fit. Tomahawk said she'd met up with him three times. "Have you ever seen this man?" Savage showed her a picture of Kushner. After a hard look, she gave an apologetic grimace. "He looks familiar, although I can't be sure. So many people come in here during the course of the day."

"So, you haven't seen this man with Crystal?"

"I would have noticed something like that."

"Okay. Thanks."

He left feeling more optimistic than when he'd arrived. A black SUV. That tallied with what Crystal's friend had said.

He burst into the Sheriff's office, startling Barbara, who was crouching down behind her desk. "Good Lord, Dalton, what's got into you?"

"Sorry. I've been following up on a lead."

Sinclair glanced up. "You found something?"

"Tomahawk found Crystal's diary. She mentioned meeting someone at a coffee shop. I visited every single coffee shop in Hawk's Landing."

Sinclair looked at him intently as he spoke.

"Nothing concrete. The woman who owns the Golden Roast knew Crystal but said she hadn't been there with an older man. She did notice her getting into a black SUV one day last week."

"That's the second time someone's mentioned a black SUV," Thorpe said. "Didn't Crystal's friend say that as well?"

"Exactly."

"Which of our suspects drives a black SUV?" Littleton asked.

"Kushner, for one," Savage said.

"I saw Connelly in one at the building site," Sinclair added.

Barbara popped her head in. "Andy Rogers from the DEA office called and left a message. He said to call him back on this number." She handed Savage a yellow sticky note.

"The DEA?" said Thorpe. "I wonder what they want."

"I called them the other day regarding Grayson Carter, or rather Max 'Burner' Wilson. Just a courtesy call, to let them know Burner filled us in on the undercover op."

Savage went into his office and dialed the number on the note. It connected to the DEA Field Office in Denver.

"Andy Rogers," came the gruff voice.

"This is Sheriff Savage from Hawk's Landing. Thanks for returning my call."

"I must confess, I was a little confused by your message," he said. "You mentioned a Special Agent Grayson Carter?"

"Yeah."

"We don't have anyone by that name working out of this office."

"What? Are you sure?"

"Positive. I'm not even sure which op you're referring to. We don't have any active operations in southern Colorado."

"I saw his ID," Savage explained, his head spinning. "There must be some mistake."

"No mistake, Sheriff. I checked on the nationwide database. Grayson Carter is not employed by the Drug Enforcement Agency. Not here, not anywhere."

"So, you're not watching the Crimson Angels?"

"This is the first I've heard, Sheriff. Carter may well be undercover, but he's not one of ours."

A pause.

Savage digested this. "Thanks for letting me know."

Bemused, he wandered into the open plan office. "The DEA says Burner isn't one of their agents."

Sinclair frowned.

"They've never heard of him."

Thorpe spun around in his chair. "What about the cover up? Didn't you say he'd assumed another man's identity?"

"That's what he told me. He knew all about the real Max 'Burner' Wilson's death and the cover up. How could he have known that if he wasn't law enforcement?"

"Was there even a cover up?" Thorpe asked. "Has anyone checked with the Denver MC gang?"

Savage hesitated. "There must have been, otherwise Rosalie wouldn't have hired him. She'd have checked him out before taking him on, you can trust me on that."

Littleton swallowed. "So, if he's not DEA, then who the hell is he?"

TWENTY-EIGHT

SAVAGE DROVE out to the Roadhouse under the pretense of seeing Rosalie. Her Harley-Davidson stood outside, glinting in the afternoon sun. Low rider, cream fenders. Parked beside it was Burner's motorcycle.

Folk music greeted him as he pushed open the door. Things were back to usual at the Crimson Angels' HQ.

As expected, Burner was behind the bar. A waitress with long blonde hair and tight jeans sashayed about, clearing glasses. He hadn't seen her before. "Can I help you?" She smiled flirtatiously.

"No, thanks." He walked past her to the bar.

"What do you want?" Burner asked, giving no indication that they'd spoken.

"Rosalie here?" He lowered his voice. "We need to talk."

"One minute. I'll tell her you're here." Burner picked up his phone and sent a text. While his head was down, he murmured, "My shift ends at five."

"Where?"

"There's a farm store half a mile down the road. I'll meet you behind it."

Savage gave a barely noticeable nod, just as Rosalie appeared out of her office. "Sheriff, this is becoming an unfortunate habit. Don't you have anywhere else to drink?"

He tilted his head. "Nowhere as welcoming."

The witchy green eyes sparkled. "What can I do for you?" She'd lost the pale, drawn look from the last time they'd met. The shock of the ambush had worn off.

"Somebody took a potshot at Jonny Star yesterday." He slid a photograph of the mobster across the table at her. "You know anything about that?"

She glanced down, her face remaining impassive. "No, who's he?"

"You know who he is, Rosalie."

She shrugged. "Just because you think I know doesn't mean I do." She played a good game, he'd give her that much.

"He's a drug dealer. We think he's the one muscling in on your business." He was pretty sure he wasn't telling her anything she didn't already know.

She leaned back and studied him. "The man responsible for the ambush?"

"Possibly."

"I see." Her eyes narrowed. "Why are you telling me this?"

"Because I want you to leave him to me. I'll take care of it. I know you feel like you've got to do something, but the last thing we need is for them to come looking for you and cause another shoot-out."

"Why? Because it makes you look bad?"

"Because I don't want anyone else to get hurt."

He felt her bristle. "This guy ambushes my men twice. Kills one of them, puts another in the hospital, and you want me to forget he's in town?" She gave a very unladylike snort.

"We're watching him." His voice was edged with steel. "If any of your men go near him, they'll be arrested. I won't be able to let them go this time."

"Your concern is touching," she said. "Is that all?"

"Back off, Rosalie. Don't start a full-on turf war. People—your people —will get hurt."

Her expression hardened. "You know I can't do that, Sheriff. There have to be consequences."

He shook his head, although he understood. Her business was at stake, her own livelihood and that of her men. Their reputation. She had more to lose than most. If Burner was right and there were parts of the club who didn't think a woman should be at the helm, then she couldn't show weakness. She was fighting a battle on two fronts. Savage didn't envy her.

"I was hoping we could work together on this." He took a step closer to her. "Taking potshots at a guy like Star is only going to cause problems."

"That was a warning," she said quietly, so only he could hear. "That was us being polite. If he chooses to ignore it, I can't be responsible for what happens next."

"Let me talk to him," Savage said.

Rosalie raised an arched eyebrow. "You think he's going to listen to you."

"No," Savage said. "But he'll know the heat is on him. Hopefully, he'll figure with you guys out for blood and us breathing down his neck, it might be too risky to continue to do business in this county."

"You think the Denver mob is going to scare that easily?"

"Probably not, but it's worth a shot."

So, she did know who Jonny Star was, and who he answered to. He wasn't surprised. Despite her lust for vengeance, Rosalie wasn't the sort of person to rush headfirst into battle without knowing her adversary. She was a planner, she mitigated the risks. That's what made her so successful. She was always one step ahead of everyone else, including Savage.

She gave an empty smile. "Good luck with that."

———

JONNY STAR LAY by the motel swimming pool, sunbathing. The water twinkled despite the constant drone of freeway traffic on the other side of the precast slab wall.

Star, plugged into an enormous set of headphones, jumped when Savage appeared in front of him. "Christ, you shouldn't sneak up on people like that."

Savage smirked. "How are you Mr. Star?"

The mobster scowled, removing his headphones.

Savage was surprised to discover the drug dealer listened to classical music. "I must say, I'm surprised to find you're still here."

Star's eyes turned to slits. "Why is that?"

"After what happened to your... sales team, I'd expect you to head back to Denver."

Star snorted. "To lick my wounds?"

"Something like that."

"I don't scare easily, Sheriff."

"I'm sorry to hear that," Savage said. He took a step closer, so the drug dealer had to arch his neck to look up at him. "Because it's in your best interests."

"To leave town?"

"Before the situation gets out of hand."

"What makes you think it will?"

"Sheriff Shelby tells me someone took a shot at you yesterday."

"Stray bullet, could have been anyone." Star shrugged.

"But it probably wasn't," Savage said. "Your life is in danger here, Mr. Star. I'd advise you to leave."

"Like I said, I don't—"

"Perhaps you didn't understand me." Savage leaned forward, blocking the sun. "I want you out of this county tonight, and I don't ever want to see your face again."

"Now you're just being mean."

"This isn't a joke, Mr. Star. Take your drug dealing thugs and get out. We don't want you here. If your boss Guy Hollander has a problem with that, he can speak to me."

Jonny looked up, startled.

"Consider this your last day in La Plata County."

TWENTY-NINE

IT WAS five o'clock when Savage drove into the farm store parking lot. Situated halfway between Durango and Hawk's Landing, it was busy with commuters stopping for groceries on their way home from work.

He couldn't see Burner's replacement Harley anywhere. Slowly, he drove around the back. There was more parking here, but other than a white van, it was empty.

Checking the rearview mirror, he couldn't see anyone milling about. Good. He climbed out of the Suburban and leaned against it, waiting. The rugged mountain cast a shadow over this side of the valley, now that the sun was lower. He could feel the temperature start to cool.

He glanced behind him, up at the jagged peaks, turning a dusky purple in the twilight. A couple of months back, he'd been traipsing around those mountains, searching for another missing girl. What a case that had turned out to be. Now that same girl was living a different life in witness protection. He hoped she was happy—at least as happy as she could be.

He turned around at the low rumble of a motorcycle engine. Gravel crunched and Burner appeared. The Roadhouse barman cut the engine and took off his helmet.

Savage walked up to the man who was definitely not a DEA agent. "Who are you?"

Burner looked surprised. "I told you—"

"Don't lie to me. I know you're not a DEA agent. I spoke to someone at the Denver field office. They've never heard of Grayson Carter."

Burner climbed off his motorcycle. Weariness seeped from every pore. Shoulders slagged, neck stooped, a hand clawed through his hair. Savage got the feeling he was trying to decide what to say.

"I am undercover," he began, placing the helmet on the seat. "I infiltrated the Crimson Angels so I could find out more about the drug smuggling operation." He hesitated. "I'm just not DEA."

Savage gave him a hard look. "Who are you then? FBI? CIA?" When he didn't reply, Savage said, "I know Max Wilson really existed. My contact at Denver PD confirmed it. He's under the impression that he skipped town."

The biker nodded. "He did."

"How could you know that?"

Burner sighed. "He was my wife's cousin."

Burner closed the gap between them and looked Savage in the eye. "I didn't lie. My real name is Grayson Carter, and I am from Denver. You can look it up. When Burner skipped town, I took over his identity."

"But why?" Savage was beginning to wonder if the guy was alright in the head.

"I had to," he rasped. "To find out what happened to my daughter."

Savage stared at him. "What do the Crimson Angels have to do with your daughter?"

"It's a long story."

Savage crossed his arms. "We have time."

Nobody knew they were there, other than his team. Out of sight, they were safe from other members of the biker club. Burner was off duty.

"My daughter was taken almost two years ago now." His voice was heavy with suppressed emotion. "Abducted on her way home from school."

An uneasiness built in the pit of Savage's stomach.

"We were living in Fort Collins." He took a painful breath, like it hurt to talk about. "One day, my daughter didn't come home from school. We talked to her friends, her teacher, and it appeared she'd left, but never made it back." He glanced down at the ground and kicked an imaginary pebble. "That's when the nightmare began."

"I'm sorry."

"They found my daughter's body four days later in a flea-bag motel."

Dread pricked his skin. He had a terrible feeling he knew what was coming next.

"She died of a drug overdose."

Savage took a sharp breath. "Like Eddie Youngblood?"

Burner's eyes met his. "Just like him."

"What makes you think the Crimson Angels are involved?"

"I don't, but I do think Apex Holdings is involved."

A chill shot down his spine. "Connolly's company?"

"Yeah. They were building a townhome complex nearby." He fixed his gaze on Savage. "My daughter walked past it every day on her way to the bus stop. She was a good girl. Studious, fun-loving, innocent. She played the violin. Wanted to be in an orchestra when she grew up." His eyes grew moist, and he blinked furiously. "She did not do drugs."

Neither did Eddie Youngblood.

"What did the autopsy say?"

"That she'd been injected with heroin. There was a lot in her system. The ME thought she'd been in a drug-induced stupor for days before she died." His voice broke. "She didn't stand a chance."

"I'm sorry for your loss," he said more gently. "What makes you think Apex Holdings is involved, other than they were operating nearby?"

"Because it was shortly after they came to town that it happened."

Savage rubbed his forehead. "That's not—"

"She was raped." Carter blurted out. "The autopsy showed she'd had sexual intercourse before she'd died. Several times. There was... a lot of... damage." He could barely get the words out. "The assault must have carried on for a long time."

Something Sinclair had said about her sister sprung to mind.

That monster kept her prisoner all night.

"Did you go to the police?" Savage asked.

"Of course, but nothing was done. They looked into the construction workers but couldn't find any leads. I didn't think it was one of them, anyway."

"Why not?"

"They were transient workers, coming and going. Hard to trace. Some were illegals, others just passing through. They all lived in the barracks on the site. The police raided, but they found nothing. It would have been difficult, if not impossible, for one of them to have taken Hannah back there unnoticed."

Savage nodded slowly. What Carter said made sense. "Who do you think was responsible?"

"I suspected it was someone on the management team." His gaze narrowed. "Connelly was hardly ever there, so I ruled him out. There was another guy, a finance geek who I'm pretty sure was gay. Then there was the Operations Manager, a hard bastard by the name of Kushner. He oversaw everything. You may have met him at the building site here in Hawks Landing."

"I know him," Savage said quietly.

"I think he's the one who drugged her, raped her, then left her to die in that seedy motel room."

"Do you have any proof?"

Burner hesitated. "He was there when my daughter went missing, and he's here now. Hasn't another girl gone missing?"

Savage gave a resigned nod.

"Sheriff, I don't believe in coincidences. Not like that."

Savage massaged his forehead. "Apex is a large company. There are bound to be other people, construction workers, project managers, and freelancers who were at both sites. There'd be trusted suppliers and service providers."

"You don't think the two cases are connected?"

"I'm not sure. There could be any number of reasons she was taken."

"How old is she, Sheriff?"

"She's sixteen."

Carter nodded. "Two years older than my Hannah."

"That doesn't mean—"

"He likes them young," Burner continued as if Savage hadn't spoken. "My daughter used to walk past the construction site every morning. This Crystal was a protester, wasn't she?"

Savage nodded.

"She'd been on the site before?

"Yeah, but that still doesn't mean she was targeted by someone working there."

"It doesn't mean she wasn't, either."

"Two girls do not make it a pattern," Savage said. "We need more than that to assume it's the same kidnapper. I'm not ruling it out, but I think we need to gather more evidence before we can make that leap."

Carter stood stiffly, his hands clenched. "What about the boy? The one who died on the site?"

"What about him?"

"Someone shot him full of meth and left him to die."

Savage couldn't argue with that. "We're doing our best to find out who's responsible."

"It's him," Carter whispered. "Kushner."

"Kushner has an alibi for the time Crystal was taken."

"He does? But I—" Burner rubbed his head. "I'm sure he's lying, or whoever gave him the alibi is lying."

"Do you think we didn't check?" Savage said.

Carter fell silent.

"Why the Crimson Angels?" asked Savage. While he felt sorry for Burner, or Carter or whatever his name was, the guy was messed up. "Why not sign up as a construction worker if you're investigating Kushner? Wouldn't that be easier?"

"I thought about it, but he'd recognize my name."

"Only if he knew your daughter."

"Exactly. I didn't want to warn him off. Once someone does something like what happened to Hannah, they don't stop. I knew there'd be another girl. It was only a matter of time."

Savage frowned. "How did you know?"

"You learn a lot about human nature being a lawyer."

"You're a lawyer?" His gaze roamed over the long hair, beard, and tattooed arms.

"I never used to look like this, you know."

It was hard to imagine what Carter would have looked like before he adopted the biker image. "I'm sorry about what happened to your daughter, but you can't go around infiltrating MC gangs and investigating suspects on your own. You have no authority here. You have no authority, period. Not to mention, impersonating a DEA agent is a criminal offense. You'll be lucky if they don't press charges."

His face hardened. "There's nothing stopping me looking into my own daughter's death."

"That's what the police are for."

He snorted. "The cops don't care. Girls go missing all the time— runaways, druggies, prostitutes. The police force doesn't have the time to look into every case, particularly a girl who OD'd in a sleazy motel room."

Savage knew this to be true. When he'd been a cop in Denver, there'd been so many missing persons they had to prioritize the most urgent ones. Even then, they couldn't do them all justice.

"What were you planning on doing when you found him, the man who hurt your daughter? You can't make an arrest."

"I wasn't planning on arresting him," he said flatly.

Savage saw a strange type of calm come into his eyes, and it scared him. Carter had accepted his fate. He would kill whoever was responsible for his daughter's death, and to hell with the consequences.

THIRTY

"I'VE GOT TO GO," Savage said, glancing at the time on his phone. "Stay away from Kushner."

Carter shook his head, like he couldn't quite believe his prime suspect had been ruled out. Savage knew what that felt like. After you'd been hunting someone for so long, it was hard to accept that they weren't guilty.

Still, Carter didn't say anything.

"Hey, Carter? Are you listening to me?"

The former lawyer glanced up. "Yeah, sorry. I was just thinking about that guy who owns the convenience store, Kevin Someone. He's the one the Angels sell the drugs to. He runs the distribution network, doesn't he?"

Savage's eyes narrowed. "Yeah. So what?"

"Maybe he knows who bought the drugs that caused that boy's death."

"He doesn't. Kevin has dealers to do the selling. He doesn't get his hands dirty."

"Have you asked him?"

"Yes. I told you, we've got this. Now go home and get some rest. You look like shit." Too many late nights had given Carter permanent shadows beneath his eyes.

Reluctantly, he climbed back on his bike.

Savage waited until he drove off, then he walked around to the front of the store. He bought a bag of fresh vegetables and a box of strawberries. Becca would love those. Then, Carter's story still fresh in his mind, he drove home.

CRYSTAL HAD BEEN MISSING for forty-eight hours when Savage pulled into work the next morning. There had been no sign of her. No sightings reported overnight.

Was she even alive?

"Any news?" he asked Barbara, as he entered the lobby. She shook her head.

He used his fob and entered the sliding doors into the office. "We need to talk about Carter."

"You know who he is?" asked Thorpe, looking up.

"He's nobody," Savage said, stopping in the middle. "He doesn't belong to any organization."

"Then why is he undercover?" Thorpe pushed his glasses up his nose.

Littleton frowned and Sinclair shook her head.

"He's just a father looking for his daughter's killer."

They stared at him.

"For real?" Sinclair uttered.

Savage told them what he'd discovered.

"That's awful." Sinclair shuddered. "Poor man. All this time he's been searching."

"But why lie about being a DEA agent?" Littleton asked. "Why not just tell you who he really was?"

"Credibility, probably," Savage said. "He didn't want us to think he was some vigilante nut job."

Thorpe frowned. "He knew a lot about police procedure. And he gave us Guy Holland. We'd never have known about him if it weren't for Burner—I mean, Carter."

"He's a lawyer," Savage told them. "Or he was before he became Burner Wilson, who's his wife's cousin, by the way. That's how he knew so much about riding with an MC club."

"What was his daughter's name?" Sinclair asked.

"Hannah. Hannah Carter."

She turned back to her computer. "I'll see if I can pull up her case."

"There are similarities," Savage said. "I'll give him that much."

"Here it is." Sinclair gazed at her screen. "She was last seen leaving school, and they found her body four days later in a motel. Cause of death was drug overdose. Heroin. There was a needle in her arm." Sinclair looked up. "On paper, it looks like she was just another junkie."

"Carter swore she didn't do drugs."

"Like Eddie?" Littleton said, making the connection.

Savage shot him a nod. "That's right."

"Can't be connected, can it?" asked Thorpe. "Eddie is male, and he wasn't kidnapped. It wasn't heroin in his system either. It was meth."

"Yeah, different drug. Different MO."

"It was a few years back," Sinclair pointed out. "Pink Soda wasn't on the market then."

"Are we saying it is related, or it isn't?" Littleton tilted his head to the side. "I'm confused."

"Carter thinks it is," Savage said. "He's convinced Kushner did it."

"Kushner?" Thorpe shook his head. "We've ruled him out."

"That's what I told him, but he's convinced. Said it had to be someone connected to the development company."

"Apex Holdings?" Sinclair frowned. "Why is that?"

"They were constructing a townhome complex in Fort Collins when his daughter disappeared. Apparently, she walked past the construction site every day on her way to school."

There was a pause.

"That is quite a coincidence," Thorpe muttered.

"And now Crystal Morning Song has gone missing," Sinclair said. "On the construction site."

"Maybe there is a link?" Littleton chimed in.

Barbara poked her head in. "Sheriff, there's a call for you on Line 1. A possible sighting of Crystal Morning Song."

Sinclair gasped as Savage reached for the phone. "Sheriff Savage." He listened, then nodded. "Thanks for letting us know."

"Is it her?" asked Sinclair.

"Maybe. A deputy over in Pagosa Springs thinks he may have seen Crystal at a diner this morning."

"By herself?" asked Thorpe.

"Looks like it. He said she was alone."

Sinclair frowned. "How did she look?"

"He didn't say. We'd better go check it out. Sinclair, you dig a little deeper into Hannah Carter's death. Let's see if we can find a link."

"Okay." She turned back to her computer.

"Littleton, I want to know who Grayson Carter really is. His employment history, his wife, where they've lived, everything."

The deputy nodded.

"Thorpe, grab your stuff. We're going to Pagosa Springs."

———

IT TOOK an hour and a half to drive east to Pagosa Springs. Savage knew the route well, as this was where Becca had her practice. As he drove, he passed the spot where she'd been run off the road earlier in the year by that bastard Axle Weston, Rosalie's ex. It was a miracle she hadn't been too badly hurt.

He'd never felt such blinding fear as when he'd seen her mangled car at the bottom of that ravine. But she'd survived. The baby had been unharmed, and here they were three months later, about to give birth.

A sense of urgency filled him. "Let's hope it's her," he said, as they passed mile after mile of state forest. The cobalt blue sky stretched out in front of them, drawing them ever closer to Crystal Morning Song. If it was the missing girl, and she was uninjured, they might be able to have her back home today.

That left Eddie Youngblood. One last murder case to solve before Becca went into labor and his life changed forever. He didn't add the turf war to the list, or the mysterious sniper who'd taken a shot at him from the hill. He'd have to take care of both those things, but neither took priority over a dead kid.

"That's the diner, over there." Thorpe pointed it out as they drove along San Juan Street. The Junction Restaurant was a brown-painted wood building with an A-frame roof. It had decking all around it with tables outside under blue umbrellas a shade darker than the sky.

Tall pines and firs created a pleasant backdrop and offered some shade from the sun that had finally succeeded in pushing through the scattered clouds.

Savage and Thorpe parked the Suburban out front and walked into the diner. There were a few customers outside, but the majority sat inside drinking coffee and tucking into the all-day breakfast, which did look kinda good. His stomach rumbled.

"The deputy's going to meet us here," Savage said, as they approached the counter. "Excuse me, Miss. Do you have any surveillance footage?"

"Um, yeah, but you'd have to talk to the manager about that."

"Is he or she here?"

"She's not in yet."

"Could you call her? It's important we take a look at those tapes." He showed her his badge and smiled encouragingly when she reached for the phone. The conversation was brief, and the waitress did a lot of nodding.

Someone called from the kitchen that an order was waiting. She hung up. "That's fine. I'll pull it up for you in a sec, it's in the back. Take a seat. Order whatever you want, it's on the house."

"Just coffee for me," said Thorpe.

Savage nodded. What he really wanted was an all-day breakfast, but they didn't have the time. "Same."

She saw to her customer and then brought them some coffee. "Give me five minutes."

The wait staff rushed around, taking lunch orders. The diner was filling up now. The coffee wasn't great, but it was strong.

"You Sheriff Savage?" asked a nasal voice behind them. Both Savage and Thorpe turned to see a short, balding deputy standing there, hat in hand.

"Yeah. Deputy Haller?"

"Yes. Thanks for coming. I saw your missing person right here not two hours ago."

"I've asked to see the surveillance material," Savage told him. "Did she look like this?" He passed a photograph of Crystal Morning Song to him. He glanced down, and Savage saw a flicker of uncertainty in his gaze. He hoped this wasn't going to be a wasted trip.

"Yeah, looks like her." The confidence wasn't there.

Savage met Thorpe's eye. "Let's review the video footage."

The waitress was beckoning from behind the counter.

They all squeezed into the back room, which wasn't big enough for two people, let alone four. Savage had to stand shoulder to shoulder with Thorpe as they peered over the waitress's shoulder at the grainy screen.

"This the best quality you've got?" Thorpe asked.

"Sorry," she said, with a toss of her head.

"What time did you see her?" Savage asked Haller.

"Roughly ten o'clock this morning."

"Could you forward the tape to that time?" Savage asked. The waitress did as he asked, and soon they were watching a young Native American girl walk into the diner. At first, Savage felt his pulse escalate. From a distance, it did look like Crystal, but as she walked to the table and sat down, he could tell it wasn't her. This girl was coarser, rougher. She had a nose piercing and a tattoo partially visible on her left arm. Crystal had neither. This was not their missing sixteen-year-old.

Thorpe cleared his throat. "This isn't her."

"She's not?" Deputy Haller looked affronted.

"No, sorry. I can see why you thought she was," Savage said, "but our girl doesn't have any piercings or tattoos." He looked down at the wait-ress. "Sorry to have wasted your time."

She gave a stiff nod, clearly annoyed. Outside, the noise level was growing as more people walked into the diner for lunch.

They filed out of the office, which she locked behind them. "You stayin' for lunch?"

"No, thanks." Savage shot her a strained smile.

She nodded and took off, back to waiting tables.

"I'm sorry to have got you out here." Haller shuffled.

"That's okay." Savage tried not to show his annoyance. "It was an honest mistake. Every lead is worth following up."

The deputy gave an uncertain nod. "I guess so."

Savage nodded to Thorpe. "Let's go."

They walked outside, sidestepping customers coming the other way. Savage felt a weight press down on his shoulders. "Shit."

Thorpe nodded. "Yeah."

They were about to get into the SUV when Thorpe grabbed Savage's arm. "Hey, isn't that Kevin Handsome?"

Savage looked across the road to where a man was exiting a hard-ware store, a bag in one hand and a roll of something under the other. "Yeah, that's him. What's he doing here?"

"Should we ask him?" He made to walk across the road, but Savage held him back.

"No wait."

The drug dealer dumped the supplies into the back of his pickup. "Is that plastic sheeting?" Savage strained his eyes.

"Could be."

They waited for Kevin to drive off, and then went into the hard-ware store. Savage marched straight up to the cashier. "Excuse me, ma'am," He flashed his badge. "That man who just left. What did he buy?"

"Which man? The tall, ugly one?"

There was no other way to describe Kevin Handsome. He gave a nod.

She pursed her lips. "Let me see." A few quick taps later and she had the till slip in her hand. "Duct tape, plastic roll, rope, hunting knife, and bleach."

Savage stared at Thorpe. "I think we need to ask Kevin a few questions."

"Yeah." Thorpe took the till slip. "Thank you, ma'am." She nodded and turned to the next customer, who was tapping his foot impatiently.

"Why would Kevin need those items?" asked Thorpe.

"He wouldn't," Savage said. "Not unless he was planning to kill someone."

THIRTY-ONE

"DO you think Kevin kidnapped Crystal Morning Song?" Thorpe asked, as they hurried to catch up with the drug dealer's pickup. He'd had a good ten-minute head start and would be on the freeway back to Hawk's Landing by now.

"Maybe. He must have gone to the store in Pagosa Springs in the hope that no one would spot him."

"We can't be far behind him."

"I know where he lives." Savage weaved in and out of the traffic, his eyes on the road.

"He could be hiding her somewhere else," Thorpe said.

"That's true. Get Littleton on the phone. Let's put a trace on his cellphone, just in case."

Thorpe got right on it.

"There he is," Savage said as they watched Kevin turn into his driveway. It was a dirt track and turning in behind him would have given him advance warning.

"Let's hang back for a few minutes," Savage said. "Wait until he gets home."

"He'll still see us coming," Thorpe said.

"But if he's inside, there's nowhere to run."

They waited until the drug dealer was inside his house, along with his packages from the back, before they drove in. Savage went slowly, keeping the approach as quiet as possible.

"Kevin doesn't have a black SUV," Savage murmured.

"I can't believe he was the older man Crystal was dating, anyway," Thorpe reasoned. "I mean, what would she see in him?"

Savage grunted. Thorpe had a point. "He never struck me as the psycho type, either. Opportunistic, but not secretive or manipulative. He doesn't have the depth for that."

Thorpe looked across. "Should I call for backup?"

"Not yet. Let's check it out first. If she's in there, we can call the others. It'll take too long for the troopers to get here."

"Okay." They crept up to the house and Thorpe kept guard as Savage bent down and maneuvered himself underneath the window. Kevin hadn't spotted the dust kicked up by the Suburban as it had come up the drive. He'd obviously been too preoccupied with what was going on inside the house.

Savage poked his head up and took a peek.

Nothing. The blinds were drawn, which was suspicious on a sunny day like today, and he couldn't see anything through the crack down the middle.

Looking back at the waiting Thorpe, Savage shook his head, then tried the other window. This time, the blinds were open, but the room was in darkness. There was no movement inside.

He ran back to Thorpe. "I can't see anything."

"He hasn't been back long. Do you think Crystal's in there with him?"

"I don't know. Maybe I should just walk up to the front door and do a knock and talk? I'll know if he's hiding anything. I might even be able to get in and have a look."

"That might be our only option. Let's put a call into Sinclair and get her to start drafting a search warrant while we stand by and hold the status quo."

Savage heard a muffled thud, followed by a cry of pain from inside the residence.

"We can scrap the need for a search warrant. Sounds like we've got our exigent circumstance." Savage ran toward the house. Thorpe followed right on his heels.

"Kevin, open up!" Savage banged on the door. Thorpe stood behind him, gun drawn. There was another shout, and a shuffling of feet. "It's Sheriff Savage. I'm coming in."

There was no response from within. Savage took one step back, giving himself adequate distance. He delivered a powerful stomp kick to the door. The heel of his boot struck alongside the doorknob. The frame let out a wicked cracking sound as the door gave way and swung inward.

Weapons at the ready, Savage and Thorpe entered the hallway. Grunts and scuffles continued from the living room to the right. They moved swiftly in that direction. Savage came to an abrupt halt, with Thorpe coming up alongside. Both men trained their guns on the sight before them.

Kevin Handsome stood in front of a man tied to a chair with zip ties. The man's back was turned toward the door, so they couldn't see who it was, but it definitely wasn't Crystal.

"Kevin, put the gun down," Savage ordered.

The tall man didn't move. He was still pointing his weapon at the man tied to the chair.

"Kevin, if you don't put your weapon down, I'm going to shoot you. I don't want to do that."

Slowly, Kevin responded. His gaze lifted, and he blinked at Savage. With a frustrated grunt, he dropped his gun.

Thorpe shot forward, kicked the gun away, and pulled Kevin's hands behind his back, snapping on a pair of cuffs. Savage went to help the man tied to the chair.

"You!" he gasped. Grayson Carter sat there, duct tape covering his mouth, his eyes angry and wild.

Kevin tried to wiggle out of Thorpe's grip. "This man attacked me. I was protecting myself."

"From where I'm standing, it looks like the other way round." Savage ripped the tape from Carter's mouth. The undercover biker hissed an expletive.

"He's mad. I came here to question him about my daughter, but he attacked me and tied me up." Carter strained at the wrist ties.

"You were sneaking around on my property," Kevin exclaimed.

"I wanted to see if you were home."

"When I asked what you were doing, you barged into my house without permission."

"You told me to get lost. I had no choice."

"Gentlemen," Savage exclaimed, cutting the plastic ties around Carter's wrists. "Let's calm down."

Carter got up, his body poised for action. "Did you kill my daughter?"

"What?" Kevin scowled at him.

"You were in Fort Collins two years ago. You were there, at the construction site. I know you were. Was it you?" It looked like he was about to lunge at Kevin, so Savage cuffed him too.

Kevin tried to shrug him off. "Hey, man. I'm the victim here."

"I don't see it that way," Savage said. "I'm arresting both of you and we'll sort this out down at the station."

That got a barrage of complaints from both men. Ignoring them, Savage called Barbara and asked for another vehicle. Littleton arrived soon afterwards.

"You take Burner," Savage ordered, handing Carter over to the young deputy. He didn't expect the vigilante father would give them any trouble. He'd purposely used Carter's fake name so as not to blow his cover. He was ensconced with the Crimson Angels, which wasn't such a bad thing. As much as Savage admired Rosalie, he didn't trust her and Carter could keep an eye on her.

Littleton nodded and led the cuffed man away. Kevin proved a lot more difficult.

"Why am I under arrest? I was protecting myself and my property. That guy's crazy. He forced his way in here, demanded to know if I'd raped his daughter. I don't even know who his daughter is. I want to press charges."

"I wouldn't be so hasty," Savage warned him. "You tied him up, then drove to Pagosa Springs to buy supplies with which to dispose of his body. Plastic sheeting? What the hell were you thinking, Kevin?"

"I'm painting the spare room," Kevin sulked.

"Bullshit. Let's go." Savage manhandled the drug dealer out of the house and into the Suburban. Thorpe sat in the back with the suspect while Savage drove back to the sheriff's station.

Kevin kept complaining. "I was protecting myself. I just wanted to find out who the guy was, that's all."

"Save it," Savage ordered. "You have the right to remain silent. I suggest you use it. Once we get to the station, you'll have a chance to get your side of the story on record."

With a huff, Kevin shut up.

When they got back to town, Savage drove down the ramp and paused in front of a large metal-coated garage door. He pressed a button on his remote and it screeched upward, and he drove into the station sally port, leaving enough room for Littleton to park beside him.

Once the garage door had been lowered, Thorpe and Littleton removed their prisoners from their respective vehicles and led them through a secure door to a small holding area containing two jail cells. These were used to detain prisoners before they were sent to the correctional facility in Durango.

Both men stood erect, bristling at each other like dogs about to pounce while they waited to be admitted to the cells.

"Someone will come to fingerprint and book you," Savage told them, ignoring the obvious tension.

Although the place was sanitized, there was still a faint smell of sweat and other bodily fluids. No amount of cleaning could fully erase that. Littleton was the only one who seemed affected, crinkling his nose.

Savage reached for the radio clipped to his waist. "Barbara, open the cells, please?"

The familiar sound of the buzzer was followed by a loud, metallic clunk as the mechanisms on the secure doors sprung open. Thorpe shoved a sulking Kevin inside, then confiscated his cellphone, wallet, and keys before removing his restraints.

"Be good," Thorpe told him, closing the door.

Kevin glanced around, unimpressed. Inside was an aluminum bed bolted to a concrete wall and not much else. "I'm gonna need those back," he barked.

Littleton uncuffed Carter and placed him in the second cell. He looked around as if only just realizing what he'd got himself into. Savage was betting the lawyer had never been inside a cell before. Carter didn't have anything on him, other than his car keys. His cellphone and wallet must still be locked in his motorcycle parked down the road from Kevin's house.

Back in the office, Barbara flicked a switch and both doors hummed. The accompanying satisfying click told Savage they were secure.

He exhaled. "Let's give them some time to reflect while we figure out a gameplan."

They walked through another door housing what looked like an oversized photocopier but was actually an AFIS machine, the Automated Fingerprint Identification System. The next room was the booking room, complete with a wall-mounted camera and photographic station for mugshots. Beyond that, a narrow hall connected them to the back of the office. Here were two doors labeled Interview 1 and Interview 2. Soon, he'd face off with both men in those rooms, trying to discover what the hell had happened at Kevin Handsome's house, and why Grayson Carter thought the drug dealer had raped and murdered his daughter.

"I really thought he had Crystal in there." Thorpe sat down at his desk. "I was not expecting Burner Wilson."

"Me neither," Savage admitted, then explained to Sinclair and Barbara what had happened. "We heard yelling, so we went in. He had Burner, or rather Carter, tied to a chair and it looked like Kevin was about to beat the shit out of him."

"How'd he get the jump on Burner?" Sinclair asked, surprised.

"Kevin's a big guy," Savage said. "And he's used to taking care of himself."

"I feel sorry for the guy," Sinclair admitted. "Burner, not Kevin. I mean, he's only trying to find out who killed his daughter. Is that such a bad thing?"

"He's going about it the wrong way," Savage said. "We can't have a vigilante causing chaos in Hawk's Landing. We've got enough on our plate with the death of Eddie Youngblood, Crystal's disappearance, and the damn turf war."

"So, how are we going to handle those two?" Thorpe nodded to the screen that showed the two men in the holding cells. Kevin was lying on the bed, resigned to await the inevitable interrogation. This wasn't his first rodeo. Carter, on the other hand, was pacing up and down, clearly agitated.

"You take Carter," he said to Thorpe. "Find out why he thinks Kevin Handsome is involved in his daughter's death. He was yelling something about him being in Fort Collins two years ago. Find out if there's any truth to that. I'll take Kevin. He'll be the tougher nut to crack."

"You need help?" Sinclair asked.

"Nah, but if you and Littleton could keep watch on the monitor and confirm anything these two say." Sinclair nodded, she knew the drill. An effective interrogation relied on the suspect's statements being verified, alibis checked, details confirmed. The watchers would report back to the interviewer via cellphone message, enabling them to control the interrogation.

"Littleton, will you prep them?" The young deputy nodded and got up. This part of the job he knew well. He'd done it enough times in the two and a half years in which he'd been here.

"Sure thing, Sheriff."

Savage turned to Thorpe. "Ready?"

The deputy nodded.

THIRTY-TWO

KEVIN HANDSOME STRAIGHTENED up as Savage entered the interview room. He'd been slouching in the metal chair, his long legs sticking out from under the table. Hooded eyes regarded Savage warily, the irises following the Sheriff like in a painting as he walked across the room.

"How are you, Kevin?" Savage dropped a manilla folder onto the table in front of him, then sat down. The thick file landed with a satisfying thud. He'd padded it with printer paper, but the drug dealer wouldn't know that.

"That my file?"

Savage patted it. "Sure is. We've got a lot to talk about."

The lanky man frowned, creasing the lines in his broad forehead. He had a strange face, wide at the top, tapering to a recessed chin with a severe overbite. Pockmarked skin and yellowing teeth completed the picture. "Do I need a lawyer?"

"That's up to you. You have anything to hide?"

"I don't know what you got on me, but I didn't do anything that wasn't within my rights."

"Held a man hostage, tied him up, beat him, and almost shot him. How's that, for starters?"

Kevin glared at Savage. "I told you, he jumped me outside my house."

"His daughter was raped and murdered," Savage told him. "Now, why do you think he thought you had anything to do with that?"

"I don't know. The guy wasn't making any sense."

One thing he had learned today was that Carter had a nasty temper. Usually, the biker was controlled, level-headed, decisive. Rosalie's loyal servant. Today, he'd let that slip. The vigilante had been fuming when they'd arrived on the scene. Savage had never seen him so angry.

"Tell me what happened. Right from the beginning."

Kevin heaved a dramatic sigh. "I got home from the convenience store, and he was waiting for me. I didn't see him at first, he was hiding behind the wall. Then, as I opened the front door, he jumped me." Kevin's pitch increased as he became more outraged. "I turned around and wrestled with him for a moment, not knowing who the hell he was. Eventually, I pulled him inside and threw him into the chair. I was just trying to figure out why he was attacking me."

Savage gave him a hard look. "You tied him up."

"I tied him up 'cos he wouldn't stop moving around. I couldn't get a word of sense out of him."

So far, Kevin's story sounded feasible. "Then what?"

"I demanded to know who he was and what he was doing on my property."

"What did he say?"

"He called me a rapist and a murderer. The guy was spitting mad. I didn't know what to do."

"So you left him there, went to Pagosa, bought duct tape, rope, plastic sheeting, and came all the way home to do what? Kill him?"

"No!" Incensed, Kevin leaned forward. "He wouldn't stop yelling, so I stuffed a sock in his mouth to shut him up. I realized I needed to get some duct tape or something, since the sock wasn't great, and the rope I used to tie him with wasn't very secure, so that's when I went to the hardware store."

"You left him alone in your house?"

"Yeah. I thought it wouldn't hurt him to stew a little. Calm the hell down."

Savage sighed. "Why didn't you just call us, Kevin?"

"The cops?" A snort.

"Yeah."

"I handle my own problems."

"Was Burner a problem for you?"

"Not really. I knew who he was, or rather, what he was. One of Rosalie's guys. The newbie."

"You were going to beat him up, is that it? Teach him a lesson?"

"I thought Rosalie had sent him to warn me."

"Warn you about what?"

Kevin clammed up.

"You're in a lot of trouble here," Savage said. "If you don't want to be charged with kidnapping and attempted murder, you'd better start talking." Although Savage already knew. Kevin was worried about repercussions from the shooting at his store where one of Rosalie's men had died.

Kevin raised his bound hands. "Okay, okay. I thought she'd sent him to take me out."

"Because?"

"Because of what happened to her guy. Because I'm buying product from the Denver mob." He leaned forward. "I tried to refuse, okay? I wanted to say no but look what happened. They shot up my store and killed Aaron."

"That's why you're working with them now? Distributing their lethal form of meth that's killing youngsters all over the county."

"What choice do I have?"

"Again, you could have come to us."

A dry laugh. "Sure. And you would have said, 'Don't worry, Kevin. We'll talk to them. Give them a slap on the wrist, so you can go back to running your gang of street dealers.'" This was the closest Kevin had ever come to admitting his drug dealing. "You think that would've worked?"

"Rosalie know you sold her out?" Savage asked.

Kevin's eyes grew huge. "You're kidding, right? If she knew I told the

Denver thugs about the drug shipment, I wouldn't be sitting here talking to you."

"I can see why you thought Burner was a threat, but when you discovered he wasn't there on Angels' business, why didn't you let him go?"

"He accused me of raping and murdering his daughter. I wanted to know why."

That made two of them.

———

DEPUTY JAMES THORPE sat opposite a disgruntled Grayson Carter. The Sheriff had briefed him on his previous encounters with the under-cover biker, but Thorpe was still unsure how to approach this interview. The man was riled, angry. His eyes burned with resentment, like a caged animal.

"Where's Savage?"

"He's busy. Name for the record."

Carter scowled. "Grayson Carter."

"What's your current occupation, Mr. Carter?"

"You know who I am."

"Current occupation?"

"Bartender."

"At Mac's Roadhouse?"

"Yeah."

"Which is owned by the President of the Crimson Angels motorcycle club, Rosalie Weston."

A grunt. Carter's cuffed hands rested on the table between them. Every time he moved, the steel cuffs scraped the metal table.

"Are you a member of this club?"

"Only because I'm trying to find out who killed my daughter."

Thorpe paused. He hadn't been expecting such a forthright reply, but he took the opening. "Is that why you were at Kevin Handsome's house? Because you think he killed your daughter?"

A low hiss. "Yes."

"What led you to that conclusion?"

"I want to talk to Savage."

"The Sheriff has asked me to take your statement."

"He interrogating that bully, Handsome?"

Thorpe refused to be distracted. "If you'll answer the question, sir."

Carter made an annoyed sound at the back of his throat. "I discovered that he was working in Fort Collins around the time my daughter disappeared."

Interesting.

Thorpe glanced up at the camera. He'd need confirmation of that. He turned back to Carter. "Yesterday, you thought Mr. Kushner had murdered your daughter."

"I see you've been speaking to the Sheriff?"

"Of course."

Carter gave an angry sigh. "That's true. Except, as you know, Kushner has an alibi for Crystal Morning Song's disappearance."

"What's that got to do with your daughter's death?"

The cuffs scraped as his fingers curled into fists. "They're related. I think the person who killed my Hannah also kidnapped Crystal."

"Kevin Handsome?"

"I didn't say it was him. I said I wanted to question him. He was there. Kevin Handsome was in Fort Collins when she went missing, and he's here now."

"A lot of people would have been working in the area at the time. The same company was managing both developments. You must have something else?"

Carter fell silent.

"Are you saying you don't have any other reason to suspect Kevin Handsome other than he was in the area at the time?"

"Look, I know how it sounds, but—"

"What does it sound like?"

"Like I'm crazy. Like I'm just trying to pin this on anyone who was there."

"Isn't that what you are doing?"

"No, goddammit!" Another rake through the hair. "Look, it's not just Fort Collins. There have been disappearances in other locations."

Thorpe frowned. "What?"

The cuffs clattered as he moved forward. "Not just disappearances. Deaths. Drug-related deaths. Rapes. Murders. It's the same MO every time."

"Are you saying your daughter isn't the only victim? That there are others?"

"Yes. There's a pattern. In every town where a development has taken place over the last five years, a girl has gone missing. In most cases, she's turned up dead from a drug overdose. Guess which company has been managing those developments?"

Thorpe let out a slow breath. "Apex Holdings."

"Bingo."

THIRTY-THREE

"IS THAT TRUE?" Savage asked once Thorpe had filled him in. "Have there been similar deaths in the other locations?"

"I'm looking it up now," called Sinclair, who typed a lot faster than Littleton.

"I'll help." Thorpe lived for data research. "Give me the locations of the developments and I'll look up missing persons or drug overdoses in those areas."

Sinclair went onto the Apex Holdings website and found a list of recent projects under their portfolio section. Her eyes trawled the list. "Colorado Springs in 2018."

Thorpe's hands flew over the keyboard. "According to Colorado Springs PD, four teenagers went missing that year. Two were recovered, one died of a drug overdose, and one has never been found."

"Let's take a closer look at the overdose," Savage said.

"Margaret Valance, 16, went missing on her way to a friend's house on Saturday afternoon. She was found three days later in a campground near Pikes Peak, a needle in her arm."

Savage's heart sank. Carter was right.

"She may have been a junkie," Littleton said.

"Call her parents," Savage barked at the young deputy. "Find out what they think. Ask them if she ever did drugs. And get me the name of the investigating officer."

Littleton gave a hurried nod and turned back to his computer.

"Castle Rock. 2017," Sinclair called out.

Thorpe punched the details into the police database. Once the page came up, he scanned the results. "Laura Palmer, 15. She disappeared on her way to a drama production at the local theater."

Savage met his gaze. "Did she OD too?"

Thorpe read on. "She was found two days later in a nearby creek. Cause of death was drowning, but she'd been shot up with heroin."

Christ.

They all looked at each other. "That's two more," said Savage, feeling slightly nauseous.

"Three, if you include Carter's daughter," Sinclair whispered.

Thorpe glanced up. "Four, if you count Crystal."

"What about Eddie?" asked Littleton.

Savage hesitated. "Eddie is the only male victim."

"That we know of," croaked Sinclair. "Should I go back further?"

Savage shook his head. "Later. Let's verify these deaths are related first."

"I'm on it," said Thorpe, turning back to his screen.

Savage felt the adrenaline hit his system. "We also need to find out which of our suspects were at those sites. I mean everyone—Connelly, Kushner, the finance guy, the foreman. Cross-reference the workforce." The words spilled out of him. "And check Kevin Handsome's history. Apparently, he spent some time in Fort Collins. He could have been at the other sites, too."

"Are we talking about a s—serial killer here?" stammered Littleton, his eyes huge.

There was a pause as all eyes turned to Savage.

"It's starting to look that way," he muttered.

While the team got to work, Savage went back down to Interview 2.

Carter was still sitting there, staring at the table. His head shot up when Savage entered. "Did you look it up?"

"We did." Savage sat down opposite him. "Why didn't you tell me about the other deaths?"

"I knew how it would sound. It makes me look like I'm obsessed."

"You are. I mean, you grew your hair and got tattoos just so you could infiltrate an outlaw gang operating in the area."

"I thought if I could find out who was distributing the drugs, I could figure out who their customers are. Maybe sniff out the killer that way."

It was an angle, though Savage wasn't sure it was the most logical angle.

"How did you find out about the Crimson Angels?"

Carter shrugged. "They're the only outlaw gang in the area. I spoke to a couple junkies who told me where they got their stash. I used to be a lawyer, remember? I know how to follow a lead."

Savage gave a thoughtful nod.

Carter leaned forward. "Sheriff, whoever is raping and killing these girls also murdered my Hannah. Did you look up the dates? Did you see how they coincide with the overdoses?"

"We're still looking into it."

Carter banged his hands on the table. "Damn it, Sheriff. Those girls were murdered, and it has to be someone connected with the organization."

Savage tilted his head back. He'd never admit it to Carter, but he had the same nagging feeling. The vigilante might be obsessed, but he was onto something. Every instinct was telling him so.

"Tell me what you know." he said.

"I started at the top with Douglas Connelly. Driven. Single-minded. Workaholic. But he cares about his daughter. He doesn't have the time to go around drugging and raping young women. Also, when Laura Palmer was killed, he was out of the country. It can't be him."

"And he was on a Zoom call when Eddie Youngblood was murdered," Savage said. "Three people vouched for him."

Carter nodded. "Kushner was a possibility until you killed that theory with his alibi. Where was he when Eddie Youngblood was murdered?"

Savage sighed. "He doesn't have an alibi for Eddie's murder."

Carter thought for a moment. "Then it can't be him. The two have to be related. It's the same pattern as before."

"Except Eddie's a boy."

Carter shrugged, as if that wasn't important. Maybe it wasn't. But what if it was?

"What about Kevin Handsome?" Savage asked. "Why was he in Fort Collins?"

"His sister lives there. I called her up, said I was an old friend. Apparently, he was only there to help her do some renovations to her house. She's a single mother and Kevin helps her out from time to time."

Kevin had a soft side. Who knew?

Carter looked down at his hands. "I wasn't going to hurt him. I just wanted some answers."

"You can see how it looks, though." Savage fixed his gaze on Carter. "Kevin's been strong-armed into buying from the Denver mob. In doing so, he's pissed off the Angels. Rosalie is mad as hell, threatening to get revenge. And then you turn up, poking your nose through his window. What the hell's he supposed to think?"

"I know. I messed up."

"This was a warning," Savage said.

Carter glanced up. "You're not charging me?"

"Not this time, but there are two conditions."

"What?"

"First, you're not going to press charges against Kevin Handsome. If he goes down for assault and kidnapping, one of the Denver thugs will set up shop here in Hawk's Landing, and I want them out of my county."

Carter gave a tight nod.

"Second, you're going to tell me everything you know about Apex Holdings and the mob."

THIRTY-FOUR

"APEX HOLDINGS IS in bed with Guy Hollander," Savage told his team. "The mob finances all of their projects. It's how Hollander launders his dirty money. They also use the property development company as a way of expanding their drug distribution network."

"That's why they shot up Kevin Handsome's store?" Thorpe asked.

"That was a warning. To make sure that Kevin plays ball. If he doesn't, they'll take him out, and if Kevin goes down, the Denver thugs will take over the distribution of drugs in this area and it'll be way worse than it is right now."

"We've got to stop them," Sinclair said through gritted teeth.

"I've convinced Carter not to press charges. Littleton, you can release both men, but not at the same time. I don't want to have to arrest them again outside the station."

The deputy nodded and left the office through the secure door that led down to the cells.

"Apparently Kevin Handsome's sister lives in Fort Collins," Savage told them. "That's why he was there two years ago."

"I can confirm that," Sinclair said. "Although I haven't spoken to her yet."

"Do it," Savage nodded at her phone. "I want to make sure we've got an accurate timeline on all our suspects."

He went over to the whiteboard and wrote Kevin Handsome's name under a list that included Douglas Connelly, Steve Bryant, Paul Kushner, and the site foreman, Angus Harmon. An piece of copier paper stuck to the board contained the names of all the construction workers, consultants, and freelancers, while another listed the names of the protesters. Only one of the workers had a star next to his name. Matteo Verona—they'd questioned him already.

"Tomahawk says we can rule out the youngsters." Savage pointed to the sheet of protesters. "They all live on the reservation and would never hurt Eddie. He was their friend and a local hero."

"Besides, they weren't in the other locations," Sinclair pointed out. "Most of them are too young.".

"What about the construction workers?" Savage asked.

Thorpe adjusted his glasses. "I've cross-referenced this bunch with the employment records from the sites where Hannah, Margaret, and Laura were taken. Several names appear on all three, but they're permanent employees of the company."

"Run those few through the database," Savage said. "See if anyone has priors."

"Already done it," Thorpe said with a rare grin. "Nothing."

"What about the executive committee?" Savage asked Sinclair.

"Bryant and Kushner were working at all four locations, including Hawk's Landing. Burner, I mean Carter, was right about Connelly. He was on vacation when Laura died. We found his hotel bill in the Bahamas."

"That rules him out." Littleton said.

Savage studied the board. "The other two are still suspects. Any news on Crystal?"

"Not yet," whispered Sinclair. "It's been—"

"I know." He didn't want to think about that. "Did you get me the number of the Sheriff departments investigating the Colorado Springs and Castle Rock overdoses?"

"On your desk."

Nodding his thanks, Savage went into his office and closed the door. As much as he hated to admit it, it was looking less and less likely they'd find Crystal alive at this point. If this was a serial offender case, he ought to get the FBI involved, but the thought of suits trampling all over his investigation was enough to make him shudder.

First up was Sheriff Coleman of El Paso County. A jovial man, he was only too happy to help. "Well, here's the thing," he began in a lazy drawl. "We found her body in a campground, the needle still in her arm. Now I know her parents said she didn't do drugs, but that's what they all say. Most of the time, their kids have been hiding it from them."

"You think it was a legitimate overdose?"

"I do. That campground's where the junkies hang out. We have a lot of trouble out there near Pikes Peak."

"I see. What did the autopsy say?"

"Just that she'd OD'd. Heroin."

"Would you mind sending me the report?"

"Sure, if you think it'll help." He paused. "It was a sad case, Sheriff. I've never seen parents so distraught."

Unfortunately, he had. Carter was one of them.

Savage gave Coleman his email address and signed off. He could see Coleman's point of view. On the surface, it did look like any other overdose. He wondered what the victim's parents had to say.

Looking up their number, he placed the call.

"Hello?" A man's voice.

"I'm sorry to bother you. This is Sheriff Savage from Hawk's Landing Sheriff's Department. Could I ask you a couple of questions about your daughter, Margaret?"

A pause. "What's this about?"

"I'm investigating a similar death in La Plata County, and I'd like to ask you some questions about the manner in which your daughter died."

"The coroner said it was a drug overdose." The man's voice was clipped, like it hurt to say the words out loud.

"I know, but I understand your daughter didn't do drugs?"

He heard a sharp intake of breath. "That's right. How did you know that?"

"I read your statement in the police report."

"Margaret never touched drugs, neither did any of her friends. They weren't like that. We could never understand why she was found at that campsite. None of it made sense."

"You said she was on her way to a friend's house. Bonny Michaels. Did you or the investigating officer speak to Bonny?"

"We did, of course. When Marg didn't come home, we called Bonny. She said Marg had never arrived."

"Is that when you went to the police?"

"Yes, but Sheriff Coleman said she hadn't been gone long enough to file a missing persons report. They didn't start looking for her until the following day."

That was a shame. Savage had nearly fallen into the same trap. It happened so often with missing teens.

He thought of Crystal. Was it too late for her?

"Was she seeing anyone, do you know?" he asked, forcing his attention back to Margaret.

"You mean like a boyfriend?"

"Yeah."

"Not to our knowledge, no. I'm sure she would've told us."

"Had she been acting differently before she disappeared? Excited? Happy? Nervous?"

"No, I don't think so. What's this about, Sheriff?"

"We've got a missing teen down here in Hawk's Landing. There are similarities with your daughter's case." He didn't elaborate.

"You're thinking they're related?" He heard the change in Margaret's father's voice.

He didn't want to get the man's hopes up. "It's just a line of inquiry we're following."

A woman's voice filled the background. The words 'excited' and 'happy' floated down the line.

"Is that your wife?" Savage asked.

"Yeah, hang on. She wants to speak to you."

A moment later, a feminine voice came on the phone. "This is Margaret's mother, Clare. You were asking if she was excited or happy before she disappeared?"

"Yes, was she?" He held his breath.

"The day she went missing, she couldn't sit still. I remember asking her what on earth was the matter, and she said she was excited to see her friend. I thought it odd at the time, Margaret was usually such a sensible child. It was unusual for her to fidget like that."

Savage exhaled. "Do you think she was meeting someone else?"

"You mean other than Bonny? I don't know. It's possible. She was wearing makeup too, which isn't something she'd normally do."

Savage felt his pulse increase. "Mrs. Valance, did you or the Sheriff ever look at the messages on Margaret's cellphone?"

"No, we never got her phone back," she said sadly. "It wasn't with her when they... found her." A strangled sob.

"I'm sorry to dredge all this up, Mrs. Valance. If you could give me Bonny's number, I'll leave you in peace."

A sniff. "Okay, one second." He heard scratching in the background and then she came back on the phone. "Do you have a pen?"

Savage took down the number. If Margaret had met someone, an older man for instance, there was a chance she'd told her best friend about it.

Bonny picked up on the third ring.

Savage introduced himself and then asked if she was free to talk.

"What's this about?" Her voice was high pitched. Cautious. He heard chatter in the background.

"Your friend Margaret."

"Margaret is dead."

"I know. I'm sorry for your loss. I'd like to ask you some questions about her, if you don't mind."

Bonny hesitated. "Hang on." The background noise quieted. "Okay, shoot."

"I believe she was on her way to your house when she disappeared."

A short pause, so quick he almost didn't pick it up. "Yes, that's right."

"What were you girls planning on doing that day?"

"I don't know. It was a long time ago."

"Margaret was wearing makeup," he said. "Were you going out? Shopping? To a festival?"

"Yeah, I think we were going shopping."

"Bonny, was Margaret using you as a cover to meet a man?"

There was a much longer pause this time. "No."

Shaky. Definitely shaky.

"If she was, it's not your fault. I know how teenage girls are. You're not in any trouble, I just want to know if she was meeting someone."

"She wasn't. When she didn't get here, I called her parents."

"You didn't call her parents," Savage said. "According to the police report, they called you when Margaret didn't come home much later that day."

Silence.

"Is that because you didn't know she was missing?"

Bonny didn't respond.

"You didn't know, because she wasn't with you. She'd gone to meet a man, an older man, someone she couldn't tell her parents about."

"How do you know that?" Bonny whispered. "Nobody knew."

A surge of adrenaline made his pulse race.

"Do you know who it was?"

"No, I never met him."

"Did he have a name?"

"She called him Peter."

Peter.

Unlikely to be his real name.

"Where did she meet Peter? Do you know?"

"No, I'm sorry." He thought he heard sniffling. "She didn't say. I think she met him at a coffee shop the first time, but after that—" She drifted off.

"Do you think Peter made her do drugs?"

"I think he may have, yes." A gasp. "I should never have covered for her."

"It's not your fault," he said quickly. "You didn't know he was—" He was going to say a pedophile. "A bad influence."

"They said she'd slept with him." Bonny spoke quickly, the words falling over each other in an effort to get out. "I was surprised at that. Margaret was saving herself for marriage. She'd never have slept with a man she'd only just met." Savage had read she'd had sexual intercourse in the police report. It hadn't been flagged as suspicious. Not for a sixteen-year-old junkie.

"Do you think she was raped?" Savage asked.

Bonny was crying now. Small sobs making it difficult to speak. "I think so. Oh, God. Why didn't I stop her?"

"Bonny, listen to me. This is not your fault. Neither of you could have known. Is there someone there with you?"

"I'm at my boyfriend's house."

She'd be nearly twenty now. "Go tell him what we talked about. Tell him what happened to Margaret. It's important you don't bottle this up. You understand?"

If Becca had taught him anything, it was to speak openly about your feelings. Keeping things locked away didn't do anyone any good. He didn't want Bonny blaming herself.

She sniffed. "I understand."

"Good. Thanks for talking with me, Bonny."

"Okay." There was one last sniffle, and the line went dead.

THIRTY-FIVE

IT WAS a similar story in Castle Rock. The Sheriff was less amiable than Coleman, but he didn't hold back. "Kid OD'd, not much more to it than that."

"She was fifteen."

"So? We got kids shooting up at twelve, thirteen. Mostly dysfunctional kids, but it does happen."

He sounded like a man who'd seen it all. Savage recognized the type. After a while, the work numbed a person. That's why he'd left Denver. Too much crime, too much violence. He didn't want to get numb. He didn't want to get to the point where it didn't matter anymore. Where it was just a job.

"You didn't suspect foul play?"

"No, why would I?

"Wasn't her body pulled out of the creek?"

"Yeah, but there was a picnic blanket beside the river, along with a bunch of drug paraphernalia. She'd gone there to shoot up."

"Had she had sexual intercourse before she died?"

There was a brief pause. "How'd you know that?"

"Just a hunch."

———

"IT'S the same MO in every town," Savage said to his team. "He grooms them for a short period of time, then arranges to meet. Once he picks them up, that's it. He takes them somewhere for a few days, probably drugs them, then dumps their bodies, making it look like they OD'd."

"What an animal," Sinclair blasted, her cheeks flushed. "Those poor girls. To think they even put on makeup for him. It's horrible."

"The detectives investigating Margaret Valance and Laura Palmer saw it as a drug overdose. Neither of them investigated further."

"Didn't the fact that they'd been sexually assaulted mean anything?" Sinclair said, angry now.

"Apparently not. In both cases, the autopsy revealed the victims had had sex before they'd OD'd. But our killer was careful. He wasn't brutal and there were no other signs of assault. No bruising, nor marks from restraints."

"That's something, at least," Thorpe mumbled.

"That's because he drugged them," Sinclair said flatly. "They were too doped up to fight him off."

Nobody contradicted her.

———

HE GOT HOME to find Becca covered in blue paint. "Why are you still up?" he asked, after kissing her hello.

"I had a spurt of energy, so I painted the baby's room."

"Blue?"

"Boundless Blue, actually."

He chuckled. "What if it's a girl?"

"It isn't."

At his arched eyebrow, she continued, "I can't explain it, I just know."

He grinned. "I believe you."

They went into the kitchen where he got a beer out of the fridge. Becca was drinking herbal tea. "You eaten?" he asked.

"Yes, I made jacket potatoes and there's salad on the counter. You might need to heat yours up."

"Thanks." He realized he was starving.

"How'd it go today?" she asked. "Are you any closer to finding that missing girl?"

Savage exhaled. "It's not just one missing girl."

"Another one's gone missing?"

"Not here, no. But we looked back at all the places Apex Holdings has worked, and a missing girl popped up in all of them."

Becca stared at him. "What does that mean? That someone connected to the company is kidnapping young women?"

"That's what it looks like. We're trying to figure out who, but they all have alibis for Crystal's disappearance, and everyone except the project manager has an alibi for Eddie's death."

"Do you think this is related to Guy Hollander?"

He frowned. "Why would you ask that?"

"You said he was connected to the mob, that's all."

Savage got himself a plate. "I don't think so. He's a silent partner. He doesn't come to the project sites."

"Then you think they're all connected?"

"They must be. The MO is the same." He told her about the grooming, the drugging, the lack of defensive wounds, the rape, and the eventual overdosing of the victims. Even though Becca wasn't law enforcement, she was a psychologist. Becca was used to working with the police on young offender profiles and rehabilitation. That was part of her job.

She frowned. "It can't be."

"You mean because Eddie's a guy?" He shrugged. "He wasn't raped before he was injected with drugs, but other than that, it's the same."

"Same drug?"

"Well, the others were heroin. Eddie was injected with meth."

"All the other victims were young women?"

"Yeah, we went back five years and found two more victims. They both went missing, their bodies found a few days later, having overdosed. If we include Hannah, Carter's daughter, that makes three, and with Eddie and Crystal, five. There are probably more, but we're going to start with those."

"And they were all sexually assaulted?"

"Yeah."

She shook her head. "A killer who sticks to an MO like that is not going to deviate and target a male. Part of what turns him on is the power he has over his victims. He drugs them to keep them compliant. He has sex with them, then when he's bored, he kills them. Eddie doesn't fit that victimology."

Savage frowned. "What are you saying?"

"I don't think Eddie was killed by the same man."

He sat in silence, letting her words sink in. Not the same killer? Two killers?

"It doesn't seem likely," he said slowly. "But what if Eddie saw something he wasn't supposed to?"

Becca gave a ready nod. "That would make more sense. If the killer's only goal was to silence Eddie, then I can see that happening. Eddie wasn't a primary target."

"It could have been a case of the wrong place at the wrong time," Savage mused. "But what did he see that got him killed?"

She took his hand. "That I can't help you with." She kissed him on the cheek, then went upstairs.

Savage finished eating, washed his plate, and joined her. Becca was lying in bed, looking thoughtful. "Dalton, let's have lunch tomorrow."

"Sure." He smiled. "Any reason?"

"It might be our last chance at a quiet meal before the baby arrives." She hesitated. "And there's something I want to talk to you about."

"You can talk to me now."

She laughed. "No, it's late, I'm too tired to talk now. And no offense, but you need a shower."

"Okay." He frowned. "It's nothing serious, is it?"

"No, just something I think we should discuss. It can wait till lunch." She rolled over and closed her eyes. "Hurry up and come to bed."

He showered and was about to crawl next to her when his phone rang. He glanced at the screen.

Tomahawk.

Becca gave him a worried look. It was too late to be good news.

"Tomahawk? What's up?"

His heart sank. "Are you sure it's her?"

Becca reached over and grabbed his hand.

"I'll be right there."

He hung up. They were too late. The heaviness pushed down on him.

"They've found Crystal Morning Song's body in a cave on the reservation. It looks like she OD'd."

THIRTY-SIX

SAVAGE HAD NEVER KNOWN such darkness. There were no lights in this part of the reservation, no houses and no roads. The dirt track had ended five hundred yards back, so he proceeded to the crime scene on foot. Even the crescent moon had disappeared behind a cloud, refusing to help.

His flashlight showed him the way over the rocky terrain. Trees and shrubs were sparse, but every now and then a twisted branch reached out toward him, or a thorny twig snagged the denim of his jeans.

As he got closer to the ledge where Crystal's body had been found, the darkness gave way to a sudden pool of light. Someone had switched on a portable lamp.

An officer glanced up as Savage approached and stuck out a hand. "Sorry, this site is off limits."

"It is okay," Tomahawk called from somewhere beyond the light. "Sheriff Savage can come through."

Savage ducked under the police tape, treading carefully to avoid shrubs and loose pebbles. Since Crystal had been found on the res, Tomahawk would lead the investigation. At best, Savage would be a bystander. At worst, he'd be left out entirely.

"She's over here." Tomahawk appeared like an apparition into the pool of light. He followed the tribal policeman around a rocky outcrop and into a cave where a second lamp had been set up to illuminate the body.

So still.

That was his first thought on seeing her. The stillness of death was unlike any other. Looking at her unmoving form, he could tell nothing was there. Even though her eyes were open, they may as well have been closed.

His second thought was how young she looked. Naked, except for the long, dirty T-shirt, her bare arms and legs were splayed out like starfish. He cringed at how vulnerable and exposed she was. "Can we cover her up?"

Tomahawk nodded. "We're nearly done here."

Two white-clad officers buzzed around her body, taking samples and photographing her in situ.

"Cause of death?"

"It looks like she overdosed," Tomahawk said, his voice brittle. "Just like Eddie."

"I'm sorry," Savage said.

Tomahawk turned away. "I haven't informed her parents yet."

Savage didn't envy him that job.

"Injection site?"

Tomahawk cleared his throat and turned back to the body. "Left arm."

"May I?"

Tomahawk nodded.

Savage pulled on a pair of latex gloves and bent down to take a closer look at her arm. There were several needle marks. "Looks like she was injected more than once."

"Yeah."

"And you're sure she wasn't a user?"

"I'm sure. Anyway, Crystal was left-handed."

Savage studied the injection sites. Unlike Eddie's, these looked intravenous. It would have been extremely difficult for a left-handed person to have done this with their non-dominant hand. Not that he needed any proof that she'd been murdered. The MO was exactly the same as all the others—except Eddie.

Becca's words resonated in his head.

Eddie wasn't the primary target.

But Crystal was.

He looked at the dirty T-shirt. "Has she been raped?"

Tomahawk gave a grave nod. "There are signs of sexual intercourse. We will know more once we get her to the mortuary in Durango."

"Did you find the syringe?" The other victims, apart from Eddie, still had the needle in their arm. No mistaking they'd shot up before they'd died.

"It was in her hand."

Close enough.

"Her right hand?"

"Yeah." Tomahawk's dark eyes probed his.

Savage exhaled. Crystal Morning Song was the heroin killer's latest victim.

Tomahawk put his hands on his hips. "Do you know who is doing this?"

"We're working on it."

Tomahawk studied him. "Did you find out who Crystal was seeing? The older man?"

"No, her friend didn't know anything and the coffee shop where they met wasn't able to ID him. We're still looking."

Tomahawk nodded. "You will tell me when you know?"

"This is your turf, your investigation."

"Except it is linked with Eddie Youngblood's death, and that is on your turf." Tomahawk released his arm. "We need to work together on this."

He was right.

Savage took a deep breath. "In that case, Tomahawk, we should talk."

"Why?"

"There's more to this than you know."

Tomahawk scowled. "What are you not telling me?"

"Let's talk tomorrow. Right now, you've got to take care of Crystal."

THIRTY-SEVEN

TOMAHAWK WAS due to the sheriff's station at ten-thirty. He never made it. Just before ten, a frazzled Barbara rushed into the office. "Sheriff, the building site. It's on fire."

They saw the smoke long before they got there. Great black billows curled into the sky, coating the sun.

"What the hell is going on?" muttered Savage, as they raced up the dirt road to the gate. It was open, the armed guards inside, rifles ready. Two fire engines hurled water at the burning office and guard's hut. It didn't seem to make any difference.

An angry crowd parted as Savage drove up, sirens screaming. Thorpe and Littleton followed in a second squad car. Tomahawk came running up.

"I cannot keep them back."

"What's going on?" Savage shouted over the din.

"They want the development gone."

There was a loud crash as the office imploded. The crowd shifted back. Savage turned to see the walls tumble inwards, the equipment alight. Inside was a mangled mess of cables and wiring, like entrails on fire. It was too late to save anything. Now the fire department had to concentrate on preventing the blaze from spreading to the barracks.

"How'd it start?"

"Molotov cocktail is my guess." Tomahawk pointed to one of the protesters, waving a bottle.

"Great. So do you want to start arresting people, or should I?"

"Not my jurisdiction," Tomahawk responded. These were his people. He wouldn't be the one to apprehend them.

What was worrying was the guards had seen the bottle too and moved forward. They were feet away from the protesters. All it took was one person to start firing, and they'd have a massacre on their hands.

Savage returned to the team. "Okay, let's take 'em in. Aim for the ringleaders. I'll take Crystal's father." The middle-aged man stood at the front, shouting at the security guards, tears pouring down his face.

Thorpe, Sinclair, and a quivering Littleton moved in on the protesters and began slapping on the cuffs. As soon as the rest saw what was happening, they scattered.

"Mr. Morning Song, I think you'd better come with me." Savage put a hand on his arm.

"Are you kidding?" The man shook it off. "My daughter was just murdered."

"And I'm sorry for your loss, but you're an accomplice for arson."

"We'll burn the place to the ground," he growled. "That'll get rid of them. Scum stealing our land, killing our children."

The grieving father was too riled up to be reasoned with, so Savage handcuffed him, then read him his rights.

Thorpe and Sinclair each had one instigator in cuffs, including the man who'd been holding the bottle. Littleton hadn't managed to arrest anyone, but the crowd had dispersed.

Two black SUVs pulled up. Connelly and Bryant jumped out of one, while Kushner climbed out of the other. The tide of protesters regathered and surged toward the vehicles. The security guards ran out, guns raised.

"Tomahawk!" yelled Savage.

The tribal police officer got there first. "Get back inside your vehicles.

It's too dangerous for you here." As if to prove it, a stone smashed into Connelly's windshield, cracking it.

"You!" shouted Littleton, pointing. "You're under arrest." The stone thrower took off in the direction of the reservation.

"Know that guy?" Savage asked Tomahawk, who shrugged, and made no attempt to go after him.

The black SUVs turned around and drove away, the shocked, white faces of their inhabitants staring out at the inferno.

Leaving the fire department to get the blaze under control, Savage and the others transported the troublemakers back to the sheriff station. He wasn't thinking about pressing charges, not when tensions were so high, but it wouldn't hurt to hold them for a couple hours until they cooled down.

The CCTV camera mounted to the roof of the guard's hut had been destroyed in the fire. They had no way of identifying who'd thrown the gas bomb.

"There's a ruckus outside the station." Thorpe's voice came over the radio. He was ahead of Savage. Sinclair and Littleton were behind him. They each had a suspect in the back seat.

"Shit." Savage slowed down to drive through the swarm of angry Native Americans. He might have guessed they'd move their protest to the Sheriff's office. A woman holding a sign that read, "Down with the Development," stood in front of him.

A scream made him glance sideways.

Becca.

What was she doing here?

Then he remembered, they'd arranged to meet for lunch. In the chaos, he'd completely forgotten. She was being shoved back and forth like a ping pong ball, and it looked like she might topple over at any moment.

"Sinclair, help Becca," he yelled into the radio. He couldn't leave the prisoner alone in his SUV.

"On it."

In his rearview mirror, he saw her jump from the cruiser. Thorpe was driving. Sinclair ran into the crowd, grabbed hold of Becca, and extricated her from the throng of people. It seemed like half the res had turned up to complain about the arrests.

He'd just driven through the garage into the sally port when his phone buzzed. It was Sinclair, saying she'd taken Becca to a coffee shop around the corner. He heaved a sigh of relief.

He texted back, "Be there soon." First, he had to lock up these guys.

———

"I'M SO SORRY," Savage said as he walked into the Bouncing Bean a fraught twenty minutes later.

Becca smiled up at him. "That's okay. Becky filled me in. Looks like you have your hands full."

He grimaced. "You can say that again."

"I'd better get back." Sinclair got to her feet. "It was lovely seeing you, Becca."

"Thanks for coming to my rescue."

Savage shot his deputy a grateful smile. "I'll see you back at the station. Use the back door to my office." He reached into his pocket and took out a key, handing it to Sinclair.

She smiled ruefully and headed out the door.

Savage sank down opposite his fiancée. "I'm sorry. I should have told you not to come. I didn't know—"

"It's okay." She placed her hands on her belly. "No harm done."

He let out a shaky breath. "When I saw you being shoved around, I panicked."

"I know, but we're fine. Really." She took his hand. "How about you? Will you be okay?"

"Yeah, but I'm not going to be able to stay long."

She smiled. "It's not important. We can reschedule."

"Was there something specific you wanted to talk about?" He looked at her quizzically.

"No, it's fine. Nothing that can't wait."

"Okay, good." He kissed her and with an apologetic glance, got up, and headed back out into the street.

———

"WHAT ARE WE GOING TO DO?" Barbara asked once she'd let Savage in the back door. He closed it behind him, slipping the lock bolt across.

"They'll go home once we've released the protesters," he said. "I wouldn't worry about it."

Out front, the noise went from a loud buzz to a roar. Savage peered out of the window. "For God's sake. It's Connelly and Kushner. What are they doing here?"

Sinclair and Thorpe raced to the front door, grabbed the visitors, and pulled them inside. Shouts of 'Murdering scumbags' and 'Get off our land' echoed behind them.

"What the hell do you think you're doing?" Savage stormed out of his office. "Are you insane?"

Connelly, red-faced and riled up, took his hat off and chucked it onto a nearby chair. "Damnit Sheriff, those maniacs burned down my building site. I want to file charges."

"Against whom?"

"Against the men you've got in custody. Against the whole goddamn tribe if I have to. I won't let them get away with this."

Kushner, surprisingly calm, stood beside Connelly.

"Another one of their own has died. Two of the tribe's teenagers have been murdered in the last week."

"I don't care. They gas bombed my site, for God's sake. Do you know how much that's going to cost to rebuild? Not to mention the lack of earnings. I demand compensation."

"Aren't you insured?"

"Not against Molotov cocktails." Connelly raked a hand through his thinning hair.

Kushner was looking around the open-plan office.

Savage sighed. "Look, we don't know who threw the makeshift

bombs. The CCTV camera was damaged in the fire, and none of the protesters are going to talk. I suggest you just forget about suing them and move on."

"You're kidding, right? Who do you think is going to pay for the damages?"

"How about your silent partner, Guy Hollander?"

Kushner's head swung around. If Connelly was surprised by the question, he covered it well.

"Mr. Hollander is not going to cover this. I'm afraid you've got the wrong impression."

"Maybe he can use some of the drug money he's pumping into the company." At Connelly's dry expression, Savage added, "We all know he's using it to launder his ill-gotten gains."

Kushner glared at him.

Connelly cleared his throat. "I wouldn't know anything about that."

"Sure you wouldn't."

"Regardless, I want to press charges." Connelly threw his hands in the air. "This is unacceptable. Your people are out of control."

"They're not my people," he said. "The reservation is not in my jurisdiction."

"You mean to tell me you're just going to let them walk out of here?"

Savage was getting tired of Connelly's self-righteous ranting.

"Probably. Littleton!" The young deputy appeared in the doorway. "Take down Mr. Connelly's complaint."

The deputy gave a wide-eyed nod. "If you'll come with me, Mr. Connelly." The business owner shot Savage an annoyed look, then followed the deputy to his desk.

Kushner gave Savage a last look, then joined his boss.

Savage went back to his office and closed the door. His desk phone was ringing. "It's Tomahawk," Barbara said. "I'm putting him through."

"Tomahawk?"

"She was raped, repeatedly," came the hollow words down the line.

Savage grunted. That was what he expected. In fact, if she hadn't been, that would have been more of a surprise. The MO was consistent.

"Cause of death was cardiac arrest and respiratory failure due to an overdose of heroin."

Shit.

"Just like the others," Savage murmured.

"What?"

"There are others, Tomahawk. Crystal isn't the only one."

"This what you wanted to tell me?"

"It's classified. If word of this gets out, your protests are going to turn into a full-out riot."

"The development company is involved?"

"It's someone at the company, yeah."

"Okay, I'm coming to you."

"Better not," Savage said quickly. "We're surrounded. I'll come to you. See you in half an hour."

It was time Tomahawk knew the full extent of what was going on.

THIRTY-EIGHT

"THREE OTHER GIRLS?" Tomahawk stared at him.

"That we know of. We're still uncovering the rest. It could go back years, even a decade."

"Holy shit." Tomahawk was as shocked as Savage had ever seen him. After a long pause during which he simply gaped at Savage, he said, "Why do you think the company is involved?"

"Because every time one of these girls goes missing, Apex Holdings is in town."

Tomahawk let out a shaky breath. "How long have you known about this?"

"A couple days." Savage didn't bother mentioning Carter, who was still undercover.

"I take it you are looking into the employees?"

"We are. So far, they've all got alibis for Crystal's disappearance, but we haven't questioned them in response to the other girls yet. Nobody knows we've linked the murders."

Tomahawk gnawed on his lip. "If it is an Apex Holding employee, you don't want them to know you're onto them."

"That's right." Savage leaned back in his chair. "You got anything more on Crystal or the man she was dating?"

Tomahawk reached into a drawer and took out a pink, sequined diary. It was the kind that changed color when you ran your hand over it. "Her parents were in the dark, and her best friend doesn't know anything. You're welcome to take a look."

Savage reached for it. Opening the first page, he read: *This Diary Belongs to Crystal Morning Song.*

The writing was typical of a teenage girl. Messy, with swirling loops for the y and g's. She'd also drawn what looked like doves all over the page.

He was hit by a terrifying image of her face. Waxy, unseeing, still. When she'd started this diary, she'd been filled with hope. A long life ahead of her. Dreams. Ambitions. Now she was gone. Those same dreams and ambitions extinguished because of some sick pervert.

———

SAVAGE TRUDGED through the embers left by the fire. Some were still burning, the rest had turned to a smoky, gray ash.

"What's the extent of the damage?" he asked Angus Harmon.

"These two structures have been totaled." The foreman's expression was grim. "There's nothing left. Everything was burned to a cinder."

Savage gave a somber nod. "Any other buildings damaged?"

"Nope. They managed to stop the blaze from spreading."

"Are you going to relocate?" Savage surveyed the mess of machinery, wires, and something that might have once been a desk.

"Yeah, to one of the outbuildings we use to store machinery. We've got to get new computers, though. Everything was destroyed."

"You lost all the files? Employment records?"

"Yeah, although a lot of that stuff is on the cloud, so it's not a problem. We lost all the hard copies, the contracts, but we have digitals."

Thank goodness for modern technology.

"Heard anything from Denver?"

The foreman frowned. "Why would I hear anything from there?"

"Because that's where the money comes from," Savage said.

"Don't know anything about that." Angus shrugged. "I take my orders from Kushner, and he gets them from Connelly." With that, the foreman strode off.

Savage took a walk to clear his head. Work had commenced on the site, and he stopped to watch a digger lazily turn as it got into position. It lowered its bucket into the ground and scooped up a load of dirt, which it then dumped to the side, before swinging back again.

He walked on. What had Crystal been doing here? Had she really gotten separated from the group? Or had the killer messaged her, asking to meet?

They hadn't found anything on her phone records. Maybe she'd had a burner phone? One he'd given her to communicate. Savage thought of the other victims, Hannah, Laura, and Margaret. No phone had been found on them either. The killer was careful. He made sure they didn't still have them when he dumped their bodies.

A lone figure caught his eye. It was Connelly's daughter, Celine. He raised a hand in a wave. She looked up and saw him, recognition dawning.

Savage strode up to her. "What are you doing out here?"

"My father's inspecting the damage." She shrugged. "I was bored, so I came along."

"How have you been?"

She looked around as if wishing she were somewhere else. "You know."

"When are you off to college?"

"Not soon enough." She glanced back toward the burned-out buildings, now hollow shells.

"I can't imagine moving around all the time is very nice for a teenager."

She rolled her eyes. "It sucks."

He gave a sympathetic grimace. "What about your mother? You could go live with her?"

The big eyes narrowed. "She's in Europe. She and my father split up years ago."

"You didn't want to go with her?"

"He wouldn't let me. She's a reporter. She moves around even more than he does."

"I see."

"Besides, my mother is more concerned with covering the latest war zone than her own daughter."

Savage sensed a lot of animosity there. "I'm sorry."

She pretended not to care. "It is what it is." In the distance, the digger's boom lifted again, before plunging down into the pit.

"How well do you know Paul Kushner?" he asked.

She glanced up, surprised. "Why?"

"I'm trying to figure out what his role at the company is. He said project manager, but he doesn't seem to have much to do with the day-to-day running of the site."

"He keeps an eye on everything," she said vaguely. Savage didn't miss the hint of bitterness.

"Even you?"

She didn't meet his gaze. "Daddy borrowed a lot of money to fund this project, so Kushner makes sure it runs efficiently."

Savage studied her. Soft brown hair, large oval eyes, pale freckled skin. She reminded him of a skittish deer about to bolt. "You know a lot about your father's affairs."

"It's hard not to, living with him. I hear things."

He'd love to know some of what she'd heard. Celine Connelly was a lot savvier than she let on. "How long has Kushner been with the company?"

"Years. For as long as I can remember." She shuddered, like someone had walked over her grave.

"You don't like him much, do you?"

Her expression darkened. "He's a brute. I mean, he doesn't treat the staff very well. He still thinks he's in the Army."

Savage raised his eyebrows. "Kushner is ex-military?"

"Yeah."

At that moment, the man in question strode over to them. "Can I help you, Sheriff?"

"No thanks. I'm taking a walk around the site."

Kushner's gaze lingered on Celine. "Is Miss Connelly helping you?"

"I was just leaving." The teenager tossed her hair over her shoulder.

"I'll give you a lift back to the hotel," offered Kushner.

Celine glared at him. "I'll get a ride with Steve."

"Suit yourself." The enforcer gave a curt nod, turned around, and stalked back the way he'd come.

THIRTY-NINE

"HE WAS IN THE MARINE CORPS," Thorpe said, gazing at his computer.

"A marine. Then he knows how to handle himself," Savage muttered. Celine had been right. A brute, she'd called him. Interesting choice of words.

"Listen to this." Thorpe said. "Kushner was investigated back in '05 after a female officer claimed he'd sexually assaulted her."

"What?" Savage spun round. Sinclair and Littleton both stopped what they were doing and looked up.

"Yeah, there was an internal investigation, but nothing came of it. Not enough evidence."

"Who was the female officer?" Savage asked.

"A Monique Henderson. She quit shortly after the inquest, saying she could no longer work with the man responsible for raping her."

———

MONIQUE HENDERSON LIVED in Philadelphia and was hesitant to talk about her experience.

"I've tried to put that behind me," she said.

"We're looking at him for another sexual assault," Savage explained, hoping that would persuade her to open up.

"Really?"

"Yeah, several actually. Would you mind telling me what happened?"

She hesitated, then gave a little sigh. "This won't be on record, will it?"

"No. Strictly off the record. I'm just trying to get the measure of the man."

"Okay." She took a shaky breath. "He was my commanding officer. I took orders from him."

"I understand," he told her. It was easy to see how the lines would get blurred.

"It was my first tour in Afghanistan. I was the only female soldier in the unit. He'd made a few passes at me, but I'd turned him down. That's when he threatened me."

"How did he threaten you?"

Her voice changed, became hollower. "There was an incident. We came under attack on a road south of Kabul. I was so scared that I froze. I hid under our vehicle and didn't move while my fellow soldiers took the brunt of it. Kushner saw the whole thing. He said he'd tell everyone I was a coward if I didn't... have sex with him." Her voice cracked. "I didn't want my unit to know I'd let them down."

"So you slept with him."

"Yeah." her voice was a whisper. "I didn't know what else to do. I thought it would only be the once, but—" She faded off.

"It happened again?"

There was a heavy pause. "Several times. He had me exactly where he wanted me, and unless I wanted to be shamed in front of my unit, I had to agree to it."

Savage tensed. "That still doesn't make it right."

"I know that. When we got home, I began having anxiety attacks. My therapist said I should report him, so I did." She hesitated. "It was a mistake."

"What he did was wrong," Savage said. "You made the right call."

"I didn't. I'd voluntarily slept with him, so it wasn't rape. I had no case. All I did was humiliate myself. That's why I left. I couldn't face them, couldn't face him."

"You quit?"

"Yeah. All I ever wanted to do was serve. Kushner ruined that for me."

"I'm sorry to hear that."

"I hope you put him away, Sheriff. I really do. But he's slippery. He'll have covered himself, you can bet on it."

"Thanks for the warning."

Not for this, Savage thought as he hung up the phone. There was nothing that covered him for this. They just had to prove it.

"SHOULD WE BRING HIM IN?" asked Sinclair.

"We need a warrant for an arrest, and no judge is going to give us that based on what we've got," Savage said.

"If he killed Eddie and kidnapped Crystal, he must be lying about his alibi," reasoned Thorpe.

"He doesn't have one for Eddie's murder," Savage reminded them. "He said he was in his hotel room at the time."

"That's easy enough to check," Thorpe said, standing up. "The key cards are linked to a digital system. I'll go down to the hotel and double check."

"I'll come with you. I want to talk to that finance guy, Steven Bryant. He provided Kushner with his alibi for Crystal's disappearance. If Kushner's lying, Bryant must be too."

Sinclair glanced up. "What should I do?"

"Come with us. I'm worried about Celine. I think she knows more about Kushner than she's letting on."

"You don't think he'd hurt her, do you?" Sinclair frowned, worried.

"I don't know. She might open up more to another woman."

He's a brute.

As Savage was pulling on his jacket, Barbara rushed in. "Sheriff, there's been a shootout at Mac's Roadhouse. One casualty."

He froze. "Rosalie?"

"No, a male. The paramedics are on their way."

He turned to Thorpe and Sinclair. "You two handle the hotel. Littleton, with me."

The young deputy jumped up. They ran outside, climbed into Savage's Suburban, and sped off to the Roadhouse.

"Who do you think's been shot?" Littleton asked.

Savage weaved in and out of the traffic. "Don't know. We'll have to wait till we get there to find out." But the same thought was going through his head. Was it Carter? Had Rosalie figured out he wasn't who he'd claimed to be? Had someone else?

He hoped not. Despite his messed up vigilante mission, Carter was a good guy. All he was trying to do was track down a killer.

He thought of Becca and his unborn child, and his hands tightened around the steering wheel. If someone hurt them, he'd also want to hunt them down and make them pay. The difference was he had a badge, Carter did not. But that didn't make the anger or the grief any less pertinent.

Sirens blaring, they pulled into the Roadhouse parking lot. The sun was setting and the whole valley was bathed in a peachy glow. In the distance, the mountain peaks grew purple as night engulfed them. A small crowd of bikers stood outside, looking grim. There was no sign of an ambulance, but the nearest hospital was in Durango, a good twenty-minute drive away.

Rosalie came to meet them. It was only when Savage got out of the vehicle that he saw she was covered in blood.

"Are you okay?" He eyed the wet stain on the front of her shirt.

"Not me," she said. "It's Scooter."

The Vice President of the Crimson Angels. Savage breathed out. Thank goodness it wasn't Rosalie or Carter. "Is he dead?"

"He will be if the ambulance doesn't get here soon."

"Show me." Savage and Littleton followed Rosalie into the bar. On the ground, by the jukebox, lay a pale-faced Scooter. Carter was holding a cloth over a bullet wound in his abdomen. It was on the right side, bleeding profusely. A sticky red puddle had formed beneath him.

"Who did this?" Savage asked, as Littleton went outside to check on the status of the ambulance.

"The Denver thugs," Rosalie spat. "That weasel Jonny Star came in with two of his goons. They wanted to talk business, but I told Scooter to get rid of them." She tossed her hair back in a defiant gesture, but he could see she felt guilty about what had transpired.

"We asked them to leave," Burner took over. "They refused. Scooter helped me show them the door. One guy pulled a gun. There was a scuffle, and the gun went off. Scooter went down."

"What did Jonny Star do?"

"He said they'd be back and left. Unfinished business, was how he put it."

"You got it on camera?" Savage asked.

Her eyes glistened. "You betcha."

"Then we can get an arrest warrant."

He called Shelby at the Durango Station and told him what had happened.

"I'll get my guys to go to the Dorchester and bring them in," Shelby said. "If they're there."

"Send Sheriff Shelby that camera footage," Savage told Rosalie after he'd hung up. "He's going to need it."

Rosalie nodded.

Things moved fast after that. The ambulance arrived, the paramedics stabilized Scooter, who was cringing in pain, his eyes squeezed shut. From what Savage could see, the slug had missed any vital organs, but was buried in the soft tissue above Scooter's right hip. The VP had yet to make a sound. He was a tough bastard.

To Savage's surprise, Rosalie climbed into the back of the ambulance with him. "I'll clean up," Burner said, as she left. She nodded her thanks.

"Something going on there?" Savage asked, as the ambulance pulled away.

"Not to my knowledge," Carter said.

"It was pretty brazen of Jonny Star to march in here," Savage said. "What did he want?"

"To talk. I think he wanted to strike a deal with Rosalie, but she wasn't interested. Nothing on God's green Earth is gonna make her negotiate with those Denver thugs."

Now that was interesting.

The bikers filed back into the bar, talking in low, angry voices.

"Everybody loves Scooter," Carter said, going inside. "He's one of the inner sanctum, along with Buck and Whitey over there."

Savage and Littleton followed. Whitey tended the bar while Carter grabbed a bucket and mop and began to clean up the blood on the floor.

Inside, the atmosphere was seething. The air felt heavy with testosterone and vengeance.

"Listen up," Buck shouted. He had long, wavy hair and a generous amount of stubble prickling his jaw. The tail end of something reptilian snaked up his neck. The bikers quieted down. Buck looked Savage's way. "You and your deputy might wanna leave now, Sheriff."

There was a snicker. Littleton shuffled.

"I wouldn't advise going after those guys." Savage raised his voice so everyone could hear. "Sheriff Shelby and his men are on their way to their motel right now to arrest them. Anyone going off half-cocked is going to get in the way, and possibly arrested."

More murmuring, but the tension had eased.

"Okay, okay." Buck regained control of the room. "Thank you, Sheriff. We'll bear that in mind."

Savage nodded. "Come on, Littleton." He strode from the bar, leaving his deputy to follow. As they got into the Suburban, Savage said, "I think the turf war just ticked up a notch."

FORTY

THORPE AND SINCLAIR arrived at the Boulder Creek Hotel just as the sun was setting. The sprawling log cabin glowed orange as it soaked in the dying rays. Behind it, the trees were falling into shadow.

"I'll go and find Celine," Sinclair said, heading down the corridor.

Thorpe nodded. "I'll meet you in the dining room." He walked up to the same fresh-faced receptionist as before. "Hello again."

It took a moment for her to register. "You're that deputy that came to see Mr. Connolly the other day."

He grinned. "That's right. Good memory."

She smiled at the compliment. "What can I help you with today?"

"I'd like to take a look at your keycard data."

She frowned. "I'm sorry Deputy, but I'm not supposed to give out that information."

"I just need to know if one of your guests was in his room last Tuesday evening. That's all."

She hesitated. "It's not Mr. Connolly, is it? Because he wouldn't like me to—"

"No, his project manager, Mr. Kushner. The big guy."

She gave a relieved nod. "He's next to Mr. Connolly in Room 9." For someone who wasn't supposed to give out personal information, she'd just given him Kushner and Connelly's room number. "Alright, I can pull some strings since you're a deputy and all."

He smiled. "Thank you."

Her nails clacked on the keyboard. A few minutes later, she looked up. "There isn't much."

"Can I see?"

She nodded and Thorpe scooted around the desk. According to the system, Kushner entered his room at 16:37. That was the only entry.

Thorpe rubbed his forehead. "That was the only time he entered his room?"

"Uh-huh. Of course, we can't see when he went out, but that's when he got back."

"He was there all evening? He didn't even go out for dinner?"

"If he did, he didn't use his keycard," she said.

Thorpe sighed. It looked like Kushner had been telling the truth. There's no way he could have left and returned to his room later that night without it showing up on the system.

A thought occurred to him. "Can we check if he ordered room service?"

"Sure, one moment." She tapped a few more keys. "Yes, he did. Brisket, fries, and a large coke."

"Right. Thank you." He turned away.

Damn, Kushner was covered. Unless he'd somehow managed to get out and back without using his keycard.

"He didn't have anyone else in the room with him, did he?" asked Savage, when Thorpe called to tell him the news.

"Doesn't look like it."

"Is there any way of keeping the door open to prevent it from locking?"

"That's a possibility, except he ordered room service at seven o'clock, which is around the time Eddie Youngblood was murdered. I don't think it was him."

He heard Savage emit a frustrated growl on the other end of the line. Their only suspect was in the clear.

Sinclair still wasn't back yet, so Thorpe went into the dining room to see if he could get a coffee. A tired-looking waitress came up to him. "Can I get you something?"

He ordered, then said, "Hey, have you been on the breakfast shift all week?"

"Yeah. I do the breakfast and lunch shifts most days. I don't work evenings. Got a kid at home."

"I see." She did look exhausted. Thorpe pulled out his phone. "Maybe you can help me. Do you remember seeing these men here?"

"At breakfast?"

"Yes."

She gazed at the pictures on his screen. He flicked between the two. They were photographs taken from the company website. Both men were wearing expensive suits and fake smiles.

"I recognize them both," she said. "They're staying at the hotel."

"Did you see them on Monday morning?"

Her forehead creased. "I don't think so."

Thorpe frowned. "You don't think so?"

She shrugged. "I don't remember seeing them, but I could be wrong. Mondays are always busy. Sorry."

"That's okay. Thanks." It was enough to make him doubt their alibis, but it wasn't enough to bank on. He could hear Kushner's defense attorney already. He'd argue that the waitress was a tired, overworked mother. She could have easily been mistaken.

———

SINCLAIR KNOCKED on Celine's door. It was next to her father's suite, but separate. She wondered if Celine had wanted it that way.

"Can I help you?" the youngster said, opening the door. She wore loose fitting clothing and had her hair up in a messy bun. Without it framing her face, her freckles were more noticeable, and so were her huge oval-shaped eyes.

Sinclair showed the teenager her ID. "I'm Deputy Sinclair," she said. "I work with Sheriff Savage."

"Oh yeah." The girl turned away from the door, leaving it open. "I recognize you now."

Sinclair hesitated, then followed her in. "You busy?"

"Nah, just reading." There was a dent in the bed where she'd been lying, and the lamp on the bedside table was on.

"What book?"

She held up a worn paperback. Simone de Beauvoir, with a French title.

"Any good?"

"It's okay. Are you interested in feminism?"

"Sure. Is that what you're going to study at college?"

"Women's studies and politics."

"You're reading in French." Sinclair nodded to the book, impressed.

"My mother's half-French." A nonchalant shrug.

The mother Celine never saw. Sinclair remembered Savage saying her mother was in Europe somewhere, reporting from war zones.

"What do you want?" Celine sat on the bed and pulled her legs up beneath her.

"I wanted to ask you about Paul Kushner."

"Him again." She rolled her eyes. "I told the Sheriff everything I know."

"He thinks you're holding back." Sinclair had decided to play it straight with Celine. She was a smart kid, and would see through any attempt to befriend or manipulate her into talking.

"What makes him think that?" She blinked, thrown.

"It's clear you despise the man. We want to understand why. Has he done something to upset you?"

"What do you mean? Like what?" The words came out fast. Too fast.

"I don't know." Sinclair glanced at the book on Celine's bed. "Has he made you feel inferior? Been rude to you?"

The girl was already shaking her head.

"Has he been nice to you? Too nice, perhaps?" She saw Celine glance away.

That was it!

A chill washed over Sinclair. Kushner had made a pass at Celine. Or worse.

"Has he hurt you in any way, Celine?" Sinclair pressed.

The girl fidgeted, but she couldn't meet Sinclair's eye. "No, he hasn't hurt me."

"You don't seem sure. Has he threatened you? Made you do something you didn't want to do?"

No reply.

She lowered her voice. "Has he had sex with you?"

Celine's head jerked up. "How do you know about that? Has someone said something?"

Sinclair's gut twisted.

Not Celine too.

She sighed. "Because he's done this sort of thing before."

"He has?" The fawn-like eyes stared up, making her look even younger.

"Yes. when he was in the Marines. He blackmailed a woman into having sex with him."

The girl's slender shoulders sank. "He warned me not to tell anyone. Said he'd make things difficult for us, for my father."

"Did he force himself on you?"

Celine bit her lip. "No."

"But you slept with him?"

A tiny nod, then a tear ran down her cheek. "I had to."

"No, Celine. That's where you're wrong. You didn't have to. You *don't* have to."

"I've got to get out of here," the teenager sobbed. "Don't you understand? I hate this place. If the company goes under, I can't go to college. Then I'm stuck here."

Sinclair nodded. "I get it, but it's not right. We could get a court order, make him stop."

She gasped. "No, don't do that." Sinclair knew she was thinking about her future, about the possibility of not going to college. "Please, you can't tell anyone that you know."

"Is it still going on?"

She nodded. "But it's fine. I don't care. Another three weeks and I'll be in Boston."

"But it's wrong," Sinclair whispered.

Celine grasped her hand. "If you say anything, I'll deny it."

Sinclair left the hotel room feeling more helpless than she ever had before.

———

THORPE HAD JUST FINISHED his coffee when Sinclair stomped into the room. She slumped into the chair opposite him. By the morose expression on her face, he could tell it hadn't gone well.

"What happened? Did you find her?"

"I found her alright. We had a very interesting talk." She was flushed with anger. He listened while Sinclair told him what she'd discovered.

"No way," Thorpe breathed, shocked. "Can't we stop him?"

"How? She's not a minor according to Colorado law, and she consented. Kushner's covered. Plus, she said she'd deny it if we said anything."

"But he's twice her age, for God's sake. He can't force himself on her like that. It's not right."

"Not forcing, but he's definitely coerced her into sleeping with him. The guy's a monumental scumbag." She swiped at a stray hair.

Thorpe shook his head. "So, there's nothing we can do?"

"Not unless we can arrest the bastard for murder."

They walked past the reception on the way out, but instead of the young brunette, an older woman with gray-blonde hair in a stylish chignon stood behind the desk. On a whim, Thorpe said, "Excuse me, about your guest in room 9?"

"Yes?

"Does he have someone else staying with him?"

She looked shocked. "Mr. Langton? No, of course not. His wife just passed away."

"Sorry, did you say Mr. Langton? I thought the room was occupied by Mr. Kushner."

"No, Mr. Kushner agreed to change rooms a couple nights ago. Mr. Langton comes to Hawk's Landing twice a year to go hiking and we're happy to accommodate him." She smiled. "He's such a gentleman."

Thorpe scratched his head. "Mr. Kushner was in room 9 but changed to a different room?"

"Yes, that's right."

"Which room is he in now?" Sinclair asked, stepping forward.

"I believe he's in room 6." She smiled. "It doesn't have a mountain view, but he very graciously said he didn't mind."

Thorpe placed his ID on the desk. "Portia," he said, reading her name tag. "It's very important that we see the keycard data for room 6 for last Tuesday evening."

Her eyes darted uncertainly from Thorpe to Sinclair and back again.

"This is a homicide investigation." Thorpe wasn't going to take no for an answer. Not after what he'd just heard. "We could get a warrant, but then we'd have to shut down the hotel and—"

"No, that's okay," she was quick to reassure him. She was slower than her assistant, her finger poking at the keyboard. Eventually, she brought up the required data. "Here you go."

Without waiting to ask permission, Thorpe marched around the desk to take a look. His eyes scanned the page. Then he paused, catching his breath. The first entry stamp was at nine thirty-seven on Tuesday night. Kushner had been out the entire day.

"WHY DIDN'T you tell us you'd changed rooms?" Savage sat across from Kushner in the interview room. The project manager had come in voluntarily, confident in his alibi. Savage had just crushed it underfoot and was enjoying watching Kushner unravel.

"Why is that important?" Kushner looked genuinely surprised.

It was a good act. Savage wasn't buying.

"We asked where you were when Eddie Youngblood was murdered. You purposely told us you were at the hotel, in your room."

"I was."

"Except, you said you were in room 9, when in fact you were in room 6."

He spread his giant hands. "So what? I forgot I'd changed rooms."

"You forgot?" Now he'd heard it all. The fluorescent light above them flickered, and he saw Kushner glance up. The bulb was wearing out, kind of like his patience.

"Yeah, the hotel asked if I'd mind moving, so I agreed. I took my stuff across the hall to the new room and left for work." He frowned. "What's the big deal?"

"The big deal is that the occupant of room 9 was at the hotel all evening, while the occupant of room 6 wasn't."

"How do you know?"

Savage leaned forward. "We checked the hotel system. You only got back to your room after nine thirty that night."

Kushner fell silent.

Savage fixed his gaze on him. "Eddie Youngblood was murdered between six and eight o'clock."

Kushner shook his head and said in a tired voice. "Sheriff, haven't we been through this?"

"Not since your alibi fell through." Savage paused, letting the tension build. "And not since we found out you're sleeping with Celine Connelly."

Kushner's eyes became slits. "Who told you that?"

"She did."

The veins stood out in his thick neck.

"She also said she'd deny it if anybody asked."

He relaxed slightly. "It's consensual."

"She's seventeen."

He shrugged.

Savage gave him a hard look. "Did you know Eddie Youngblood was in love with her?"

Kushner stiffened. Savage had hit a nerve. "They were meeting in secret. She liked him but was holding back, for obvious reasons."

Was that a smirk? Could the hulking project manager have been jealous of Celine's feelings for Eddie?

Savage continued. "Eddie received a text message from Celine that night. That's why he was there at the construction site."

The hulk shifted. "I don't know anything about that."

Savage sensed he was making progress and pushed harder. "I think you do. I think you knew exactly where he'd be because you sent him the text from Celine's phone."

It was a calculated guess. They hadn't been granted a warrant to look at Celine's phone records, but stealing Celine's phone would have been easy enough for Kushner, considering he'd been sleeping with Celine. She may not have known he'd used her phone if he'd sent the text, then deleted it.

"Sheriff, this is nonsense. I had nothing to do with that boy's death."

"I think you did. You lured him out there because he'd seen something, hadn't he? He knew what you were doing to Celine."

"What? That is bullshit. I want to speak to my lawyer." He scowled, tension radiating across the desk.

"Celine told Eddie there was something she needed to talk to him about. It wasn't that she'd agreed to date him, it was to tell him what you were doing to her."

Kushner said nothing. He was fuming.

"You couldn't have that, could you? If Connelly found out you were sleeping with his daughter, there'd be hell to pay."

"He couldn't do a damn thing about it," Kushner spat. "I don't work for him. I work for Guy Hollander."

"The man funding the project. You know, I think Connelly would put his daughter before the project, even if it meant losing everything. He'd cause a lot of trouble for you."

Kushner was silent.

"Is that why you killed Eddie? Is that why you shot him up with Pink Soda that you bought from Aaron, Kevin Handsome's dealer?"

Kushner glared at him. "Lawyer."

FORTY-ONE

"TODAY I WANT to talk about Crystal Morning Song." Savage faced Kushner and his lawyer, a man who'd introduced himself as Nathan McMann, across the table. Above them, the light was still flickering.

Last night, he'd arrested Kushner on the suspicion of Eddie Youngblood's murder so he could hold him overnight. To say the project manager was pissed was an understatement. Savage couldn't care less.

Becca had been packing and repacking her hospital bag this morning. He trusted her instincts. The baby was imminent, and he still had this case to wrap up.

"Make sure you've got your phone on you," she told him, before he left.

Even though he was excited to meet his newborn, he couldn't help but hope the baby would hold off for a while longer. Just a couple more days, that's all he needed. Then he could take some time off and be a father, satisfied this raping, murdering scumbag was behind bars.

Kushner's silver-haired, buttoned-up attorney glanced at his client. "Who?"

Kushner gave an emphatic shake of his head. "You're not pinning that one on me too."

"Who is Crystal Morning Song?" McMann leaned forward, now directing his question at Savage.

Interesting that Kushner hadn't spoken to his lawyer about Crystal. What did that mean? Too big a secret?

Savage placed Kushner's file on the table. "She's a Native American girl whose body was found on the res a couple of days ago. She'd been drugged, raped, and murdered. The cause of death was a drug overdose, just like Eddie Youngblood."

Kushner thumped his massive hands on the table. "I don't know anything about that girl, and I ain't no goddamn rapist."

Savage shot him a harsh look. "No, you just blackmail young women into sleeping with you."

Kushner sat back in his chair, scowling.

"So, given your predilection for young girls, I must ask. Where were you when Crystal Morning Song disappeared? In case you've forgotten, that was on Monday."

"I already told you. I was at the hotel having breakfast with Steve Bryant. He vouched for me." According to the hotel system, Kushner had re-entered his room a little before nine a.m. which corroborated his story. Still, Kushner had fooled them before, and Savage wasn't leaving anything to chance.

"My deputy interviewed a waitress at the hotel restaurant who remembers neither you nor Bryant being there that morning."

"She's mistaken. Of course we were there. We're there every morning."

"She recognized you," Savage admitted with a nod, "but said you weren't there Monday morning."

"I can't help it if she's half asleep." He pressed down on the table. "What can I say? We were there."

"My deputy has asked for the CCTV footage from the hotel lobby for that day, so we'll know soon enough."

Kushner glanced across at his lawyer.

Something wasn't right. Following his gut, Savage pressed harder. "If there's something you want to tell us, now would be the time. If we find out you're lying, it's only going to make you look guilty."

There was a sullen silence. Savage could sense the unease in the suspect. It seeped off him like a bad smell. "How long have you been working for Guy Hollander?"

The change in direction unnerved Kushner, who 'umm'ed and 'ahh'ed before he said, "Almost twelve years."

"Since you left the military?" Savage put his hand on the file lying on the table.

We know all about you.

An anxious scowl. "Yeah."

"Did you know that at almost every project Apex Holdings has been involved in over the last five years, a young girl has gone missing and later turned up dead?"

Kushner's eyes narrowed, but he didn't look surprised. Not as surprised as he should have. Not as surprised as his lawyer, who had a thin layer of perspiration forming on his forehead. "I didn't know that. No."

Liar.

"Is this true?" McMann asked, wiping his forehead on the back of his shirt sleeve.

"Yes," Savage cut in. "In every case the girl died of a drug overdose, just like Eddie and Crystal."

Kushner's scowl got deeper until his eyebrows met in the middle.

Savage honed in. "Unless you want to spend the rest of your life in prison, you'd better start talking."

Kushner pursed his lips, thinking, then leaned back in his chair. "I'd like a word with my lawyer. In private."

———

"DID YOU GET THE CCTV FOOTAGE?" Savage strode back into the squad room. He had Kushner exactly where he wanted the hulk of a man. With a bit of luck, they'd get a confession and could charge the bastard.

"We did." Thorpe's cheeks were flushed. "There is no record of him entering the dining room the morning Crystal disappeared. The only time he appears on camera is when he left the building just after nine o'clock."

Savage frowned. "Then he was there."

"Yeah, until nine."

Crystal had already gone missing by then. Savage shook his head. "There must be some mistake. Is there any way he could have left earlier, returned to the hotel and walked out the front door at nine o'clock?"

Thorpe scratched his head. "Maybe. There is an exit through the kitchen, but there aren't any cameras there, so we wouldn't be able to verify that. It's cutting it a bit fine, though, isn't it?" He looked at Savage.

It was. Would Kushner have had time to drive to the building site, abduct Crystal Morning Song, get back to the hotel to walk out the front door like nothing had happened at nine o'clock?

"If the protesters were at the site around seven o'clock, which is when the security guards say they were, Crystal was abducted around eight, after the gang had dispersed. He may have had time to get back to the hotel." But even Thorpe looked doubtful.

"What would he have done with her?" Littleton asked. "I mean, he didn't take her back to the hotel."

It was a good point.

"He could have drugged her and left her in the trunk of his SUV?" Sinclair suggested.

Savage gave a decisive nod. "Let's get a warrant to search his vehicle. If there's any DNA belonging to Crystal, I want it found."

"On it," said Thorpe, reaching for the phone.

"I'll call Ray and Pearl," Sinclair said.

Savage turned around to head back to the interview room. "I want to know as soon as they find anything."

———

"MY CLIENT HAS AGREED TO TALK," McMann said.

Savage sat down.

Here it comes. Would the ex-Marine confess to the deaths of the missing girls, as well as Eddie's?

"Let's hear it."

"I wasn't having breakfast with Bryant the day—" Kushner broke off, frowning. "The day that girl went missing."

Savage nodded. They already knew that much.

"I was in Celine's room. With her."

"What?" he blurted, unable to help himself. *That*, he hadn't been expecting.

"You can ask her. I went to her room early that morning and left around eight thirty. I returned to my suite, showered, got dressed, and left for the site office just before nine."

Savage slumped in his chair. Was this true? It did tally with what was on the CCTV camera in the lobby. "She'll vouch for you?"

"Ask her."

Savage glanced at the interview room camera suspended from the ceiling. "Don't worry. We will."

At that moment, Sinclair would be leaving for the hotel. If the teenager backed up Kushner's story, then their prime suspect was nowhere near the building site when Crystal disappeared.

Savage's desire to wrap up the case evaporated, and with it, his patience. "Why'd you say you were with Bryant then?"

"I didn't. He did."

Savage shook his head. "You just said—"

"It was Bryant's idea," Kushner interjected. "He knew about my relationship with Celine, so he told you he was with me in the dining room to help me out."

"Why would he do that?"

"To prevent his boss from finding out. Like you said, if Connelly knew what was going on, he'd go apeshit. He dotes on Celine. She's his little girl."

It made sense. It also meant Bryant had perjured himself.

Savage stood up. "You're going to stay here until we check out what you've told us. Then we'll talk again."

Kushner crossed his beefy hands over his chest and shot him a sour look. His lawyer nodded and got up. Savage didn't say a word as he led him down the corridor, past the booking room, and through the squad room to the front door.

————

AN HOUR LATER, Sinclair rushed in. "Celine confirmed it. Kushner was with her on Monday morning."

"She's sure?" Savage frowned. "There's no mistake?"

"Nope. I promised I wouldn't say anything about their affair, but only if she told us the truth."

"Shit." Savage thumped his fist on the desk, making Littleton jump. "It wasn't him."

Thorpe swiveled around in his chair. "Just because he didn't kidnap Crystal, doesn't mean he didn't kill Eddie."

Becca's words came back to haunt him.

I don't think Eddie was killed by the same man.

Had she been right all along?

Savage exhaled. "If we go by the theory that Kushner killed Eddie Youngblood because Eddie found out he was sleeping with Celine against her will, then who the hell kidnapped and murdered Crystal?"

"And all those other girls," Sinclair added.

There was a brief silence as they pondered this.

Savage said quietly, "Kushner said Bryant fabricated the alibi to prevent his boss from finding out about the relationship with his daughter, but what if that wasn't the reason?"

"What do you mean?" Littleton asked, his forehead creased in confusion.

Thorpe's eyes lit up.

Sinclair watched him intently.

Savage took a deep breath. "What if Bryant fabricated the alibi in order to give himself one?"

FORTY-TWO

IT WAS mid-afternoon before Pearl finished her analysis of Kushner's vehicle. They'd had it picked up and taken to their forensic lab in Durango.

"Anything?" Savage asked, when the call eventually came through.

"No and yes," Pearl said,.

He frowned. "What does that mean?"

"No evidence of your girl," Pearl said. "Not a shred of DNA in that motor vehicle belonged to her. No skin cells, hair, blood, or other bodily fluids."

"Could he have cleaned it?"

"Judging by the rest of the dust and dirt we found in there, no."

Savage's heart sank. "Crystal Morning Song was never in that vehicle?"

"I can say with a hundred percent certainty that she was not."

Goddamn. Although he didn't know why he was still hoping. They'd already ruled Kushner out.

"Thanks Pearl."

"Hang on a minute. I haven't told you the yes, yet."

"There's more?" He felt a surge of energy. "Shoot."

"While we were searching, we found a bag of insulin syringes hidden under the driver's seat. The same brand used to inject Eddie Youngblood."

Savage's heart leaped. "You're sure about that? The same brand?"

"Identical. In fact, the syringe you found in the forest near to where he died probably came from the same batch."

Savage let out a slow breath. "We've got him."

———

"THIS PROVES that Kushner killed Eddie Youngblood," Littleton said, once Savage had told them what had transpired.

"It's still circumstantial. His lawyer will argue that there are a hundred other reasons why he had those syringes in his car. But it'll go a long way to convincing a jury that he did it. And maybe help get a confession out of him."

"He's not diabetic, is he?" Sinclair asked.

It was a good question. That would cast considerable doubt on his conviction.

"Not according to his military medical records," Savage replied. He had already checked that out, just in case.

Thorpe walked in, smiling. "You were right, Sheriff. Kevin Handsome found an entry for the Pink Soda in Aaron's notebook. There's no customer name, only the initials PK."

"Easy to pin it on the dead guy," muttered Sinclair.

"Aaron was his primary dealer," Savage confirmed. "Do we have this black book?"

Thorpe held it up. "I enter into evidence one black notebook."

"Excellent." He rubbed his hands together. Things were starting to fall into place.

"Kevin nearly blew a gasket when I said I was taking it. It's got a lot of names in it." Thorpe slapped the book down on the desk. "However, I reminded him that if he didn't give it up, he'd be arrested for drug dealing and sent back to prison."

"Great work, Thorpe." Savage picked up the notebook and thumbed through it. It was mostly initials, quantities, and dollar amounts.

"I've marked the page," Thorpe said.

Savage scrolled to the entry for the Pink Soda. There it was. PK.

Even though his lawyer would argue there were a hundred other men with those initials in La Plata County with the syringes they'd found in his car, it was pretty compelling.

"Kushner," he murmured. "You're going down."

———

"DO YOU KNOW WHAT THIS IS?" Savage asked, as he sat down opposite Kushner and his lawyer for the second time that day. He held up the black book.

Kushner frowned. "No."

"It's a notebook belonging to the drug dealer, Aaron Sheldon."

Kushner swallowed. It was the first time Savage had seen him really nervous.

Good.

"It's got your name in it." He didn't hand over the book, since he wanted their suspect to think they had him. As expected, Kushner didn't ask to see it. His lawyer did, though.

Reluctantly, Savage handed it over.

"This doesn't prove anything," the attorney said. "It's all initials."

"And dates," Savage amended.

"Still, you'd have a hard time proving this." The lawyer scoffed as he handed it back. Kushner started to smile, a slow grin that spread over his face. "You've got nothing."

"I wouldn't say that exactly. That notebook will go a long way to proving you killed Eddie Youngblood, along with the pack of syringes we found in your SUV this morning."

The smug smile vanished.

"Did I forget to tell you? We searched your vehicle. Very revealing. I wonder what a jury is going to make of the syringes we found under your seat. You're not diabetic, are you?"

Kushner glared at him.

"Let's not forget you also had access to Celine Connelly's phone because you were sleeping with her, even though she's barely legal."

Kushner's dark eyes bore into Savage's steely ones, his face twisted with rage.

Savage ignored him. "It's not looking good, is it?"

The lawyer cleared his throat. "I'd like a word with my client."

————

"HE CONFESSED TO EDDIE'S MURDER!" Savage said when he returned to the squad room.

There was a round of applause. The team already knew as they'd been glued to the screen during the final stages of the interrogation.

"Great work, boss," Littleton said, smiling.

"You got him!" Thorpe nodded, pushing his glasses up his nose. They always slipped down when he got excited.

"Serves him right." Sinclair said, hugging Barbara. "That bastard deserves nothing less after the way he treated Celine, and poor Eddie who didn't even know why he was killed."

Kushner had explained how he'd lured Eddie to the building site after they'd knocked off for the day. Eddie had thought it was Celine he was meeting. When he'd found out it was Kushner, he'd known something was wrong and tried to run, but by then it was too late. Kushner overpowered him and slid the needle into his arm.

"It wasn't even hard," Kushner had said during his confession. "The kid didn't put up much of a fight."

Savage hoped he got the full length of his sentence.

"We still don't know who killed those girls, though," Sinclair said, running a hand through her hair. "It wasn't Kushner, so who was it?"

"Let's give Steve Bryant a call." Savage scratched his beard. He desperately needed a shave. "We don't want to warn him, so let's pretend we need him to give evidence against Kushner and get him to come in voluntarily."

"I'll do it," Thorpe said.

Savage gave a grateful nod. "I'm going to clean up, then we'll find out why he lied to protect Kushner."

FORTY-THREE

STEVE BRYANT SWALLOWED THE BAIT. He arrived at the Sheriff's station in his black SUV, dressed in a navy suit and an arctic blue shirt that matched his eyes. "You wanted to see me?" Calm, confident, and controlled, he studied Savage curiously. "I thought I'd already given you what you wanted?"

"Let's go through to the interview room."

The flicker of uncertainty in his gaze told Savage he'd been caught off guard. "I was under the impression this was a casual chat."

"We like to follow procedure." Savage opened the door leading down the corridor to the interview suites.

Such was Bryant's confidence—or curiosity—that he followed Savage through.

"We thought you'd like to know that Paul Kushner has been arrested for the murder of Eddie Youngblood," Savage told him after they'd taken a seat.

It was warm in the interview room, perhaps from the body heat of the people who'd sat there before.

Bryant took off his jacket, hung it on the back of the metal chair and loosened his tie. "Good God. Has he really?"

"Yes, he confessed after we found evidence in his vehicle." Savage paused. "Which leads us back to his alibi."

Bryant didn't flinch. The light did, flickering several times in a row.

"The alibi you provided for him. You said he was having breakfast with you in the dining hall the morning Crystal Morning Song was abducted."

"He was."

"No, he wasn't. We spoke to the waitress on duty that morning who doesn't recall either of you being there. The CCTV in the lobby backs that up. In addition, Kushner has admitted he was with Miss Connelly at the time."

Bryant relaxed. "You know about that, then?"

"Yeah, we know."

He shook his head. "I was paranoid that Douglas would find out. He adores his daughter. It would really derail the project."

"That why you kept Kushner's relationship with Celine a secret?"

"I had to. If I'd told Connelly, he'd have lost it with Kushner. Guy Hollander would have been upset—and that's never a good thing. It would have dire consequences for the project."

"Why do you care so much?" Savage asked.

"It's my livelihood," he said simply. "I've been with the company for a long time. I know Douglas well. I don't want to have to look for another job at my age."

"How long has it been?"

"Fifteen years."

"But not all with Apex Holdings?" Savage had done his homework.

"No, I was employed by Guy Hollander first, and seconded to Apex during their first development. It worked out well, so Connelly employed me, and I've worked for them ever since."

"But you report to Hollander."

He gave a smirk. "Everybody reports back to Hollander."

"If neither of you were in the dining hall that morning, where were you?"

"In my suite."

"All morning?" Savage frowned.

"Yes, I work from there. Occasionally, I go to Douglas's suite for meetings or to discuss something, but most of the time I work out of my own."

"Can anyone vouch for you?"

"I don't know. Monday, wasn't it? I'm not sure I saw anyone that morning. There was a lot to catch up on after the weekend." He shrugged. "I can't remember to be honest with you. I may have spoken to Douglas on the phone."

"Can we see your phone history?"

He hesitated. "Don't you need a warrant for that?"

"Why? Do you have something to hide? I'd have thought you'd have wanted to clear your name."

"What exactly am I being accused of?"

"Didn't I say? The abduction, rape and murder of Margaret Valance, Laura Palmer, Hannah Carter, and Crystal Morning Song, just for starters. I'm sure there are more we don't know about yet." Savage placed four large full-color photographs of each girl down on the table, facing the suspect.

Bryant stared at them, apparently at a loss for words. When he did speak, it was in an even, tempered tone. "I'm sorry, you're mistaken. I don't know who any of these people are. Except the last one. I heard about her. She was found recently, wasn't she?"

"Mr. Bryant, were you grooming Crystal Morning Song?" He pointed to the photograph of Crystal. It was taken from her social media profile. A sunny, smiling photograph showing warm eyes, high cheekbones, and a small gap between her front teeth.

"Excuse me? Grooming?"

"She told a friend she was secretly dating an older man. Was that you?"

"Of course not." He even managed a wry grin. "What would a girl like that see in an old guy like me?"

Savage glared at him across the table.

Bryant spread his arms. "Sheriff, I've never met this girl before."

"We've got an eyewitness who says she saw you with this girl in a coffee shop not so long ago." That was a lie, but he figured it was worth a shot.

Another flicker, then it was gone. "She must be mistaken. It must have been another graying, middle-aged man in a suit."

He was cool, Savage gave him that much.

"You have no alibi for the morning of Crystal's disappearance."

"Why do I need an alibi? I didn't do anything."

Savage shook his head. If he'd expected Bryant to buckle, he was mistaken. The man had nerves of steel. He was totally calm despite the pressure he was under. There wasn't even a hint of a sweat mark underneath his arms.

"Let us see your phone log, then?"

A sigh. "Suit yourself. But for the record, I object to the invasion of my privacy." He slid his phone across the table.

Savage glanced up at the camera and gave a nod. A moment later, there was a brief knock on the interview room door.

"Excuse me. You can have this back after the interview." Savage picked up the device, then opened it. Littleton stood there, waiting. Savage passed him the phone, bent forward, and whispered something in his ear. The deputy gave him a look of surprise, then nodded, turning on his heel and disappearing down the corridor back to the squad room.

Bryant shrugged. "You won't find anything on there."

"Then you have nothing to worry about."

———

MUCH TO HIS ANNOYANCE, Savage had to let Bryant go. The finance geek had successfully skirted every trigger Savage had laid down. They didn't have enough to hold him, and he knew it. When he'd left, it was with a cold arrogance that made Savage grit his teeth.

The call history on Bryant's phone had shown one seven-minute call to Douglas Connelly before nine a.m. on Monday morning.

"If he did kidnap her," Thorpe said, "he was on the phone while he did it."

"What about that other thing?" Savage asked, turning to Sinclair. "Did you get it?"

"Yeah, I got it. But we can't use it, you know that."

"I know, but I wanted to do it before he had a chance to get his vehicle cleaned. Now he knows we're onto him, he'll take steps to get rid of any evidence."

Sinclair placed several plastic evidence bags on Savage's desk. "Those are samples from the passenger seat, back seat, and trunk of Bryant's SUV. Pearl is on her way to collect them," Sinclair said, walking back to her desk. "I don't like him. He's far too self-assured."

"That doesn't mean he's guilty," Thorpe pointed out, ever the voice of reason.

"He gives me the creeps." She gave Thorpe a knowing look.

"Let's see what Pearl says," Savage said. "If we can get a rush on the results, that would be good. If it is Bryant, we don't want him to make a run for it."

"He's not the type to run," Sinclair said. "He's arrogant enough to think he'll get away with it."

"Maybe," said Savage, running a hand through his hair. "Maybe not."

FORTY-FOUR

SAVAGE MET Rosalie at her house rather than at the bar. Her suggestion. "The men get anxious when the cops start showing up," she'd said. "No offense."

"None taken," Savage had replied. "See you at six."

Rosalie was sitting on the porch when he arrived, gazing out over the hazy peaks, a glass of bourbon in her hand. She didn't get up, simply gestured for him to join her.

He took the vacant chair, a whiff of vanilla and jasmine wafting over to him. She filled a second glass and handed it to him. "Cheers." He raised it up.

"What are we drinking to?" she asked.

"Our collaboration."

She laughed, deep and throaty. "You're funny."

"I'm serious."

Her eyes sparkled. "Do you honestly think the Crimson Angels are going to cooperate with the Sheriff's Department?"

"They might—if they don't know it's my idea. What if they think it's yours?"

"You want me to lie to my own crew?"

"To get rid of the competition once and for all? Yeah." He looked at her over his glass. "It's not like you haven't done it before."

There was a pause. She took a sip of bourbon, swallowing slowly. "I'm listening."

"I want you to contact Jonny Star and make a deal with him."

Her eyebrows shot up. "You're kidding."

"Hear me out."

She shook her head as if he were crazy.

"Tell Jonny you're ready to play ball. You've had enough bloodshed. Mention there's a shipment coming in and after what happened last time, your guys are nervous about making the journey up from Mexico with the merchandise. The DEA are watching you, ready to move in."

"That true?" She narrowed her gaze.

"I have no idea."

She snorted.

"Tell him your guys will pick it up. You need their help to get it into Southern Colorado."

"Then what? You want me to hand over our merchandise to those thugs? Are we ever going to see it again?"

"Probably not. But it's a small price to pay for getting Jonny and his gang put away."

Her eyes gleamed. "You're going to bust them with the merch?"

He gave a quick nod. "That's the plan."

"So it's a setup?"

"*You're* going to set them up."

"Who's going to bust them? You?"

"I'm going to call my pal at the DEA office and alert them to the incoming shipment. They'll swoop in and pick up the Denver thugs. Then I'm going to contact Guy Hollander and tell him to find somewhere else to peddle his wares. My county is closed for business."

"You think that'll work?" She raised a plucked eyebrow.

"I think it will. Once all his men are either dead or in jail, his business venture is over."

"And you want me to convince my guys that this was my idea?"

"Why not? You're smart enough to have come up with it yourself."
He grinned, aware he was patronizing her. "They'll believe you."

She pursed her lips and studied Savage for a very long time. He
waited, sipping his drink.

Eventually, she leaned forward and said, "It's worth a shot, I guess."

————

"DON'T TAKE this the wrong way," Becca said, after he'd kissed her
hello. "But you smell of perfume, and it's not mine."

He frowned, confused. Then he remembered. "Rosalie." Vanilla,
jasmine.

"That biker woman?" Becca frowned. "Axle Weston's ex-wife?"

"That's the one. She runs the Crimson Angels now."

"She's taken over the outlaw gang? Isn't that a bit unusual?"

"Yep. She sold him out. It was partly thanks to her that we caught
Axle and put him behind bars."

Becca shook her head. "A woman scorned and all that."

Savage raised his eyebrows. "Indeed. Now more importantly, how
are you doing?"

"So-so. I think this baby is ready to come out."

"You still having cramps?"

She nodded. "I can't work out if they're normal or not. The doctor
said there'd be some mini contractions, but this feels worse than that."

"Perhaps you're right. Maybe he is coming." Savage had picked up on
Becca's hunch and begun calling their unborn child a *he*. Goodness
knows what they'd do if she had a little girl. Even the room was painted
blue. Still, he knew better than to question a woman's intuition.

"Maybe."

His cellphone rang, and he got up to answer it. "Savage."

"It's Shelby."

"What's up?"

"Listen, I have some news for you regarding that sniper. The one who
took that pot shot at you in the mountains."

How could he forget? "Yeah?"

"Well, they've done the autopsy. It turns out the guy had a knee op a couple of years back, and the metal plate inside him had a serial number on it. We were able to trace it back to a hospital in Denver."

"Denver?" Savage felt an icy chill shoot down his neck.

"According to the medical report, the guy's name is Santiago Hernandez."

"Doesn't ring a bell."

"Savage, this guy's a gun for hire. Someone put a hit out on you."

FORTY-FIVE

SAVAGE GOT to work late the next morning. What with Becca not feeling well and the news Shelby had delivered, his head was spinning.

"I don't like leaving you alone," he'd said to Becca, before he'd gone and done just that. She'd thought he was worried about her condition, and he was, but he was also worried about his own assassination attempt. Was the price just on his head, or the head of his pregnant fiancée too? The thought made him sick to his stomach.

"I'll be fine," she'd replied. "It's more important you catch this guy now. That way I'll have you home when the baby arrives."

"I wish there was someone you could call to come and stay with you. You know, like a friend or family member."

"There isn't." She hated talking about her family. Her parents had died several years back, but from what she'd said, they weren't close. She had no siblings. "You know my college friends are all working in the city."

He tried to push the worrying thoughts from his mind as he pulled into his parking spot outside the sheriff's station. An ancient station wagon caught his eye. It was Pearl's.

He got out of the Suburban and walked over to the forensic expert.

"Pearl. This is a surprise."

"I've got something for you."

"You could have called."

"Not about this. I wanted to tell you in person."

He frowned. "You found evidence of Crystal in Bryant's SUV?"

"And then some."

He caught his breath. "Really? She was there?"

Pearl nodded. "I found hair and fibers from her skin and clothing on the passenger seat of the car. I'd say she'd been in there more than once too."

An adrenaline surge sent his heart racing. "That's great news. Or rather, not so great news."

"What do you mean? You've got him. This is enough for an arrest."

"I had you obtain those samples illegally." He ground his jaw.

"Oh." She shook her head. "Why'd you do that?"

"Because I didn't want to wait until after I'd questioned him and given him a chance to clean the car. If he didn't know he was a suspect in the multiple killings, he does now."

"Multiple?"

"Yeah, Crystal isn't the only one. There have been others." He rubbed his forehead. "Lots of others."

She stared at him. "Holy crap."

"Yeah, and we had nothing."

"What are you going to do?"

Savage drew in a deep breath. "I'm going to go after him with everything I've got."

"GOOD MORNING." Savage walked into the interview room, a manilla folder tucked under his arm. Seated were Steve Bryant and his lawyer, Nathan McMann. Clearly, Apex Holdings, or was it Guy Hollander, used McMann to sort out all their legal problems.

"Why am I here, Sheriff?" Bryant was irritated now. His usually cool demeanor was sparked with annoyance. He still didn't look anxious, just put out.

"We've conducted a search of your vehicle to see whether Crystal Morning Song's DNA was in it," Savage said, watching the other man.

Instead of the attempt at disputing the fact, or covering it up, Bryant didn't react at all.

His lawyer chimed in. "How did you obtain such evidence?"

"I had my deputy take some samples while you were questioned yesterday."

"That is unethical and inadmissible in court," erupted McMann. "We want to lodge a complaint."

"I don't think they'd take it very seriously," Savage said. "Given that Crystal Morning Song's DNA was all over your car."

Bryant leaned over and said something to his attorney, who nodded in response. Then he looked at Savage. "Her DNA was in my car because I gave her a ride home from the building site a couple of times. I've also given rides to Celine Connelly on multiple occasions. Did you find her DNA in my car too?"

Savage cringed. Of course he'd come up with something like this. "When did you give Crystal these rides home?"

"A few weeks ago. I gave her and a friend a ride after a protest, then again on the day that boy was found dead."

"Eddie Youngblood?"

"That's right. She knew him and was shaken up."

"A protester got into a company vehicle?" Savage couldn't keep the incredibility from his voice.

"Despite what you think of me, Sheriff, I'm a nice guy. If I see a young person walking back home, clearly upset, I offer them a ride. Most of those kids were from the reservation. It's a long walk home."

"Why didn't you mention this before?"

"It didn't seem important."

Savage was seething. "We also found dirt on your tires that matches dirt taken from the construction site."

"I would have expected that," Bryant said. "Since I've been there several times in the last week. You yourself have seen me there."

The guy had an answer for everything.

McMann spoke up. "Sheriff, my client has been nothing but cooperative. He came in voluntarily, he handed over his cellphone when you asked, and he provided you with plausible explanations for the findings of your *illegal*,"—he emphasized the word—"vehicle search. If there's nothing else, we'll be on our way."

McMann gestured for Bryant to stand up. Savage had no choice but to sit there and watch them leave.

————

"SHERIFF, could I bother you for a ride back to the hotel," Bryant said, when Savage got back to the squad room. McMann had gone, but his client was still there.

"Where's your ride?" he snapped.

"McMann had another appointment on the other side of town. He couldn't stay."

Savage's blood boiled. The audacity of the man. Given the way he was feeling right now, he couldn't trust himself not to lay into Bryant on the way home. He looked around at his team. Thorpe was out running an errand and Littleton wasn't up to the challenge. Besides, he was digging into Bryant's work history.

"Sinclair, won't you give Mr. Bryant a ride back to the hotel?"

She glared at him. "Sure."

For a moment, Savage wondered if he was doing the right thing. Sinclair had been more vocal in her feelings toward Bryant than any of the others, even him. Then he shook it off. She was an experienced officer and Bryant was on his best behavior, trying to fool them all into believing his "nice guy" narrative. Besides, she was a professional

————

SINCLAIR TRIED to keep her emotions in check, but she wasn't very good at it. Something about Bryant made her skin crawl. Maybe it was his icy blue gaze that gave her the chills, or his casual demeanor that seemed to mask something more sinister. Either way, he gave her the creeps.

Still, she was a law enforcement officer, and this was part of her job. Everything Bryant had said had made sense. It was plausible Crystal's DNA had gotten there because he'd given her a ride. Perhaps she was overreacting.

Also, a question they'd never found an answer to was where had the killer kept Crystal in the two days she'd been missing? If it was Bryant, he hadn't taken her back to the hotel. Someone would have noticed.

"You know Hawk's Landing well?" she asked casually, as they drove across town.

"Not really."

"How long have you been here?"

"Just since this project started. About three months now." He glanced across at her. "But I think you already knew that."

"Just trying to make conversation," she said airily, keeping her eyes on the road. She hoped he wouldn't notice just how white her knuckles were as she gripped the steering wheel.

"Do I make you nervous, Deputy Sinclair?"

She straightened her shoulders. "Of course not."

"You're not a very good liar," he said softly.

She glanced across at him. "I don't trust you."

"Why? Because your Sheriff thinks I murdered those girls?"

"I know you did," she said quietly.

He chuckled. "Then prove it."

Sinclair froze. "Are you admitting it?"

"I'm sorry to disappoint you, but I didn't kill those girls."

Don't let him get to you.

Sinclair guided the cruiser around some lazy, open bends that led up to the Boulder Creek Hotel. Now the town was behind them, the firs and pines took over.

"Thanks for the ride," Bryant said, when they were a few minutes out. He fished in his pocket for something, presumably his hotel keycard. While he pulled it out, Sinclair noticed something drop into the footwell. Small, round, and amber-colored, it bounced once, then rolled to a stop by his shoe.

Keeping her eyes on the road, she watched in her peripheral vision as Bryant bent down to retrieve it. He didn't say anything, but she could feel his demeanor change. He went very still. Even his chest stopped rising and falling.

She felt his gaze on her face.

"What?" she said.

He didn't reply. With a start, she realized that the bead that had fallen out of his pocket was from Crystal Morning Song's necklace. Hadn't she seen one just like it around Crystal's neck in the photograph her father had given them?

Sinclair gasped as the terrible realization hit her.

It was him.

Before she had time to react, Bryant lunged for the steering wheel, twisting it toward him. The car skidded across the road.

"Hey, what are you doing?" Sinclair tried to overcorrect, but it was too late, the car was swerving back and forth like it had a mind of its own.

As she wrestled to get it under control, Bryant reached for her holster, grabbing her gun. She took her hand off the wheel to stop him. It was then the car hit a rock at the side of the road and flipped over.

Sinclair screamed as they went into a roll—over and over until she was dizzy. Finally, the world stopped spinning, and she heard a terrifying screech of metal as it skidded across the asphalt on its roof. Finally, there was a spine-chilling smash as it crashed into a tree.

FORTY-SIX

SINCLAIR OPENED her eyes and groaned.

Her head was squashed between the car roof and door, and her shoulder burned like a red-hot poker was stuck in it. The seatbelt had prevented her from hitting anything with full force, but it had trapped her inside.

Beside her, Bryant was motionless. At first, she thought he was badly hurt, but then he sucked in a deep breath of air. He struggled against his seatbelt, then somehow managed to release the clasp. He sank down, curling into a ball, before exploding outward, kicking hard with both feet, smashing out the cracked windshield in front of him.

Turning toward her, a devious smile on his face, he lunged for her holster. Sinclair tried to thwart his efforts, but with one arm pinned, she could only manage to press down on the butt of her Glock.

Bryant delivered several vicious blows to her ribcage, sending a shock of pain through her damaged body. Sinclair fought to remember the weapon retention exercises drilled into her at the academy. But this was unlike anything she'd trained for.

The final blow landed on the side of her neck with a dizzying effect. She felt her grip loosen. Bryant worked feverously, prying back her fingers as he thumbed the hood release on her level two holster. He ripped the weapon free.

Sinclair now faced down the barrel of her own gun. A fear unlike any she'd ever known flooded her. "Don't shoot," she whispered, hating herself for begging. "Please." She didn't want to die. Not here. Not by the hands of this monster.

His index finger hovered over the trigger. "You know, ten years ago, you would have been just my type." The laugh that followed sickened her stomach.

A moment later, he began to make his egress. There wasn't much space, but Bryant managed to wriggle through, legs first. That's when she noticed a smear of blood on the seat where he'd been sitting. He was injured. Good. It served him right.

"You won't get far," she called out, trying to reach for her ankle holster. Her body's position wouldn't give her the leeway she needed to grip the backup weapon.

A hot rage settled over her as she watched Bryant free himself from the confines of the overturned vehicle.

The monster laughed. "Goodbye, Deputy Sinclair. Next time, trust your instincts."

With a frustrated cry, she bucked against the seat belt, but it wouldn't budge. Tears of pain and frustration sprung to her eyes as she watched Bryant disappear into the trees.

———

SAVAGE COULDN'T FOCUS on what he was doing. Bryant's arrogant smile was worrying him. He looked over at Thorpe. "You hear from Sinclair?"

"Not since she left."

"She should have checked in by now. See if you can get her on her cell."

Thorpe tried, then shook his head. "She's not picking up."

"But it's on?"

"Yeah, it's on. Rings out."

Littleton swung around on his chair. "I could trace it." It was a new skill he'd learned. Thorpe had spent the last few weeks instructing him on it.

Savage hesitated. He didn't want to keep tabs on his own deputies, but his gut was telling him something was wrong. "Yeah, do it."

Next, he called the hotel. "Could you put me through to Steve Bryant's room, please?" The receptionist connected the call. It rang and rang.

No answer.

"Bryant's not picking up either." After a beat, he made a snap decision. "I'm going after her."

Thorpe frowned. "You think something's wrong?"

Savage gave a curt nod.

"You want me to come?"

"No, you stay here and let me know when you find a trace."

"If you're sure."

It was only a twenty-minute drive to the hotel, and the route was simple. Through the center of town, out the other side, and along a winding road to where the state forest began.

Savage was almost there and beginning to think he was overreacting when he spotted Sinclair's crumpled cruiser upside down and buckled around a tree.

Shit. Shit. Shit.

Heart racing, he skidded to a stop and jumped out of the Suburban, leaving the door ajar.

"Sinclair!"

Please let her be okay.

Sprinting toward the car. "Becky, are you in there?"

He heard banging, like a shoe against the door, or the roof. Thank God, she was alive. But in what condition?

He crouched down to look in the driver's window, which had cracked but was still intact. "Becky, are you okay?"

"Dalton, get me out of here."

Relief flooded his body.

"Are you hurt?" The front windshield was completely smashed, but the slanting hood of the car prevented him from getting near it.

"My shoulder. I think it's dislocated, but otherwise I'm fine. Bryant escaped."

"Let's get you out of the car."

"You'll have to kick the side window in. I can't move. I'm stuck and I can't undo the seat belt."

"Can you protect your face?"

"Yeah, it's facing the other way. Go for it."

He put a hand on the chassis of the car to support himself, then gave the side window a kick. It buckled, and fragments collapsed inwards. He kicked some more, clearing the frame. When there was no glass left, he bent down to take a closer look. All he could see was the back of Sinclair's head, her shoulder pinned to the ground, her arm trapped beneath her. It looked painful.

"I'm going to cut through that seatbelt." He took out the folding knife he always kept on him. "Ready?"

She grunted.

Savage sawed through the high tensile polyester until it snapped. There was a thud as Sinclair's body weight toppled onto her disjointed shoulder, no longer supported by the seatbelt. She yelped in pain.

"I've got you." Savage tried to support her as best he could, but it was an awkward angle. "I'm going to pull you out now. Are you sure your head and neck are okay?"

"Yes, it's my damn shoulder. Just get me out of here."

He pulled her out gently, head and shoulders first, so the rest of her body collapsed onto the passenger seat.

"Thank God," she muttered, as the cool air hit her in the face. Savage laid her on the ground beside the cruiser. She closed her eyes momentarily.

"I'll call an ambulance."

She grimaced. "I'm fine."

"No, you're not. You're in pain and that shoulder doesn't look good."

She gently stretched her neck, then grimaced. "It's not too bad, really. We have to go after Bryant. It was him, Dalton."

Savage held up his phone. "You're not going anywhere." He made the call for an ambulance, then sat down beside her. "Tell me what happened?"

Her eyes blazed. "The bastard did it. He freakin' killed Crystal and those other girls. He admitted it to me after he wrecked the car."

Savage stared at her. "He admitted it?"

"Yeah." She clenched her jaw.

"But why? He was a free man. You were supposed to give him a lift back to the hotel."

"He pulled something out of his pocket and a bead fell on the floor. It was a bead from Crystal's necklace. You remember the one she was wearing in that photograph?"

He stiffened. "I remember."

"Bryant knew I'd seen it. There was this terrible moment when I didn't know what he was going to do. Then, he grabbed the steering wheel. We hit a rock at the side of the road and flipped over. I remember the car rolling for what seemed like an eternity, and then we slid on the roof until there was this almighty smash."

"You hit a tree," he said.

She let out a shaky breath. "Bryant escaped, but he's injured. There's blood on the seat."

Savage grunted. "That should slow him down."

Sinclair's voice was strained. "Before he left, he said, 'Next time, trust your instincts.'"

"Arrogant bastard." Savage shook his head. "He'll pay."

Sinclair gave a weak nod. "Savage, he's got my duty weapon. I tried to stop him, but--"

"Don't you beat yourself up over it. You're alive and that's what matters. Did you see which way he went?"

"Into the forest."

"He wouldn't go back to the hotel, not now that he knows we're looking for him." Savage surveyed the vast expanse of forest. "He'll probably head for the mountains. I'll get a search team together."

"It'll be dark soon," she said dismally. "You'll never find him."

Savage glanced up at the deepening sky. "Sun doesn't set for another two hours. That'll be enough time."

"Enough time for what?"

"For Tomahawk to track him." He took out his phone and made a call.

Savage spoke to the tracker, then nodded at Sinclair. "He's on his way."

Next, he called Thorpe.

"We'll be right there," the deputy replied. "I'll call the State Police and fill them in on the way."

"We're gonna need as many officers as we can get."

It wasn't long before Tomahawk skidded to a halt next to the upturned car. After greeting Savage and Sinclair, who was now sitting in the Suburban awaiting the ambulance, he took a look at the mangled hunk of metal. "It is remarkable you survived."

"I know. I was lucky." Sinclair was pale. Savage could tell she was still in pain.

"So, he really did it?" Tomahawk gazed at them. "The gray-haired finance guy is a murdering pedophile?"

Savage nodded. "It's him alright. He's had an hour head start, and there's about an hour and a half of daylight left."

"He's bleeding, you say?"

"There's blood on the seat, although we're not sure how badly injured he is."

"Doesn't matter. It'll make him easier to track."

"How?" asked Sinclair.

"He'll be limping, which leaves a more distinctive pattern. He'll also be holding onto things for support, resting more often. There's more disturbance in the undergrowth. We have a shot at catching up to him."

"I want to come too," Sinclair struggled to her feet. "You need as much help as you can get."

"You sit tight," Savage instructed. "Wait for the ambulance. You need to get checked out."

With a huff, she sat down again.

"Alright then." Savage did a press check on his Glock, ensuring it was in battery before going on the hunt. "Let's go."

FORTY-SEVEN

TOMAHAWK STOOD where Bryant had exited the car and gazed at the treeline. "How well do you know this man?" he asked Savage.

"Not well, why?"

"Is he a seasoned hiker? Is he used to being outdoors?"

"I doubt it, he's an accountant."

"That helps." Tomahawk set out toward the thickest part of the treeline.

"How?" Savage followed him.

"Because an inexperienced person who doesn't want to be found will start off in the direction they want to go, while an experienced person evading capture won't."

As if to prove his point, Tomahawk crouched down and studied the vegetation. "Blood. He entered this way."

"Let's go after him," Savage said.

"He might be more badly injured than we think." Tomahawk set off, eyes to the ground.

"Good. I hope it slows him down." Savage zigzagged between the elongated tree trunks growing close together. It made moving in a straight line impossible.

"Boot print." Tomahawk pointed to the muddy ground. The front of a shoe could be seen clearly in the dirt. "And another." Savage watched Tomahawk inspect it. He knew he was taking in the length of the man's stride. That way, if they lost track, they could measure out a pace or two until they picked it up again.

"His weight is on his left foot," Tomahawk said. "I'd guess it's his right leg that's injured."

Savage took a closer look. The indent was indeed deeper on the left side. "How far ahead of us is he?"

"I would guess half a mile."

It was slow going, and the canopy of trees made it seem darker than it was. Already, long shadows lunged out at them while twisted roots and hidden branches hindered their progress. The only consolation was that Bryant was encountering the same problems.

A freshness in the air and the forest seemed to get damper the deeper in they went. Savage heard rushing water, finding himself and his counterpart at a creek a short while later.

Tomahawk pointed to a faint red smudge on a rock. "He crossed here."

They waded in, Tomahawk first, followed by Savage. The rushing water reached thigh height in the middle, but the danger was losing their footing rather than drowning. They held their weapons and phones above their heads, crossing carefully.

It was freezing cold, coming from the mountains, already scattered with snow. Savage took a sharp breath and kept going.

"This way," Tomahawk called, as they emerged on the other side. At least their top halves were still dry, because without the sun, it would get pretty darn cold.

Savage's radio crackled. It was Thorpe. "I'm here with the troopers. We're setting out now. What are your coordinates?"

"We've just crossed the river." Savage sent through their location via his cellphone, which remarkably still had some coverage. He knew it wouldn't last, though. The deeper they went, the worse the signal would become. This wasn't the first time he'd hunted a man in the forested foothills of the Rockies.

Tomahawk moved with ease, barely making a sound. Every couple of paces, he crouched down, inspected the foliage, grunted or nodded to himself, and took off again. Savage tried seeing what the tracker saw but couldn't. The subtle nuances of tracking took years of experience to master. The broken branches, crumpled leaves, indents in the ground that were barely noticeable to the untrained eye. Tomahawk was an expert. He'd once told Savage that tracking was in his DNA, passed down through the generations.

"There is a trail here." Tomahawk pointed to the ground. "It's faint, but discernible. See how the leaves are flattened and the branches are bent back?"

Savage nodded. "So, he's not the only person who's come this way?"

"That's right. This could be a hunting trail, or an informal track that connects to a trailhead."

"You think he used it?"

Tomahawk shone his flashlight on the ground. "Yes, these leaves have been freshly traversed."

They continued for the better part of an hour, stopping now and then to check they were on the right path. There was less blood, but the limp became more pronounced.

"He has managed to stem the bleeding," Tomahawk said. "It's still giving him pain, though."

Savage was glad to hear it. "Look at that," he hissed.

They peeked through the trees at a dark shape hiding amongst the pines. The hidden cabin was very rustic. Not more than a small, log shack in the middle of the forest, probably used by hunters or park rangers as a refueling point or shelter.

Tomahawk held up a hand. "He is in there. Look."

"What am I looking at?" Savage squinted at the ground.

"The porch."

He stared hard. There were faint wet footprints on the wood leading to the front door. Tomahawk had excellent eyesight. "If he's injured, he might be looking for medical supplies, or food and water."

The tracker nodded. "Do you want to go around the back, or should I?"

They were following police procedure. Savage would approach the cabin from the front, while Tomahawk would cover the back. Likely, the suspect would attempt to flee. They had no idea if there was a back door, but there would probably be a window he could climb out of.

"I'll take the front."

They split up. Tomahawk disappeared into the foliage. Savage gave him a couple of minutes to get into position, then took cover behind a wide tree. From here, he had a great view of the front of the cabin.

He stared hard at the windows, trying to detect movement. Was that a shadow shifting inside? The darkness didn't help. Savage watched till his eyes burned.

There!

The blinds moved. Savage caught his breath. Their killer was in there.

He got on the radio. "Thorpe, how far out are you?"

"Probably twenty minutes," came the static reply.

"We've got him pinned in. There's a cabin about five miles west of the hotel. Dropping you a pin now. He's hunkering down there."

"Can you wait for backup?"

"Not sure. If he runs, we'll have to take him down."

"Roger that. We'll be there ASAP."

Savage poked his head out from behind the tree to take another look. A shot rang out. He hit the ground, taking cover. A bullet whizzed past with a soft pew and embedded itself into the trunk behind him.

Shit, that was close.

"Bryant, we know you're in there. You're surrounded. Come out with your hands up!"

Another shot rang out. Where the hell was he shooting from?

Then Savage saw it.

The window to the left of the front door had a tiny hole in it. A dark shape protruded through the hole, a barrel of a gun.

Given his position, Savage figured his own visibility would be better than Bryant's. A flicker from the cabin told him the killer had a gas lamp or a candle burning. By contrast, the trees were almost black, making it easier for Savage to stay hidden. A fact that was confirmed when another bullet whizzed past, going wide.

Bryant was taking defensive shots. He didn't know Savage's location.

Savage aimed his Glock at the hole in the window and fired a shot back. The window cracked, and the shadow ducked out of sight.

Had he hit Bryant?

There'd been no cry of pain, but that didn't mean much. Bryant could be inside bleeding to death, or he could be fine. There was no way to tell without going in there.

He tried again. "Bryant, if you want to get out of this alive, come out with your hands up."

Still no response. He hadn't heard a thing from Tomahawk, either.

Savage waited, but there was no more movement from inside the cabin. He poked his head out from behind the tree. Nothing.

I'm going in, he texted Tomahawk, and got a thumbs up in reply.

Ducking into a crouched position, he moved stealthily towards the cabin. He kept low, his eyes on the windows looking for shadows, for movement, anything that would tell him Bryant was about to fire on him.

He'd nearly reached the porch when the sound of falling glass made him glance to the left. Bryant was at the window, his gun pointed in Savage's direction.

Savage dove for cover, just as a barrage of gunshots echoed over his head. He rolled under the lip of the porch. It was wide enough to protect him from the worst of the onslaught.

The front door swung open. Bryant, still firing, made a beeline for the trees. He hadn't gone out the back at all.

"Tomahawk!" yelled Savage, shooting at the fleeing figure. The darkness, the trees, the moving target. He kept firing until he was out of bullets.

Shit.

Now their positions were reversed. If Bryant turned around, he'd have a clear shot.

Bryant wasn't stupid. As expected, he reached the shelter of the trees, spun around, and smirked at Savage. Even from where he was lying, Savage could make out the smug grin on his face.

He couldn't defend himself. This was it. He was going to die here in the forest by the hand of a psychopath serial killer. He'd never see Becca again. He'd never see his baby come into the world. He'd broken his promise.

Heart thumping, he braced for the bullet he knew was coming. Bryant raised his gun. Savage tensed as the shot rang out.

FORTY-EIGHT

FOR THE SECOND time in as many weeks, Savage opened his eyes, expecting to be shot. There was no pain, no blood. Had Bryant missed? Then he saw a slender figure emerge from the trees.

Sinclair!

She held a gun in her hand and stared down at the unmoving Bryant. Savage scrambled to his feet and ran over.

"Is he dead?" She was trembling from head to foot.

Savage kicked the gun clear just to be sure, then bent down and felt Bryant's pulse. "Yes."

She fell back against a tree. Her face was as pale as the silver crescent moon that had risen above the mountain peaks.

"What did you use?"

"My backup." She showed him her extra Glock.

Tomahawk came running up. "I heard the shots. What—?" He broke off when he saw Sinclair leaning against the tree. Then his gaze flickered to Bryant's body. "You?"

She fought back tears. "Yeah, I got him."

"Bastard was about to take me out," Savage said. "He made a run for the trees."

Tomahawk nodded at Sinclair. "You did good."

"Thanks."

"I'D BETTER TAKE THAT." Savage reached for her gun, the small subcompact Glock 26 she'd kept as a backup. She handed it over, still shaking. "You okay?"

She gave a watery smile. "I've never shot anyone before."

That was a feeling he understood. He slipped her gun into his pocket and tucked his into his holster. "You did your job. He was about to kill me."

"I took a life," she whispered, her gaze back on Bryant's body.

"No, you saved a life," Tomahawk corrected.

She gave a weak nod, closed her eyes, and sank down the tree trunk to the ground. Savage picked up Bryant's weapon and tucked it into the back of his jeans. There'd be an investigation into the shooting, and the powers that be would need to analyze both Bryant and Sinclair's guns.

"Is that why you came after us?" Savage asked.

"Yes. I knew you and Tomahawk would need backup. Thorpe and the Troopers were too far away."

"Thank you." Savage held out his hand to help her up. "We should head back. Your shoulder needs treatment."

She didn't argue.

"Hello!" called Thorpe's voice. There was a rustle as the deputy and troopers arrived. "We heard gunshots. Is everyone okay?"

"Yeah, thanks to Sinclair."

Brent Radley, the officer who'd been at the shootout in the mountain pass, stepped forward and inspected the dead body. "You got him?"

Savage nodded. "Do you think you can take care of the body? I need to get my deputy to a hospital. She's injured."

"Sure, leave it with us."

"Thanks. I owe you."

The State Trooper grinned. "That's what we're here for."

"Can you walk?" Thorpe asked Sinclair.

She grimaced. "I'll manage." Savage put an arm around her, and the three of them set off, Tomahawk leading the way.

SAVAGE WALKED through the front door to find the house eerily quiet.

"Becca!" he yelled. When there was no reply, he checked the hall cupboard and saw her overnight bag had gone.

Crap!

Had she gone into labor? Was she alright?

Racing into the kitchen, he was about to call her, when he saw the note. "I wasn't feeling well, so I've gone to the hospital as a precaution. Didn't want to distract you on a job. See you when you get here."

All he saw was '*wasn't feeling well*' and panicked. Was something wrong with Becca? With the baby?

He grabbed his keys and dashed back out of the house, almost forgetting to lock the front door. The roads were deserted at that time of night, so it took him less than ten minutes to get to the hospital.

"Becca Sommers," he panted at the night duty nurse. "Is she here?"

The woman consulted her screen, then nodded. "Yes, sir. She came in two hours ago. You'll find her in the maternity ward."

"Where is that?"

"Fourth floor. The elevators are—"

He was off before the woman could finish, running toward the stairs. He took them two at a time up to the fourth floor and arrived, panting and unable to speak, at the ward desk.

The nurse gaped at him. "Can I help you? Do you need a doctor?"

"I'm looking for Becca Sommers. I'm her partner." For once he forgot to be a Sheriff.

"She's in Ward H. Down the hall to your left."

Savage charged down the corridor, not waiting for her to finish.

E-F-G...

He burst into Ward H, his heart pounding. Becca sat upright in a hospital bed, her baby bump in front of her. He heaved a sigh of relief. It wasn't too late.

The other patients in the ward woke up, surprised at his sudden entrance. There was a murmur of alarm.

Becca shook her head. "Dalton, what's wrong with you? Why are you barging in here like we're being held hostage?"

He glanced around, then smiled sheepishly. "Sorry, I thought you were giving birth and I didn't want to miss anything." That made the women around him relax. He even got some approving smiles.

He pulled up a chair and sat down. "Are you alright? What's happening? I got your note."

"I'm okay. I was having some cramps, so the doctor thought it best if I came in. They've run some checks and the baby's fine."

He exhaled, falling against the back of the chair.

"You look terrible." She took in his dirty clothing, scratched arms and legs, and wrinkled her nose. Then her eyes widened. "Is that what I think it is?"

"Don't worry, it's not my blood."

"Shh. Lower your voice." He was getting strange looks again. "I'm just glad you're okay and you're here."

"Becca," he said, taking her hand. "This is not how this works."

"What do you mean?"

"I don't want you not to tell me things because I'm working. If anything happens to you or the baby, you tell me immediately. I will make a plan to get back to you, no matter what I'm doing. Is that clear?"

She hid a smile. "Yes, that's clear."

"Good. Because I don't want to be the last to know if—"

"I said, that's clear."

He stopped talking and squeezed her hand. It felt so good to be here. To stop moving for a moment.

"Did you get him?"

He gave a somber nod. "Sinclair shot him while he was attempting to flee. She's pretty cut up about it."

"I'm sure. Was it her first?"

"Yeah."

Becca nodded. "Tell her if she ever wants to talk, I'm available."

"You sure?" He nodded at her bump. "You've got a lot on your plate right now."

"I'm sure. I'm just waiting around for this baby to make an appearance, I may as well help someone."

"I'll let her know."

She gave his hand a squeeze. "I'm glad it's over."

"That's over," he said, "but there's still the matter of the drug war, but that's under control. I've got a plan."

FORTY-NINE

"THEY'VE PICKED UP THE SHIPMENT," Littleton told Savage, his voice squeaky with excitement. Littleton had been waiting in Las Cruces at a roadside cafe since seven o'clock that morning. It was now a little after ten.

"Copy that." Savage breathed a sigh of relief. Rosalie's guys were on schedule. He had DEA Agent Andy Rogers on standby. As soon as the Angels had made the switch, Savage would tell them to move in.

Agent Rogers had flown in from Denver with a special task force to apprehend the Denver mobsters. "We've been looking for a reason to bring them in for a long time," he'd told Savage when they'd spoken earlier in the week. "I just wish we had enough evidence to bring in Guy Hollander too."

"Maybe Jonny Star will talk," Savage suggested.

Rogers laughed. "That'll be the day. Star knows better than to rat out his boss. Besides, Hollander keeps his nose squeaky clean. And he does so much for charity that nobody will touch him. He's even supporting the mayoral campaign."

Savage was relieved he no longer worked for Denver PD. The politics used to drive him mental.

"Thorpe, you in position?"

"Yeah. Nothing yet."

"They're on their way up from New Mexico," Savage told him. "Sit tight."

Thorpe was positioned at the drop point in Santa Fe. The bikers were going to pull into the truck stop, offload the merchandise, and the Denver thugs would pick it up. Once they were on their way, Thorpe was going to let him know.

After that, the DEA would swoop in and search their vehicle, find the drugs, and arrest them.

Rosalie had given him a little shopping list:

5 pounds of heroin

3 pounds of methamphetamine

3 pounds of cocaine

4,722 DU of fentanyl pills

4 pounds of marijuana

It wasn't their biggest shipment—they were going to lose all of it anyway—but it had to be believable enough for the Denver thugs to want in on the deal.

Barbara made countless cups of coffee while they waited for the bikers to make the drop. It took a little over four hours to drive from Las Cruces to Santa Fe, more on a motorcycle, so Savage wasn't expecting them to get to the truck stop until earliest three o'clock.

At two-thirty, they got a text from Thorpe. "Still nothing."

"Come on," Savage muttered. "Where are they?"

His phone beeped again. Maybe this was it. Instead, he saw Becca's name on his screen. Frowning, he opened the message.

Just gone into labor. How soon can you get here?

He must have paled because Sinclair said, "What's wrong? Is it Becca?"

He nodded, his throat dry.

"What are you waiting for?" Barbara scolded him. "Get to the hospital."

"I can't, the sting is going down now. They're almost at the truck stop."

"We can take care of it," Sinclair said. She was on light duties, thanks to the investigation into the shooting. Her dislocated shoulder had been popped back and was now in a sling. The doctor had given her strict instructions to rest it.

Savage felt torn. Of course he wanted to go to the hospital, but this was the culmination of days of careful planning, and he wanted to see it through.

"Go," Sinclair said. "I've got this."

"We'll keep you updated," Barbara said. "Go."

He nodded, grabbed his jacket, and made for the door.

––––––––––

SINCLAIR DIDN'T TAKE her responsibility lightly. She may have sounded confident to her boss, but she knew the gravity of the situation. The outcome of this sting would see the Denver thugs arrested and stop the flow of lethal drugs into the county.

The Crimson Angels were small-time drug smugglers. This was a side hustle for them. They used it to supplement their lifestyle and had no plans to expand. Rosalie was risk averse. She didn't want to end up in the slammer with her ex.

The Denver mob, on the other hand, wanted the MC gang's Mexican contacts so they could expand distribution all over the county. They didn't care what kind of product they imported, not even if it was killing kids.

Savage's cellphone buzzed. He'd left it on the desk since everyone was using that number. Sinclair glanced down.

Thorpe.

They've just pulled into the truck stop.

She caught her breath. "It's happening."

Barbara rushed over and the two of them hovered over the cellphone, waiting for further news.

Another vibration.

The swap has been made. Denver is heading home.

That was it. That was the cue. Thorpe followed up with the make and model of the car, as well as the number plate. With trembling hands, Sinclair picked up the landline and called DEA Agent Andy Rogers.

He answered on the first ring. "Yeah?"

"Deputy Sinclair," she said. "Jonny Star and his men have picked up the merchandise and are heading north toward the state line."

"Excellent. Car make and model?"

"Dodge Dart. Silver. Colorado plate." She read him the number.

"How many men?"

"Three."

"Copy that. We'll let you know when we have 'em."

She put down the phone, then looked at Barbara.

Now all they could do was wait.

FIFTY

One week later

SAVAGE STOOD in the middle of his office and looked around. It'd be strange not coming back here for a while. Nine weeks felt like a very long time.

"It'll fly by," Barbara said. "You'll wonder where the time went."

"She's right." Shelby grinned. "Don't worry. I'll keep an eye on your crew." Savage nodded his thanks. It didn't make leaving any easier.

He'd just gotten off the phone with Carter, who'd promised to stop by and thank the team in person. Savage couldn't swear by it, but it had sounded like the undercover biker had been crying when he'd heard how Sinclair had shot Bryant in the woods.

"I never suspected him," Carter had admitted, once he'd pulled himself together. "I thought he was gay."

"A carefully cultivated façade," Savage had told him.

"I can't thank you enough."

"What you gonna do now?" Savage had asked.

"I don't know. Take a break. Maybe go and visit my ex-wife." Savage hadn't missed the longing in his voice.

He followed Barbara and Shelby into the squad room where the team was assembled. "We just heard," Sinclair said. "Hollander has withdrawn funding for the development. He doesn't want anything to do with this county anymore."

That was the second-best news he'd heard all week. "What does that mean for Apex Holdings?" he wondered.

"I don't know, but the construction has come to a stop. Connelly is closing up shop.

Savage frowned. "What's Celine going to do?" The teenager had so desperately wanted to move back east.

"Apparently, the college has offered her a financial aid package. She's already in Boston." Sinclair smiled. "I saw her before she left."

"That's great. How's Connelly taking it?"

"He's in shock. I don't think he can get his head around the fact his longtime colleague and friend was a serial killer." That would take some time to get over.

"Bryant fooled all of us," Savage muttered. "He even made a phone call to Connelly when he had Crystal in the car to put us off his scent."

Sinclair shook her head. "He was a monster."

"All's well that ends well," Barbara said, lightening the mood. Shelby grinned at her. He was doing a lot of that lately.

"You can always call me if there's a problem," Savage said. "I'm only a phone call away."

"I'm sure we'll cope." Thorpe hid a grin.

"Don't worry about a thing." Sinclair gave him a bright smile. "We've got everything covered. Now the Denver thugs have been arrested, things should quiet down around here."

He hoped she was right.

Andy Rogers had briefed him on the outcome of the bust. "At first, they played dumb, but when we found the drugs in the hidden compartment under the seat, it was game over. The older one tried to run. Jonny

Star, I think his name was. We shot him in the leg, but you'll be pleased to know he's going to be well enough to stand trial."

"I'm glad to hear it."

Littleton, Thorpe, and Sinclair had done well, and Savage couldn't be prouder of them. Still, they were a young team, and a lot could happen in nine weeks. At least they had Shelby standing by. He was a good man. Barbara clearly thought so too. Sinclair had been right about that development.

Even Tomahawk had stopped by to thank them. "We had a memorial for Crystal last week," he'd told them. "At least her parents can rest easy knowing the man who did this is dead."

"He had a lock-up," Savage had said. "We found the keys on him. That's where he took Crystal after he kidnapped her. There was a dirty mattress on the ground where she'd been held."

Tomahawk had shaken his head. "Death was too good for him."

Savage didn't disagree.

Sinclair had seen Becca to talk about what had happened. Even though Becca planned to take her full maternity leave, he secretly thought she enjoyed the mental stimulation. They'd planned more sessions in the not-too-distant future.

The front door opened, and Becca walked in with baby Connor in his carry cot. Barbara and Sinclair swarmed around them. "He's got his father's eyes," Sinclair said, smiling.

"Look at those chubby cheeks." Barbara reached in and shook his rattle. Connor, who was half asleep, scarcely registered.

"Ready?" Becca asked.

Savage took one last look around the office. "Yep."

"Let's go home."

Nodding goodbye to his colleagues, he took Becca's hand and the three of them left the station.

As Savage walked away, he couldn't help but think about the sniper who'd had him in his sights. He looked down at his baby boy, and made a solemn vow that whoever wanted him dead would never have another opportunity.

***

Dalton Savage returns in **COLD SKY**! Click the link below to grab your copy now!
https://www.amazon.com/dp/B0BTMJWWJX

Join the L.T. Ryan reader family & receive a free copy of the Rachel Hatch story, *Fractured*. Click the link below to get started:
https://ltryan.com/rachel-hatch-newsletter-signup-1

Love Savage? Hatch? Noble? Get your very own L.T. Ryan merchandise today! Click the link below to find coffee mugs, t-shirts, and even signed copies of your favorite L.T. Ryan thrillers! https://ltryan.ink/EvG_

ALSO BY L.T. RYAN

Find All of L.T. Ryan's Books on Amazon Today!

Beyond Betrayal (Clarissa Abbot)

Noble Judgment

Never Cry Mercy

Deadline

End Game

Noble Ultimatum

Noble Legend

Noble Revenge

Never Look Back (Coming Soon)

Bear Logan Series

Ripple Effect

Blowback

Take Down

Deep State

Bear & Mandy Logan Series

Close to Home

Under the Surface

The Last Stop

Over the Edge

Between the Lies (Coming Soon)

Rachel Hatch Series

Drift

Downburst

Fever Burn

Smoke Signal

Firewalk

Whitewater

Aftershock

Whirlwind

Tsunami

Fastrope

Sidewinder (Coming Soon)

Mitch Tanner Series

The Depth of Darkness

Into The Darkness

Deliver Us From Darkness

Cassie Quinn Series

Path of Bones

Whisper of Bones

Symphony of Bones

Etched in Shadow

Concealed in Shadow

Betrayed in Shadow

Born from Ashes

Blake Brier Series

Unmasked

Unleashed

Uncharted

Drawpoint

Contrail

Detachment

Clear

Quarry (Coming Soon)

Dalton Savage Series

Savage Grounds

Scorched Earth

Cold Sky

The Frost Killer (Coming Soon)

Maddie Castle Series

The Handler

Tracking Justice

Hunting Grounds (Coming Soon)

Affliction Z Series

Affliction Z: Patient Zero

Affliction Z: Abandoned Hope

Affliction Z: Descended in Blood

Affliction Z : Fractured Part 1

Affliction Z: Fractured Part 2 (Fall 2021)

ABOUT THE AUTHOR

L.T. RYAN is a Wall Street Journal, USA Today, and Amazon bestselling author of several mysteries and thrillers, including the Wall Street Journal bestselling Jack Noble and Rachel Hatch series. With over eight million books sold, when he's not penning his next adventure, L.T. enjoys traveling, hiking, riding his Peloton,, and spending time with his wife, daughter and four dogs at their home in central Virginia.

* Sign up for his newsletter to hear the latest goings on and receive some free content ➜ https://ltryan.com/jack-noble-newsletter-signup-1
* Join LT's private readers' group ➜ https://www.facebook.com/groups/1727449564174357
* Follow on Instagram ➜ @ltryanauthor
* Visit the website ➜ https://ltryan.com
* Send an email ➜ contact@ltryan.com
* Find him on Goodreads ➜ http://www.goodreads.com/author/show/6151659.L_T_Ryan

***

BIBA PEARCE is a British crime writer and author of the Kenzie Gilmore, Dalton Savage and DCI Rob Miller series.

Biba grew up in post-apartheid Southern Africa. As a child, she lived on the wild eastern coast and explored the sub-tropical forests and surfed in shark-infested waters.

Now a full-time writer, Biba lives in leafy Surrey and when she isn't writing, can be found walking through the countryside or kayaking on the river Thames.

Visit her at bibapearce.com and join her mailing list to be notified about new releases, updates and special subscriber-only deals.

Made in the USA
Las Vegas, NV
27 December 2023

83543389R00164